I

Uno

ILLUSTRATION BY

Ruria Miyuki

Reign
of the SEVEN
SPELLBLADES

"Well spotted. I knew you were a good piece of meat."

Cyrus Rivermoore

"So...what can I do for you, Rivermoore?"

Pamela Gorton

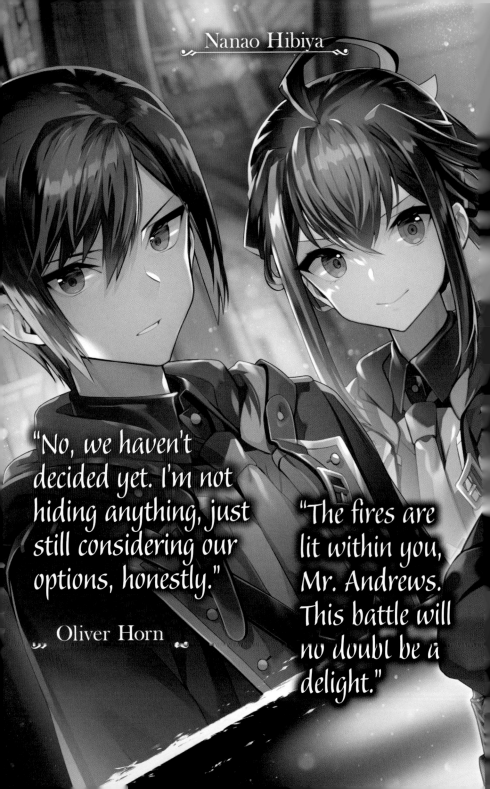

Nanao Hibiya

"No, we haven't decided yet. I'm not hiding anything, just still considering our options, honestly."

Oliver Horn

"The fires are lit within you, Mr. Andrews. This battle will no doubt be a delight."

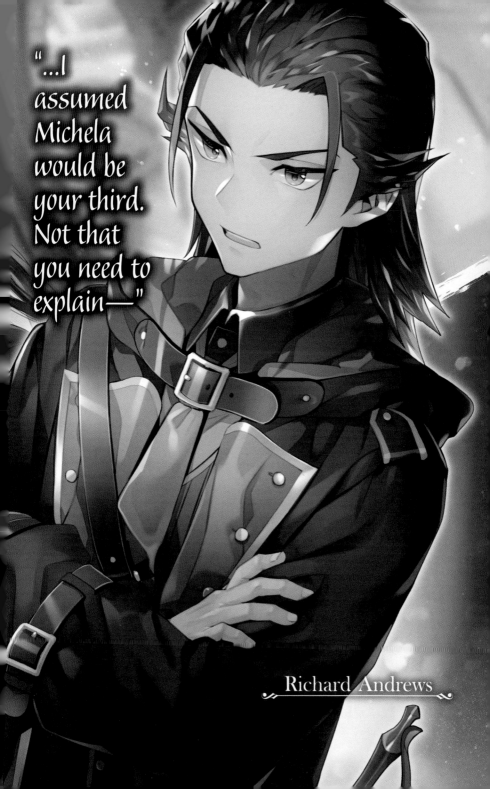

"...I assumed Michela would be your third. Not that you need to explain—"

Richard Andrews

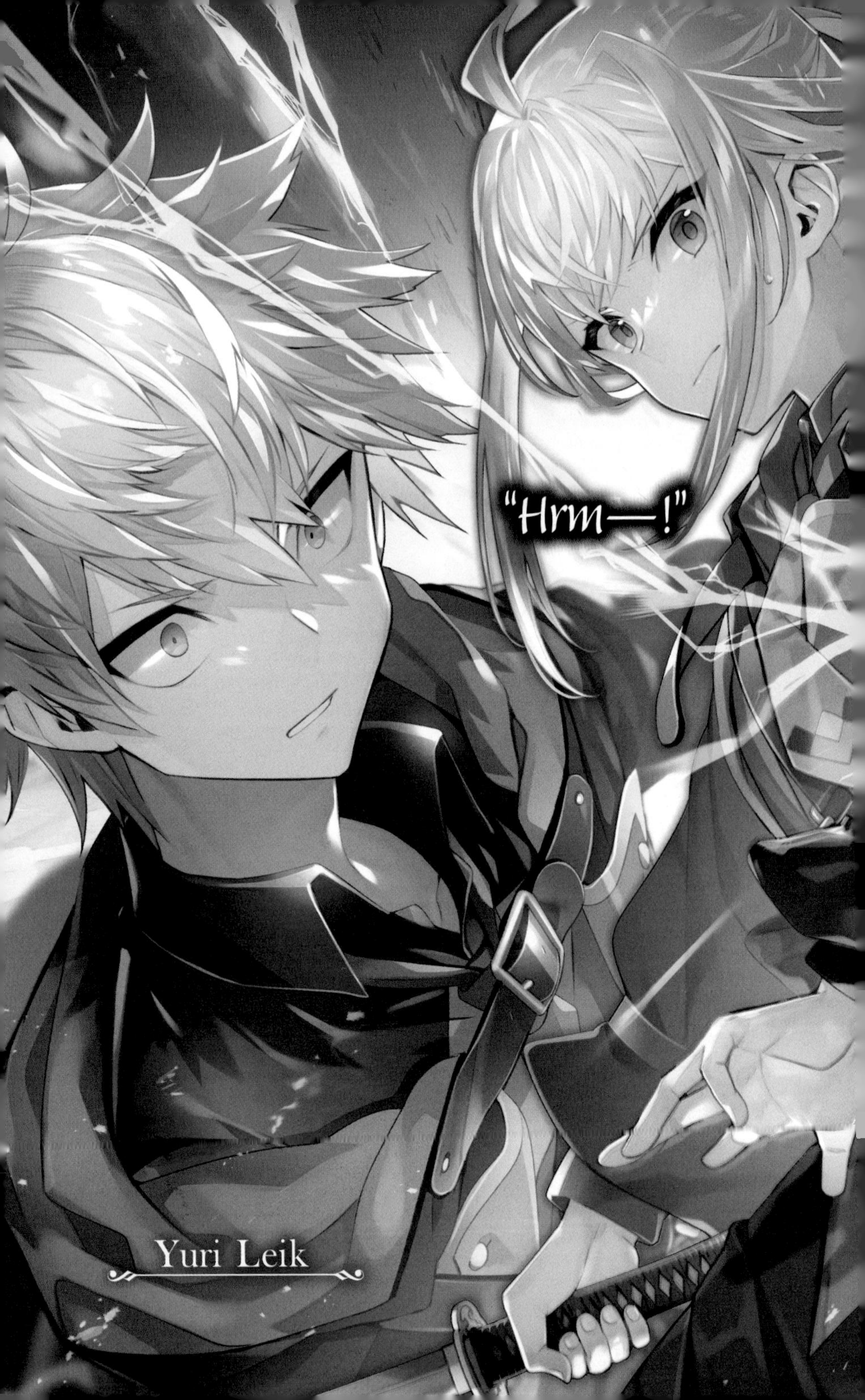
"Hrm—!"
Yuri Leik

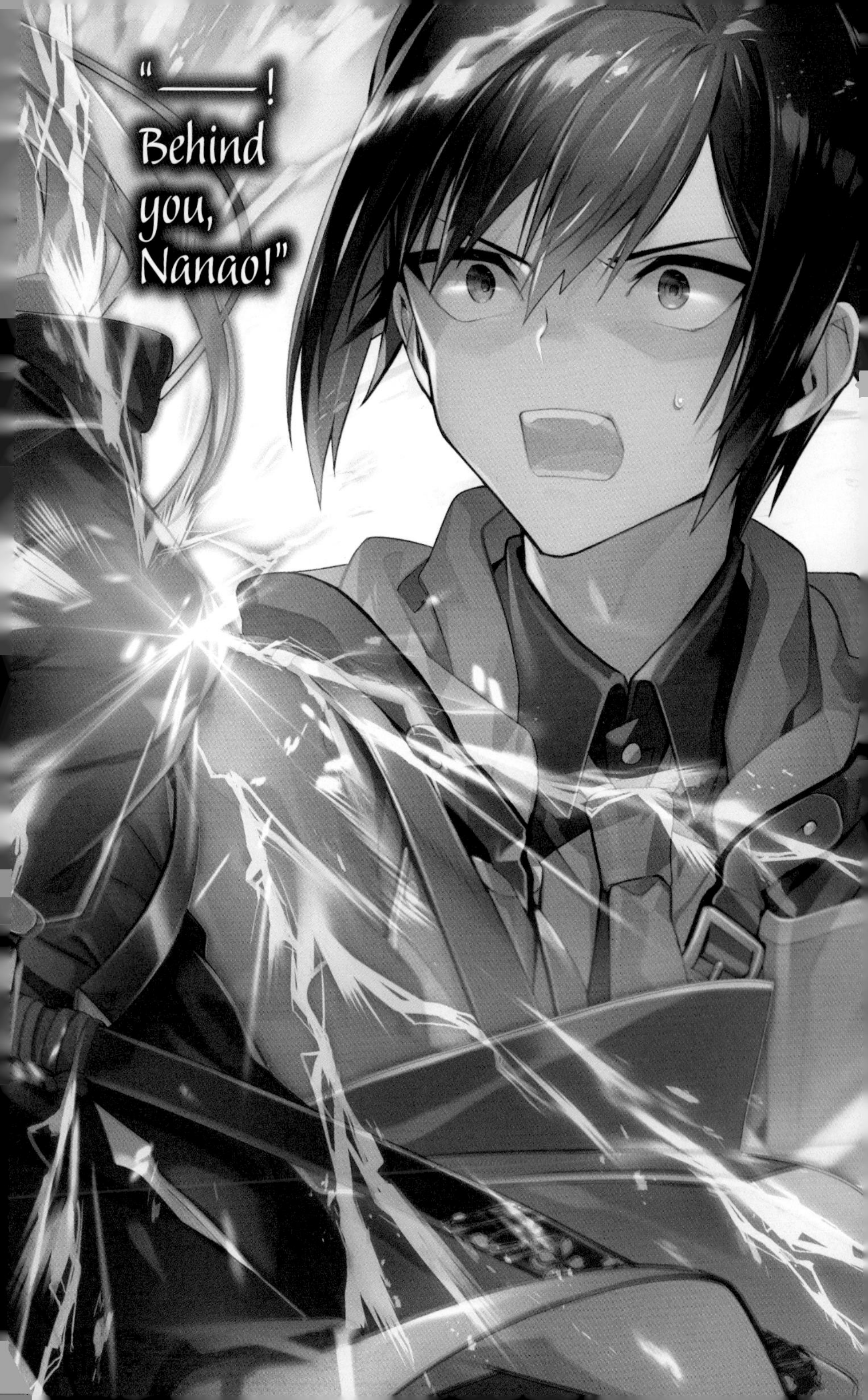
"——! Behind you, Nanao!"

CONTENTS

Reign of the Seven Spellblades
Bokuto Uno

Reign of the SEVEN SPELLBLADES

VII

Bokuto Uno

ILLUSTRATION BY
Ruria Miyuki

YEN
ON

New York

Reign of the Seven Spellblades, Vol. 7
Bokuto Uno

Translation by Andrew Cunningham
Cover art by Ruria Miyuki

NANATSU NO MAKEN GA SHIHAISURU Vol. 7
©Bokuto Uno 2021
Edited by Dengeki Bunko
First published in Japan in 2021 by KADOKAWA CORPORATION, Tokyo.
English translation rights arranged with KADOKAWA CORPORATION, Tokyo
through TUTTLE-MORI AGENCY, INC., Tokyo.

Yen On
150 West 30th Street, 19th Floor
New York, NY 10001

Visit us at yenpress.com
facebook.com/yenpress
twitter.com/yenpress
yenpress.tumblr.com
instagram.com/yenpress

First Yen On Edition: December 2022
Edited by Yen On Editorial: Rachel Mimms
Designed by Yen Press Design: Andy Swist

Yen On is an imprint of Yen Press, LLC.
The Yen On name and logo are trademarks of Yen Press, LLC.

Library of Congress Cataloging-in-Publication Data
Names: Uno, Bokuto, author. | Miyuki, Ruria, illustrator. | Keller-Nelson, Alexander,
translator. | Cunningham, Andrew, translator.
Title: Reign of the seven spellblades / Bokuto Uno ; illustration by Ruria Miyuki ;
v. 1–3: translation by Alex Keller-Nelson ; v. 4–7: translation by Andrew Cunningham.
Other titles: Nanatsu no maken ga shihai suru. English
Description: First Yen On edition. | New York, NY : Yen On, 2020–
Identifiers: LCCN 2020041085 | ISBN 9781975317195 (v. 1 ; trade paperback) |
ISBN 9781975317201 (v. 2 ; trade paperback) | ISBN 9781975317225
(v. 3 ; trade paperback) | ISBN 9781975317249 (v. 4 ; trade paperback) |
ISBN 9781975339692 (v. 5 ; trade paperback) | ISBN 9781975339715
(v. 6 ; trade paperback) | ISBN 9781975343446 (v. 7 ; trade paperback)
Subjects: CYAC: Fantasy. | Magic—Fiction. | Schools—Fiction.
Classification: LCC PZ7.1.U56 Re 2020 | DDC [Fic]—dc23
LC record available at https://lccn.loc.gov/2020041085

ISBNs: 978-1-9753-4344-6 (paperback)
978-1-9753-4345-3 (ebook)

10 9 8 7 6 5 4 3 2 1

LSC-C

Printed in the United States of America

Characters

Third-Years

Oliver Horn

The story's protagonist. Jack-of-all-trades, master of none. Swore revenge on the seven instructors who killed his mother.

Nanao Hibiya

A samurai girl from Azia. Believes that Oliver is her destined sword partner.

Katie Aalto

A girl from Farnland, a nation belonging to the Union. Has a soft spot for the civil rights of demi-humans.

Guy Greenwood

A boy from a family of magical farmers. Honest and friendly. Has a knack for magical flora.

Pete Reston

A studious boy born to nonmagicals. Capable of switching between male and female bodies.

Michela McFarlane

Eldest daughter of the prolific McFarlane family. A master of the pen and sword, she looks out for her friends.

Tullio Rossi

A lone wolf who taught himself the sword by ignoring the fundamentals. Lost to Oliver in a duel.

Yuri Leik

A transfer student. What he lacks in sense, he makes up for in boundless curiosity. Chummy with everyone.

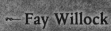

— Fay Willock

— Joseph Albright

— Stacy Cornwallis

Third-Years

Jasmine Ames

Has distinctively long bangs. While she claims to lack confidence, her sword art skills are among the best in her year.

Rose Mistral

His every move is oddly showy, like a stage performer. Bedazzles with a blend of magic and deceit.

Richard Andrews

A proud youth from a prestigious family. Recognizes Oliver's and Nanao's talents and considers them worthy rivals.

Second-Years

Teresa Carste

Oliver's closest vassal, aiding his revenge as a covert operative. Moves on her own terms and shows few emotions.

Seventh-Years

Alvin Godfrey

Student council president. Nicknamed Purgatory by his peers. Boasts incredible firepower.

Cyrus Rivermoore

A necromancer who controls the bones of the dead. Has not shown himself on campus in a while…

Fifth-Years

Pamela Gorton

Known as the Labyrinth Seller, she runs a shop in the labyrinth's depths. Shares the tenacity and techniques of her mentor, the Survivor.

Leoncio Echevalria

Leader of the previous student council's faction. Once battled Godfrey for the presidency and received burns to the right side of his face, which he refuses to heal.

Instructors

Esmeralda

Kimberly's headmistress. Proudly stands at the apex of magical society.

Enrico Forghieri DECEASED

Magical engineering instructor. Prone to outrageous lessons designed to maim students.

Theodore McFarlane

Chela's father and the man who sent Nanao to Kimberly.

Vanessa Aldiss

Magical biology instructor. Feared by her students for her wild personality.

- ∞ Demitrio Aristides
- ∞ Frances Gilchrist
- ∞ Luther Garland
- ∞ Dustin Hedges
- ∞ Darius Grenville DECEASED

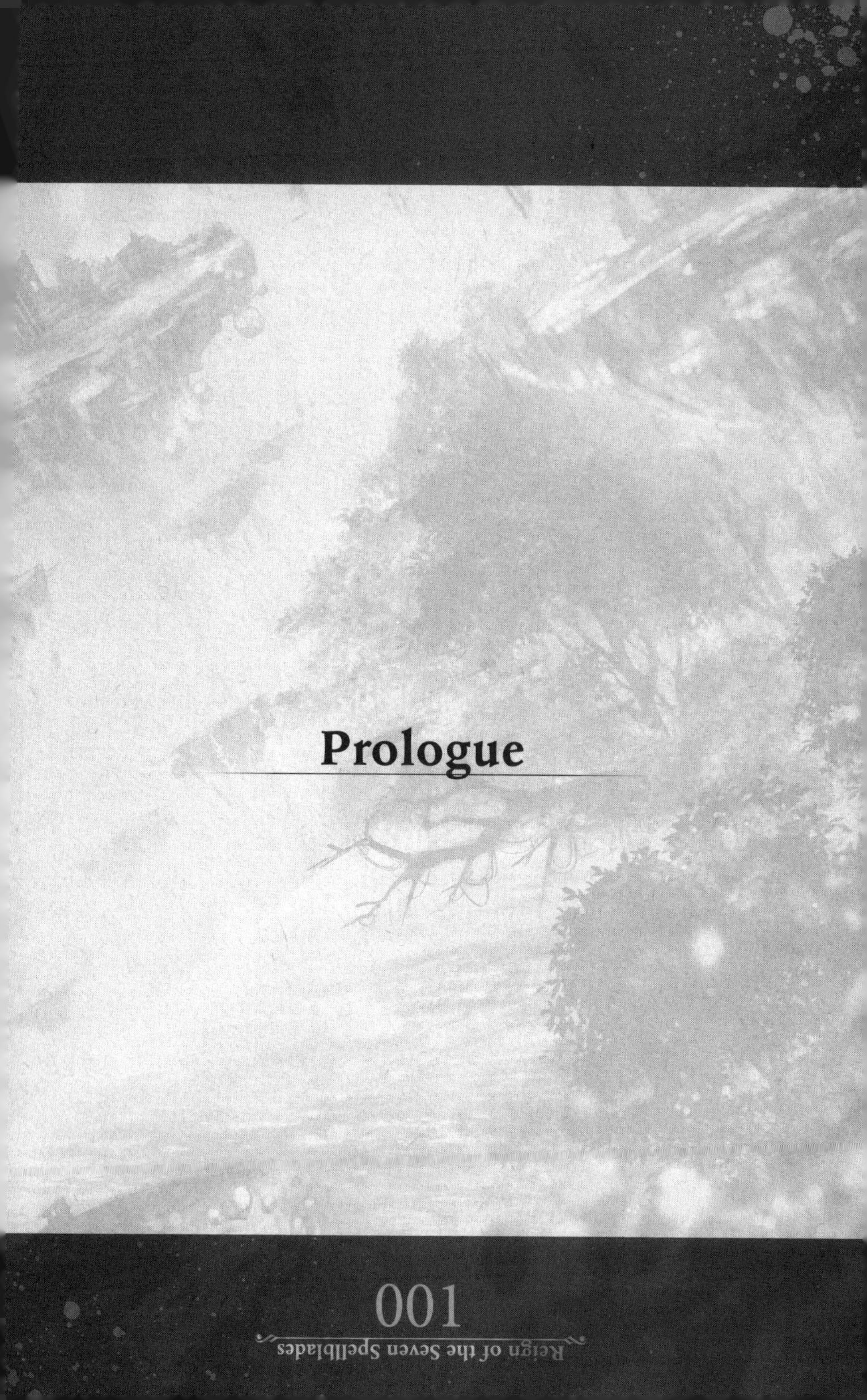

Prologue

Where there is risk, there are rewards. Hence the students of Kimberly delve into the labyrinth's depths.

Rare flora and fauna, precious minerals, even ancient writings—to a mage, the labyrinth is a veritable treasure trove. The density of resources is simply like no other. One might have to search the whole wide world to find a material on the surface, yet down below, that same thing could be found on any given layer.

But claiming that bounty requires considerable skill. Coming back alive is merely the premise—the true test lies in locating the specific item sought within the labyrinth's sprawl. Distinguishing medicine from poison, identifying mineral deposits, tracking magical beasts, and hunting them efficiently—master *all* these skills, and the labyrinth's gifts are positively abundant.

"...Nee-ha-ha! You'll not escape us so easy!"

A fifth-year student, Pamela Gorton knew a lot about feasting on the labyrinth's plenty. On a far corner of the third layer, the Miasma Marsh, she was leading a group of younger students in pursuit of a richman. An amphibious magifauna, its fins could be sold as high-quality spellstones. The fish itself used these fins to maneuver through the wind, sailing across the bog below. Pamela's crew was just barely keeping up.

"It's turning! Hit it, Hugh!"

"Tonitrus!"

Their relentless pursuit had made the richman flinch—it banked left, just as the beaters had planned. A group of students was lying in wait; one hit it with a spell. The richman landed flat on its side, not moving, and two hunters tackled it, holding it down. The caster poked their head out of the brush nervously.

"Did…did I get it?"

"Yep! It's snagged!"

"Whew…!"

Like Gorton had taught them, one stabbed a vital spot, finishing it off. The kids hoisted their catch high, cheering.

Many beasts would attack on sight, but on the labyrinth's lower levels, that just made them easy to hunt. Cautious creatures that lay in hiding—those tested a hunter's skills. And the majority of labyrinth fauna fell in the latter category. This group had spent *days* tracking this richman.

"Brilliant," Gorton called, smiling at the hunters' celebration. "It's a big lug, but bring the meat back, too. The part 'round the tail is prized, and the Gourmets'll pay a pretty penny."

"This thing's edible?!"

"I'd rather not…"

"They'll eat *anything*."

Grumbling, they dressed and packaged their catch, each shouldering their share.

Gorton turned her back toward them. "You guys go ahead," she said.

"Mm?"

"What's wrong?"

"Gonna take a gander 'round this layer. You handle my share of the catch."

She waved them off. Her party shrugged but moved on. When she was sure they were out of earshot, she spoke again.

"So…what can I do for you, Rivermoore?"

The ground in front of her welled up. From the mud rose a sinister sphere constructed of innumerable bones. And within: a grinning warlock, possessed of a clerical gravitas that boded well for no one.

"Well spotted," he said. "I knew you were a good piece of meat."

"We're off to a grand start already. You sure know how to flatter a lady." Pamela kept her sarcasm light, but her eyes never left him. "You after grub? I'm selling at fair market prices."

"Your catches are well worth it. You know how to make a clean finish. But I'm here on other business today."

Rivermoore shook his head as he ran his eyes over Gorton's form, peering through her clothes, past her skin, and beyond the muscle.

"I'm after your second lumbar vertebra. Name a price and I'll consider it."

"Don't be daft. My body ain't for sale." Her tone grew harsher. She was well aware this entire interaction was a ticking bomb. "I told you last time I wasn't selling. If you're still gunning for it, then you're a thief."

"Fair," Rivermoore admitted. He turned his gaze in the direction her party had run. "You knew this would happen and got them to clear out? You're a regular mentor now. How time flies."

"Don't it, though? I'm already a fifth-year. Can't stay scared of you forever."

Even as she spoke, she remembered their last encounter, when they were still in the lower forms. The man who'd saved her that day had said, *"Make yourself stronger. Next time, it'll be you keeping the kids safe."*

"I'm the Labyrinth Seller, Pamela Gorton. Star mentee of the Survivor, Kevin Walker. Ready when you are!"

She drew her athame—and the warlock's lips twisted into a ghoulish grin.

"*Impetus!*"

The Seller threw the first spell. Rivermoore calmly let her gust spell slam against his bone barrier.

"Hrm," he grunted. He'd spotted a bottle at Gorton's feet—hidden by her robe. She'd placed it there as they spoke, without his noticing. It was nearly empty—so whatever it contained was already loose. But to what end?

Before he came upon an answer, the results presented themselves. Rivermoore found himself surrounded by creatures with spindly bodies and translucent wings, the sheer number of them severely limiting his vision. As their number increased, Rivermoore snorted.

"Skyfish. You scattered a lure scent on my bones."

"I ain't a match for your power, sir. But I know more about the third layer than you do!"

Gorton grinned. The bottle at her feet had contained a vaporized potion that the wind had carried toward Rivermoore. Even if he'd blocked her spell, the potion still wound up on his bones. All this had done was lure in a swarm of insects, but if this many creatures gathered anywhere on the third layer—it would attract interest. Rivermoore spotted several other marsh magifauna closing in, and he narrowed his eyes.

"Wind snakes drawn by their favorite snack...and longtongue lizards to eat the snakes. You've activated the full food chain. Which means—"

Even as he whispered, the ground nearby erupted, and something giant leaped out. A wyrm—the largest predator of the third layer. Rivermoore dodged the attack from the back of his bony serpent, genuinely impressed.

"—you *do* fight like the Survivor. You've learned well, Gorton."

"Know your environment, harmonize with it—and then *use* that! Survival basics, sir. Here, your bones don't belong."

Gorton had forced Rivermoore into the food chain effect but kept herself outside, free to fling spells from the sidelines. He was no longer just up against the Labyrinth Seller but the entire third-layer ecosystem. Gorton spoke the truth, and it made him wince.

"You've got me there," Rivermoore replied. "But do you know what *used* to rule this layer?"

As if in answer to his call, a chunk of the ground liquefied, whirling—and a giant toothy bone maw emerged. Gorton leaped back, and the flow pulled in the wyrm—where it was bitten clean in half. The last thing the Seller expected to see here.

"...?!"

"The apex predator of yore. Only its bones remain."

That was not the sole table that had turned. The second coming of the long-dead ruler put flight to every creature's heels. Wyrms and skyfish alike scattered like newborn spiders. And in the deserted space they left behind stood Rivermoore—and the skeleton he controlled.

"The ancient terror lives on within them," he growled. "You spend your days rummaging through corpses, all you can see is the past."

He spun slowly. Gorton had long since stopped firing and was out of sight—but Rivermoore caught the faint sounds of her receding footsteps. Three skeletal creatures assembled themselves at his feet and darted out across the bog; one of them locked its jaws around his target's leg.

"Gah…!"

"I knew you'd turn tail and run the moment things turned against you."

He rode out on his serpent and soon found where his bony beasts had the Labyrinth Seller pinned. The serpent's tail slapped the athame from her hand—her last resistance.

Rivermoore slid down from his skeletal mount. One hand took a firm grip on Gorton's throat, hauling her body upright.

"Meat that lives with all its might leaves better bones behind. I'll help myself to just one small piece of your life, Gorton."

"…The interest's…gonna be a bitch…!"

But words were the sole resource the Labyrinth Seller had left. Rivermoore savored them with evident pleasure—and slid his athame into her flesh.

A few hours later, in the cave just past the end of the second layer—where the Battle of Hell's Armies took place.

"This time, I just sailed straight through. Shame! Clear it once, and you've gotta wait a whole year to try again! And it was so much fun."

Muttering to himself, Yuri Leik moved through darkness. Each passing day took him farther into the labyrinth's depths, and half the third layer was already in his range.

"The Library Plaza sounds pretty neat, too, but I bet soloing that would kill me. Wonder if Oliver would be up for— Mm?"

His thoughts were interrupted, and he paused his advance. There was something on the ground ahead. Spotting a uniform, he ran over.

"A student? Hellooo? Are you alive?"

There was no answer, so he bent down and looked her over. It was a girl from the upper forms, unconscious, her complexion pale. Yuri recognized her distinctively large mouth. He'd bought things from her shop on the first layer.

"Gorton, fifth-year. No visible injuries…"

He peeled her robe back for a quick inspection but saw nothing that needed urgent healing. However, something struck him as odd. He probed at that feeling a moment and then whispered:

"Hmm…it's like something important's been taken out of her."

Meanwhile, on the Flower Road leading into Kimberly, the spring warmth had the buds starting to loosen.

"So I said, 'Yo, you've got that spell all wrong. An ordinary's shiny bald head ain't gonna sprout hair just because you chant Progressio. It's not like you scattered seeds on it.'"

A man stood before the dahlias, surrounded by students of his year, speaking with enthusiasm. It was the student body president, Alvin Godfrey himself. He was performing a classic magical comedy routine, but both his voice and gestures were oddly stiff, ensuring that the humor of it was entirely lost. He was, quite frankly, being a giant ham.

"And he said, 'Makes sense. Next time I'll sow some seeds first. But what seeds should I use? Some sort of dense vine?' I couldn't stand listening to another word of this nonsense and left him to it. But the next morning—"

"Ugh, enough."

"Go away. Next!"

The dahlias were *not* about to sit through the whole routine and mercilessly sent him packing. Godfrey stood frozen for several seconds, then turned away, shoulders heaving. He sat down next to Lesedi, who'd long since taken her turn, and his head did not lift.

"…Ngh…!"

"You're straight-up shaking there."

"I practiced…for six months…"

"You're such a try-hard," Lesedi said with a snort.

It was very Godfrey to go all out on these things, even if nobody asked him to. He'd been like that since she first met him and had grown no better at navigating the world. Grinning, she turned her eyes back to the performers ahead.

"Well, the dahlias have always been a tough crowd. But this does bring it all home. Once upon a time, it was us coming down the Flower Road. And here we are, casting the spring spell."

Her tone was light, but the meaning was weighty. They'd survived six whole years at Kimberly but knew far too many students who hadn't. And the missing faces included those who'd been precious friends.

Seeing them once more in his mind's eye, Godfrey clenched his fists tight.

"I don't want much from our last year. But at the least…"

He opened his eyes. The burden of the presidency was resting squarely on his shoulders.

"…until I graduate, I don't want *anyone* else to die."

CHAPTER 1

Selection

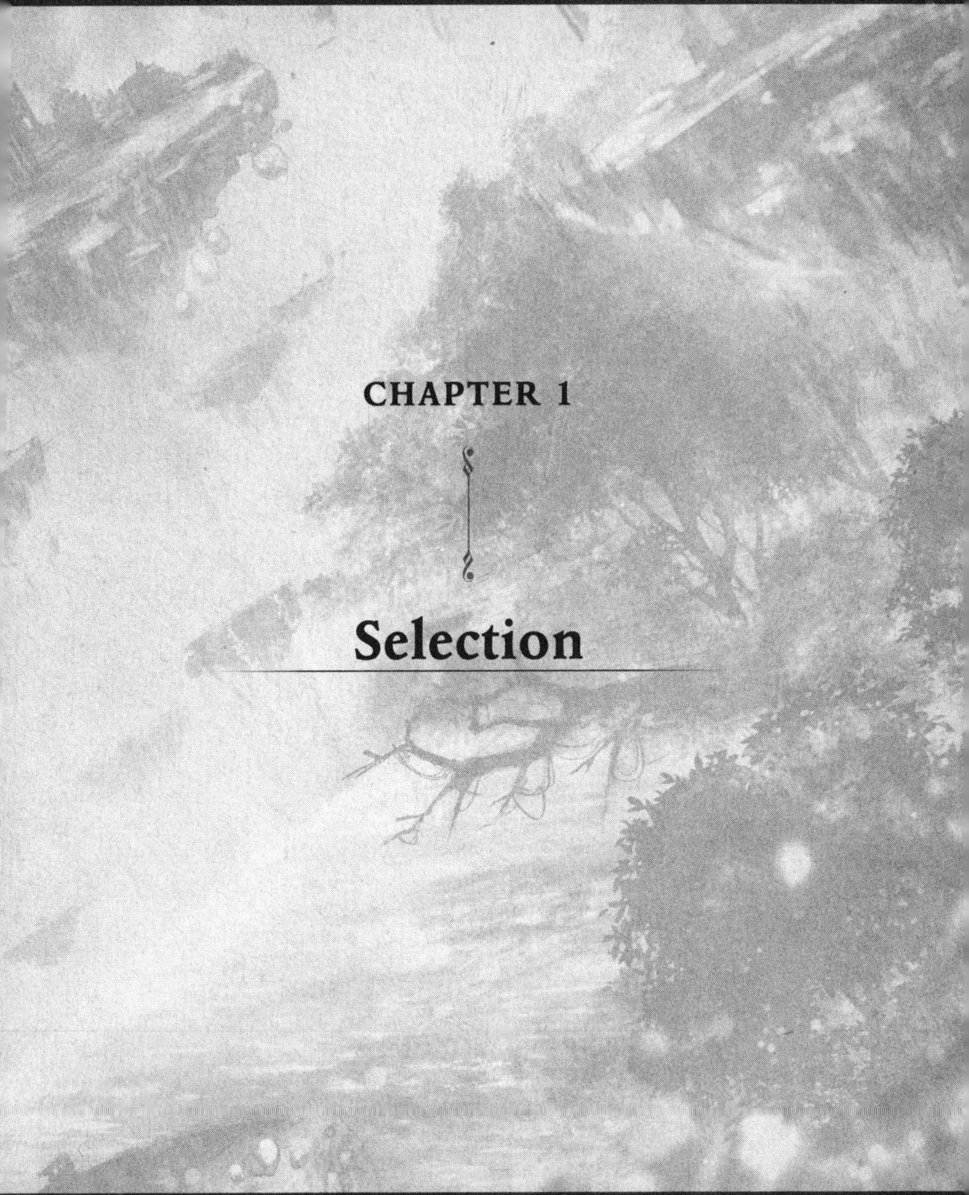

Don't give them an inch.

While the strength of this conviction varied by the individual, the core mentality was shared by the majority of Kimberly freshmen. The means to that end depended on the mage's personality and the cards they'd been dealt. Some imagined themselves shining in class, others in schoolyard fights, and still others merely spun tall tales with abandon.

"Heh-heh-heh…"

There were those who chose an even showier approach. The girl walking the halls accompanied by a magical beast several times her height was one of these. A snake's head, from which gleamed vicious fangs, and green fur in which lurked virulently poisonous spikes—the new students around gulped at the sight.

"Yikes, what is that thing?!"

"A peluda? I've never even seen one before!"

"A first-year with *that* as a familiar?!"

She acted like she heard none of these comments but was smirking inside. *Yes. Gasp in awe. Quiver with envy. Fear me. Look upon this beast and know I am better. It was well worth pushing myself to get it trained in time.*

"____?"

But then she wandered around a corner—and stopped. Her path was blocked by the bulk of a demi-human. A troll, crouched down with its back to her.

"…Hello?" the girl said, peeved. "Get that troll out of my way."

"Mm."

The troll turned toward her, at a loss—but it didn't move. That enraged the girl, who raised her voice.

"I said, out of my way! I'm coming through!"

"Urgh...sorry. But now, here...bad."

Her next words stuck in her throat. *Did it just* talk? *Human language?! Goblins, sure, but...what troll species can do* that?

The girl started running through her magifauna knowledge but quickly decided that wasn't what mattered here. What mattered was that this was Kimberly, other students were watching, and she could not afford to give anyone an inch. With that in mind, she raised her voice once again.

"...So...so what? Let me through! Or else—"

"Heyyy!"

The girl was about to order her familiar to issue a threat, but a boy came running in. From the color of his tie, he was a year above her. She blinked at the second-year, and he spread his arms, as if protecting the troll.

"What's your problem, first-year? Don't be mean to Marco!"

"Urrr...Dean..."

The troll's face visibly relaxed. Things weren't going the girl's way, and she was starting to panic, but she did her best to appear calm.

"...I-I'm not being mean. This troll is simply blocking the path for no good reason. This is a public space! My familiar and I have a right to walk where we please."

"He's blocking your path for a *very* good reason. Did you even ask him why?"

"A-ask? A troll?! Don't be ridic—"

The girl felt downright dizzy. But as she tried to argue—a shadow passed overhead, blotting out the sun.

"Hold it right there!"

A new girl's voice rang out, and manavian wings spread wide. A griffin descended from a height. It landed right before them, its glare so fierce that the first-year girl took a step back despite herself.

"…Eek…?!"

"JAAAAAAAAAAAAA!"

As the girl flinched, her peluda screeched, instinctively making a show of strength.

Here, the figure on the griffin's back hopped down. A third-year girl with curly light-brown hair—Katie Aalto.

"Sorry, there are pot weasels nesting here. We'll have that moved in no time!"

Katie pointed over the troll's shoulder. The girl looked that way and saw a dome-shaped nest in the branches of a sapling with several weasellike creatures inside. This species nested in trees they'd grown themselves—and at last, the girl realized why the troll was here.

This was one too many twists for her mind, and she found herself standing stock-still. Leaving her to it, Katie turned to the other student present, flashing a brilliant smile.

"You're looking after Marco for me? Thanks, Dean! You're such a good boy!"

"I—I—I just did what anyone would!"

This griffin was *very* intimidating, and Dean was doing his level best not to let his knees buckle. Katie's beloved manavian had grown quite a bit over the last year and was noticeably larger than the first-year girl's peluda. It gave Dean flashbacks of the beast that had once captured him—but he could *not* let that fear show. He was bluffing with all his might.

Here, Katie's gaze turned toward the first-year's creature. Her eyes lit up, and she stepped closer.

"Wow, a peluda! Female, maybe five years old? What an adorable familiar!"

"Ador—?!"

The girl couldn't believe her ears. What could possibly lead anyone to describe this hideous beast in those terms? Beside her, the peluda was screeching away, threatening both Katie and her griffin. It was no longer acting on the girl's orders but driven entirely by fear. And the ruckus was drawing other students to them.

"H-hey! Stop that screeching!"

The girl hastily started trying to talk her familiar down. With no overt hostility directed their way, failing to stop the ruckus would reflect poorly on her. But the beast was too agitated to listen. The peluda had its claws extended and was growling—this was too much for the girl, and she reached for her white wand, seeing no solution but a spell.

"Don't draw," Katie cautioned, putting a hand on her arm. "Sorry, let me talk to her a moment. Lyla, stay right there."

That last comment was addressed to the griffin behind her. Empty-handed, she stepped right up to the peluda. The girl couldn't believe her eyes—what was she *doing*? Even a third-year would be helpless if a beast like this attacked them while wandless.

"JAAAAAAAAA…!"

The peluda roared right in her face—which Katie let pass with a smile. Moving slowly, she reached out and touched it. The peluda flinched. Mindful of the poisonous barbs in its fur, Katie stroked the creature, reassuring it.

"…You're still not used to being around people, are you? And you there: You've done nothing but implant your familiar with fear—to excess. Trying to tame her quickly, no matter what?"

"…?!"

The girl's face tensed. Katie had seen right through the methods used after observing the peluda for only a handful of seconds.

"…Don't worry—I'm not your enemy. Not me, not Marco, and not Lyla," Katie whispered to the peluda.

With each word, the creature's growls grew fainter. Its master stood stunned—until hands clasped around hers. Before her stood the older girl—someone beyond her comprehension.

"I'm Katie Aalto, Kimberly third-year. Nice to meet you! What's your name?"

*   *   *

Meanwhile, in a remote corner of the school building's first floor, a little scuffle had broken out.

"...Ha! Is that all you got?"

Three students were lying on the ground, and one boy was standing over them—all first-years. They simply hadn't liked the look in one another's eyes; that was all it took to start a fight if everyone really wanted one. It was a great way to strut your stuff, and it just happened that he'd had the most stuff to strut.

"You should've warned me you're this weak. I'd have let you go three-on-one."

"...Unh..."

"Dammit..."

Three fights running, yet they'd been unable to gain the upper hand. The trio of first-years was left lying on the floor, groaning as the boy sneered down at them.

"Pardon me."

"...Eh?"

Someone had stepped out in front of him, standing by the fallen freshmen. The new arrival was on the small side, but the necktie was the third year's color. The face and voice alone weren't enough to nail down a gender. As the victor's frown deepened, the newcomer busily set about tending to the losers' wounds.

"No need to hide your fights. Make sure you've got an older student observing. That way, someone can step in to heal you up after."

This was meant as fair warning to the younger students, yet the boy read it as scorn and pointed his athame at the new arrival.

"Thanks for the advice, asshole. But I don't remember giving you permission to *heal* anyone."

The edge in his tone was enough to make the third-year—Pete Reston—turn around. The eyes behind Pete's glasses were very cold— far more intimidating than the first-year boy had anticipated. He almost flinched, but he'd committed to this approach and wasn't backing down easily, no matter how much older the foe. He put on his best glare.

"The fight's over. What's the problem?" Pete asked.

"Victor's rights. Figured they'd be good targets to practice my pain spells."

"...So you *want* to hurt people?" Pete sighed, then narrowed his eyes. "In that case, this is no longer a fight. If you insist, I'll take you on."

That makes things easy, the boy thought. His lips curled into a taunting smirk.

"You mean...you'll take their place? Suffer in their stead?"

"Practice all the pain spells you like. *If* you can beat me."

"...Hmph."

The air grew tense. The boy measured the distance between them. He was two steps outside one-step, one-spell range. But his foe hadn't even reached for his athame. The boy was certain—even against a third-year, he could win.

"*Tonitrus!*"

The boy cast first. Lightning coiled at the tip of his blade—and his vision was scorched by blinding light and heat.

"Gah...?!"

He couldn't see a thing. Backing away, he waved his blade around wildly, catching nothing—and then he felt something pressed against his throat. The chill of a metal blade. The boy froze, and a calm voice spoke in his ear.

"Think you're a quick cast? It was like you weren't even moving."

"...Ngh...! Wh-what did you even *do*...?"

"You saw it. I threw a burst orb timed to the cast of your spell."

The truth sent a chill down his spine. He'd *timed* that? The third-year had waited for him to chant and swing his athame, *then* thrown out the burst orb? But he'd seen no signs of that motion—

"If you failed to spot it, that's the limit of your current skill. Train some more and try again."

"You motherf—!"

Unable to accept the loss, the moment his vision recovered, he swung his blade. You couldn't give *anyone* an inch here. If this third-year was good at spell length, then if he tried sword arts—

But even as the thought crossed the first-year's mind, his athame was clattering along the floor.

"Count yourself lucky it was *me* you fought. Some students here would've done far worse than a mere pain spell."

"...Ah..."

Pete caught the look in the boy's eye and calmly put away his blade. He went back to healing the kids on the floor. When that was done, he turned and walked off.

"I'm Pete Reston, third-year. You want a rematch, come at me whenever. Duel rules suit me fine," he told the boy. "But don't diminish what time here does to someone—to you or to anyone else. I was born nonmagical, and this is what two years here have done to *me*. That's what you've signed up for at Kimberly."

"It's definitely bearing fruit. What do you make of it?"

Meanwhile, in a corner of the garden filled with all manner of magiflora, Guy was showing a teacher a tree he'd grown. The smooth gray bark had a sheen to it, like it was coated in varnish. Its thick trunk split in three, spreading in each direction, and at the tip of every branch hung a voluminous blue fruit. The garden's proprietor—David Holzwirt—looked it over thoroughly.

"...It's in good health. Congrats, Mr. Greenwood. Lanternblue are an endangered species...and it's been five years since a student managed to raise one from seed to bearing fruit."

"Thank you, sir. It's certainly a prickly customer, but I took my time and worked with it—and it turned out okay."

Guy grinned, and the door to the conservatory flung open. A girl a year younger came running in.

"Appleton, s-second-year!" she said. "Um, I heard the lanternblue bore fruit!"

"Come on over, Rita. Take a gander!" Guy boasted. "Ain't they lovely?"

Rita eagerly jogged up to him, looking the tree over and nodding.

The instructor let his students bask for a moment before speaking again.

"…You kept logs of the growth?"

"'Course I did."

"Mm… Pair that with your findings and give me a write-up two weeks from now. Once I've read it—we'll discuss the contents in my workshop."

And with that, David departed the greenhouse. They watched him go; then Rita turned to Guy, cheeks flushed.

"Wow!" she exclaimed. "That's amazing, Guy! Instructor David almost never invites anyone to his workshop. He's supposed to be really hard to get along with…"

"Yeah? From what I've seen, that ain't true at all. He just doesn't waste time thinking about anything except magiflora."

Guy shrugged. A thought struck him, and he grimaced.

"I have a friend like that already… Might actually be easier to get on with the instructor. I've got a green thumb to begin with, and *he* don't start any arguments."

That cut Rita to the quick. His tone of voice made it clear who he was talking about—and how much he cared for this friend.

"…You mean Ms. Aalto?" she asked.

"Yeah, she's hard to miss these days. She's finally got that griffin on her side and can't stop herself from riding it around. She's seriously terrorizing the new kids."

This was the kind of griping you did only about people with whom you were genuinely close. Unable to bear hearing any more of it, Rita interrupted—aware that doing so was more than a bit awkward.

"…I-I'd better go. The teacher wants to see me."

"Mm? About your research? Whatcha growing? I could come along—"

"No."

Looking grim, she raised both hands to stop him.

Guy blinked at her, and she hastily explained.

"I, um…I didn't do well on the last written test. Gotta take makeup classes."

"Oh. Well, if you need help, feel free to ask. You're doing great otherwise!"

He plopped a hand down on her head. She'd planned to leave at once, but the warmth of his palm was awfully nice; Rita lingered, eyes on the ground.

"I… Yes, I'll do that," she whispered.

"You're all making a name for yourselves."

Miligan had taken one sip of her tea and dropped that line on her cohort of underclassmen. They were in their secret base—clearly, she'd heard the stories.

"That's hardly new for some of you, but Katie, Guy, and Pete—you're each starting to really pull ahead in your respective fields. Makes me so proud."

"I entirely agree," Chela proclaimed. "I have not embraced you nearly enough."

"You stay down, Chela!"

"We are *done* with the celebratory hugs!"

Guy and Pete both started squawking the moment the ringlet girl stood up. The three of them began circling the couch, with the boys attempting to maintain a safe distance.

"I appreciate the praise." Katie sighed, looking up from the paper she was reading. "But I don't *feel* like I'm getting anywhere. The walls I'm banging up against seem so much bigger than the problems I've managed to solve."

"With research, that is *always* the case," Miligan said, smiling at her. "Katie, never let it get to you. For all your protests, your growth is clear to everyone."

Meanwhile, Guy had tried a double feint to escape Chela's reach, but she'd seen it coming and snared him. He let out a screech, but her hug's vise grip clamped down upon him.

"Even well-trained griffins rarely let people ride them," Oliver said, nodding and side-eyeing the commotion. "That's a much bigger deal than you realize. And it proves your approach is effective."

"I-it does? Well, good."

Katie blushed at this, then shuffled the papers on her knees into a neat pile. She stole several more glances at Oliver...

...a fact not lost on Nanao, who was sitting right next to her.

"Oliver!" she announced. "Katie desires a celebratory hug."

"Uh, Nanao?!" Katie yelped.

"Oh, my apologies. I should have known."

As bidden, he rose from his chair. Nanao grabbed Katie's hand and pulled her off the couch. The curly-haired girl let out a squeal, but the free-hug rule they'd implemented last year applied here, and she soon found herself in Oliver's arms.

"Hwahhh..."

The moment she felt that squeeze, Katie went docile. Then Nanao pounced on her back. Behind the couch, Chela had caught Pete and was doing the same thing to him.

"You no longer hesitate to express your affection," Miligan said, beaming. "Heh-heh...will any of it spill over to me? I'm wide open!"

She spread her arms, but Katie and Chela shot daggers at her. The Snake-Eyed Witch quickly put her hands down and changed the subject.

"A pity about Nanao. You were one match from a prize in the broom fight league."

"'Tis a pity indeed. I did what I could, but the upper forms are formidable."

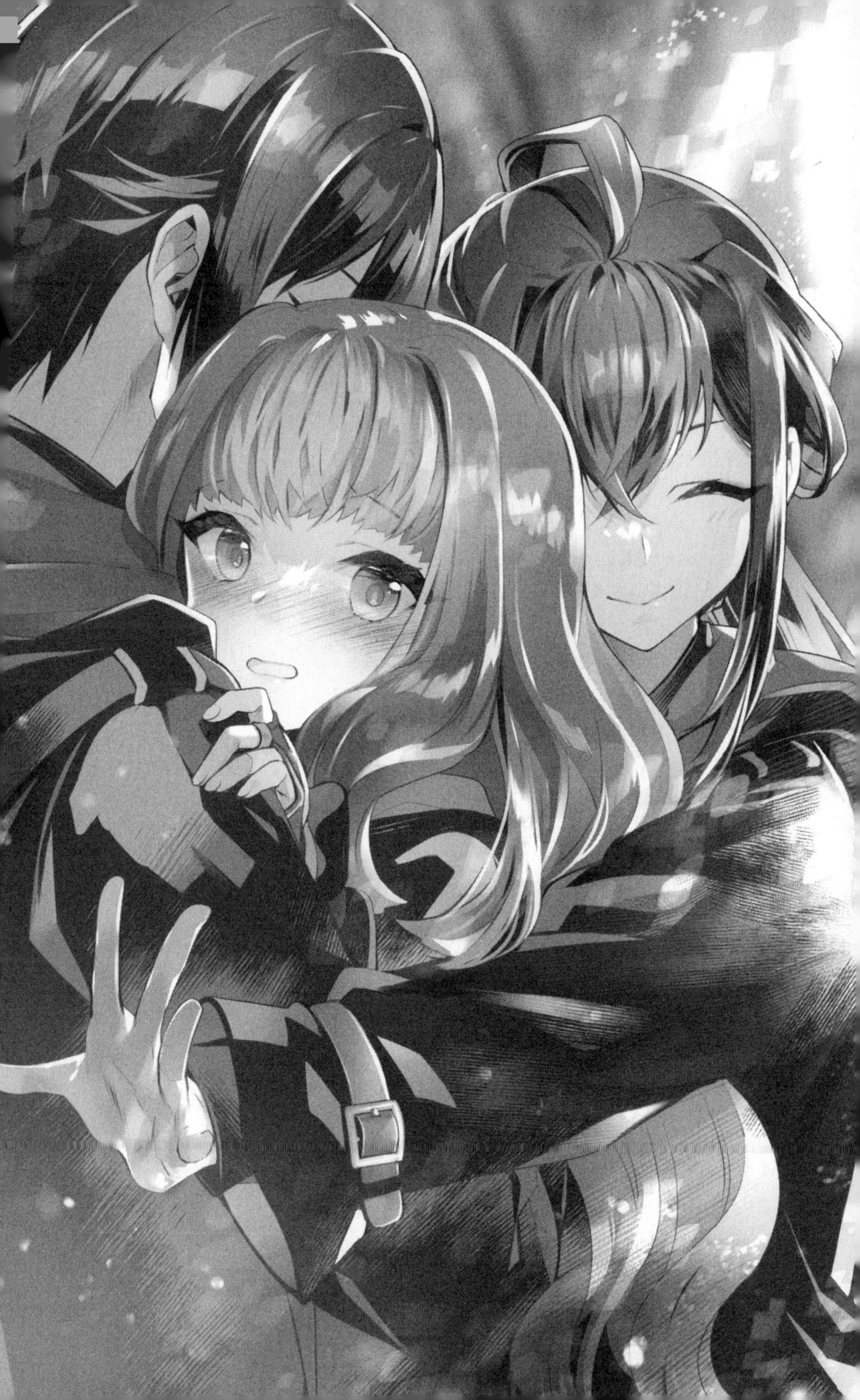

"Don't be like that, Nanao," Oliver said. "The bounty was unprecedented, and Ms. Ashbury's exploits left everyone feeling competitive. The gaps in your experience and technical skills were considerable, but you hung on for as long as you could."

Oliver's hands had slipped forward to embrace her *and* Katie.

"Well put!" Miligan added. "And from my perspective, you did *exactly* what I needed."

"You mean when she downed Mr. Whalley?" Chela purred darkly.

The Snake-Eyed Witch grinned.

"Our position is less than desirable, if I'm being honest."

Elsewhere on the first layer, in the base of the previous student council, Gino Beltrami (aka Barman) was reporting on the current election standings. His voice was calm and collected.

Leoncio listened quietly.

"As it stands, no one candidate has managed a clear advantage. Which means the swing votes remain impossible to predict. We're in a deadlock."

"…What do you say to that, Percy?" Leoncio asked.

"……!"

Percival Whalley, candidate for the next student body president, could only gulp. He was kneeling by the side of Leoncio's chair, the man's pale fingers lightly brushing his neck. There was pleasure in it, mingled with fear—should the man be so inclined, he could easily snap Whalley's neck.

"Ha-ha! Don't torment the boy, Leo," the seventh-year elf Khiirgi Albschuch said. "I sparred with her myself; the girl is not one easily measured. *And* she's the type who blooms in the thick of things. Meanwhile, Percy's the type who wins by margins; he's doomed to struggle with her ilk."

Whalley was incensed, and he glared at her. Had she done more in the past, he wouldn't have needed an assist here. The source of his frustration was obvious to all—Khiirgi's whims had disrupted his plans far more than their enemies had.

"That said, she is a foe you *could* have beaten. Your experience and broomsport skills should have given you the advantage, Percy."

"Fair enough. Percy's final standings were higher than hers, enough to claim a prize. I know it's all hindsight, but what led to your downfall was an abundance of caution, the knowledge that you could not afford to lose."

Gino was trying to be helpful, but this made Leoncio frown.

"So I am to blame for placing that pressure on him," Leoncio muttered. "Hmph."

"...Ah...!"

His fingers left Whalley's neck. The boy glanced up, tentative, searching his mentor's face for answers, and Leoncio addressed him head-on.

"I have no intention of replacing you. Win the next one, Percy."

"...Yes, sir."

As Miligan gave them the rundown, Guy brought out one of his pound cakes—a confectionary avidly sought after across campus. They washed that down with tea, and when their cups were empty:

"And that's where we stand. No one has a clear advantage, but that means my candidacy continues to serve its purpose."

With that summation, Miligan scooped up the last bite of cake, looking sorry to see it go. Her familiar, Milihand, was walking around the table, collecting dishes.

After due consideration, Chela said, "Then the final surge will be decided by...the combat league?"

"I'm afraid so. If we're matched elsewhere, then the greatest show of strength will win. That's how Kimberly works."

"So if you clean up, you've got it in the bag!"

"It's not that easy, Guy," Miligan said, pursing her lips. She was good, but hardly the best in the upper forms.

Well aware of that, Chela suggested a more achievable goal.

"The grand prize may be out of reach, but a finish in the money after defeating Mr. Whalley's team…that's probably your best bet. How do you like your odds?"

"One-on-one versus Whalley, our odds are dead even. But Kimberly changes the combat league rules regularly. There's no guarantee it'll be that simple this year. And they've upped the prize considerably—so honestly, I'm not sure what the faculty has planned."

"Are we in agreement, then? We can call this plan final?"

A meeting room on the first floor of the main building. Theodore had passed out a proposed set of combat league rules with the utmost confidence. Several other instructors were reading it over.

"…It sure is elaborate," Ted Williams said, finishing it up. He was the alchemy instructor.

"I simply thought it should be worth the fifty-million-belc prize," Theodore proclaimed. "It's hardly festive if the event itself is nothing to write home about."

"But getting the lower forms mixed up in this… Instructor Garland, your thoughts?"

Ted turned to the sword arts instructor, looking for an assist. Garland paused before answering…but his smile failed to conceal his enthusiasm.

"…It'll be a league for the ages."

"I knew you would agree!" Theodore beamed.

Ted abandoned his feeble resistance. If Garland was into this plan, there was no use arguing it further.

With everyone on the same page, the faculty's collective gaze turned to the head of the table. And the headmistress dropped her decree:

"Very well. Announce the rules to the students first thing tomorrow and begin preparations."

*   *   *

The next morning found the Campus Watch Headquarters positively crackling with tension.

"...I don't like it," Lesedi Ingwe muttered, pacing the room. A dark-skinned seventh-year, she was one of Godfrey's closest companions. She, Godfrey, Tim, and the rest of the Watch had all seen the combat league rules posted on their arrival that morning and made a beeline for their HQ.

"An unprecedented rule set," Lesedi added. "Victory requires strategies beyond your own year. What exactly is the faculty plotting?"

The same thoughts were on every mind.

"The scale is as immense as it is complex," Godfrey said. "But that doesn't work against *us*."

He'd put all other concerns aside, always inclined to find the simplest solution—specifically, what did he want to do, and how could he do it?

"There's no need to involve the lower forms. We just have to get out there and win. Nothing more, nothing less."

"These rules sure are a *snarl*."

At the same time, in the Fellowship, the Sword Roses had gathered to discuss the same topic. The papers had put out extra issues covering all the rules, and once their bellies were full, each started reading over the complete details.

"First off, there's three divisions," Pete explained. "Lower forms are limited to second- and third-years, while the upper forms are split into a fourth-and-fifth-year group and a sixth-and-seventh-year one. Participation requires forming a team of three within your division. The league itself is a prelim, a main round, and a clincher. The prelim is a group event in which everyone participates, the main round is a free-for-all with multiple teams involved—and the format of the clincher has yet to be announced. Freshmen can't participate, but anyone else can."

Oliver took over here, stroking his chin.

"And in each division, the older teams' advantage is offset by a significant handicap. In the lower league, any team with two or more second-years is given a proportional advantage. There's a lot of specifics still unannounced, but the existence of teams and the merger of two school years both seem significant."

It might matter less in the upper forms, but the gulf between the second and third year was huge. It was only natural to give the older students a handicap if they were in the same division. The team angle was much thornier—far more intel to process than a one-on-one fight and that much harder to predict the outcome.

"The money and prizes will be paid out to each division in full. Which means even we have a shot!" Guy said.

"Or rather, anyone does," Chela mumbled. "This is no longer something one enters for *fun*. These rules will motivate students who normally sit the league out—and that's likely what the faculty *wants*."

She turned toward two of her friends, looking crestfallen.

"This pains me more than you can know, but I should be up-front about it. Oliver, Nanao, I'm unable to form a team with you this time."

"Mm? Whyever not?" Nanao asked, blinking at her.

Oliver folded his arms, surmising the reason. "Ah. Theodore's involved in the league management. Is he behind these extra rules?"

"Precisely." Chela sighed. "Nearly all of them are my father's proposals. Which places me in an awkward position. He has not gone so far as to ban me from participating, but it would be ill-advised for me to join with anyone in the upper echelons of our year—with anyone likely to win. It would be difficult to shake the impression of a rigged contest if my team made it to the podium."

There was a moment's silence; then Katie looked up.

"Guy, Pete—wanna team up with me?"

Surprise showed on all five of her companions' faces. Pete and Guy gave her a searching look.

"Heh…going for that fifty mil?" Guy asked.

"I don't think I'll get it. But not even trying would feel…wrong."

"I'm shocked. I thought you hated violence."

"I do! But…that doesn't make it avoidable. Not here."

Katie sounded sure of herself, and Chela quickly connected the dots.

"Ah!" she said. "You specifically want to team up with them. Not me, not Nanao or Oliver."

"Right," Katie replied. "If I team with any of you—I'll just…*rely* on you. This has to be on our terms, our strength."

The prizes were a secondary concern. She wanted to test what she'd gained over the last two years, and the determination in her eyes had Pete convinced.

"I was thinking the same thing," he said. "Didn't expect you to suggest it first."

"You're *both* fired up! Well, if you put it like that, no way I can bow out."

With Pete and Guy equally eager, one team was already formed. Oliver decided he couldn't just sit still. He had to determine his stance on this league and, if he was entering, find a team. But as he mulled it over, someone outside their table spoke up.

"Michela, a moment?"

All six friends turned and saw a girl with her manservant. Chela immediately averted her gaze in embarrassment.

"Oh, Stacy? How can I help you?" she asked.

"Go on, Stace," Fay prompted.

"…I was wondering if you've finalized your combat league plans. If you have, then never mind."

Stacy spoke in barely a whisper, and she was fidgeting with the hem of her robe. Oliver hid his smile. It was all too obvious what she wanted.

"Go with them, Chela," Nanao said before Chela herself could answer. The others nodded, and that got her to her feet.

Chela, Stacy, and Fay left for another table. Guy began nodding.

"…Ohhh. If you're as good as Chela, people'll start trying to recruit ya."

"Yes," Oliver replied. "The fights begin with team selection. And Chela has always had a connection to Ms. Cornwallis. If she's not with us, she'll likely team up with them."

Even as he spoke, he made up his mind. His eyes turned to the Azian girl beside him.

"Nanao, if you intend to join the league, I'd like to team up with you. I won't press the point…but I'd very much like you to agree."

"But of course."

Nanao didn't even hesitate. Relieved as he was, Oliver nonetheless felt a pang in his chest. If they were on the *same* team, then they wouldn't have to fight *each other*. That above all was why he'd moved to recruit her. This condition mattered far more to him than the outcome of the league itself.

"Oh-ho! Then you'll be needing a third!"

Someone else outside of their table spoke up. It was the usual suspect, so no one was surprised. Oliver and Nanao turned to face him: last year's transfer student, smiling brightly.

"A fine morning to you, Yuri," Nanao said.

"…Leik, will nothing correct this habit? Are you compelled to barge into *every* conversation?"

Well aware this was a waste of time, Oliver said it anyway—and Yuri just clapped a hand on his shoulder. In his other hand, he had a paper with the league rules.

"I got back from the labyrinth, and all kinds of fun broke out!" he said, grinning. "This place never lets you get bored."

"You're thinking of entering?"

"You betcha. I love anything festive! Things like this bring you in contact with so many people and so many mysteries."

He looked proud of himself. It was very Yuri to care nothing for the money or prizes and everything about the people he met along the way. Oliver couldn't stop himself from smiling. He rather envied that outlook on life.

"I can't promise we'll join forces with you—but it's certainly true we'll need to find a third teammate."

He took Nanao's hand, glanced at the other three Sword Roses, and got up to leave. Yuri said not a word but clearly intended to follow.

"Let's go scout," said Oliver. "I want to know what other teams are forming."

To no one's surprise, Nanao and Oliver were hit with a flurry of solicitations the moment they stepped away from their table.

"Ms. Hibiya! Wanna join us for the league?!"

"Mr. Horn, be our ace! …No? No matter what?!"

Oliver was turning people down left and right, and when they didn't give up, he was forced to push his way past. Watching this go down, Yuri whistled.

"You two are in *hot* demand! I wonder why no one's asking me?"

"For starters, no one knows how good you are. Otherwise…well, you'll have to take a good look at yourself."

They made a circuit of the room, parrying invites while seeking out the best in their year. Along the way, a question came to mind.

"What have you been up to anyway?" Oliver asked. "Still wandering the labyrinth and campus willy-nilly?"

"Well, sure, but I've got real goals now! I've found two mysteries worth probing."

"Mysteries?" Nanao asked.

"Yep. The Case of the Missing Teachers and the Case of the Stolen Bones."

Yuri had a finger raised high and was not lowering his voice at all. Clearly not caring who heard him.

"You're looking into the teacher thing on your own?" Oliver asked, glaring. "That could get you killed. Even the Watch is staying out of that one."

He was being deliberately harsh, trying to get through—and it at least made Yuri stop goofing around and straighten up.

"Yeah, I'm aware," he admitted. "But…I'm sure you both have things you won't budge on, won't ever back down on, no matter what anyone else says. In my case, that's solving mysteries. I don't know why that is myself—but I'm driven to do it. By the blood flowing in my veins, by the nature of my very soul."

He was getting downright *deep* there, and Oliver could hardly argue. People didn't easily change the way they lived. Especially not a mage.

"But just to be clear, I'm not interested in taking out the culprit or making sure they get punished. No interest in that whatsoever. I just wanna know who, why, and how. Or maybe where it's all going. That knowledge is everything, and I have to probe further."

"You clearly won't be dissuaded. But what's this stolen bones thing—?"

"Oh, there they are! Mr. Horn and Ms. Hibiya," a curt voice cut in.

They turned to look—and found a female upperclassman, on the short side. None of them recognized her. Despite their befuddlement, she came right over.

"Lend me your ears a sec. It's important."

"Um…who are you?"

"Huh? Whatcha talking about? It's me—we've met several times, yeah?"

Oliver's bewilderment grew. The uniform had so many added frills; essentially no trace of the original garment remained. No one this distinctive could possibly have slipped his memory. Had she looked dramatically different when they first met? With that thought, he focused his gaze on her face. Even then it took several seconds—but the gleam in the eyes behind those long lashes rang a bell.

"Mr. Linton? From Godfrey's crew?"

"Obviously! Damn, you look like you just saw a ghost or something. Or wait—is this the first time you've seen me like this?"

Oliver nodded several times. Tim hadn't changed *how* he spoke at all, but the outfit and voice were totally different—everything was screaming *girl*. Even a shape-shifter couldn't change this dramatically overnight. Seeing Oliver gape, Tim pursed his pink lips and shrugged.

"…Well, my bad, then. For reference, I do drag when I feel like it, which is often enough. And I'm cute, right?"

Tim blew him a kiss. The gesture itself was bewitching, and the knowledge that this was *the* Toxic Gasser made Oliver feel downright dizzy.

"G-got it," Oliver said, aware that letting any of this show might just infuriate Tim. "So, uh…what brings you here?"

"Combat league stuff. Wanna check if you're in, who you're with—so spit it out! I mean, answering's voluntary, but don't opt out; it's a headache."

There were a lot of contradictions in that statement, but it would all be public knowledge the moment they registered, and there was no point in keeping their participation a secret from the Watch in the first place.

"…All I know right now is that Nanao and I are in," Oliver said. "We're considering our options for a third teammate."

"Cool. Lemme know as soon as you choose someone, and I mean the instant you decide. Voluntarily!"

That last word was clearly an afterthought. Then Tim grabbed Oliver's collar and pulled him in close. Oliver blinked at him.

"Word to the wise—just talking to myself here—the outcome of this combat league could have major sway on the election. But the faculty has gone and jacked up some rules the likes of which we ain't ever seen. No clue what's coming at us. You catch my drift?"

"…Yeah."

"If you're in, play to win. And don't screw up your third pick. All voluntary, of course!"

With that, Tim slapped him hard on the shoulder and stepped back. Since Oliver had told him where Nanao stood, Tim turned his gaze to Yuri.

"Mr. Leik, our transfer student. Who're you backing in the election?"

"I'm undecided. Gonna keep a close eye on what everyone does and vote for whoever dazzles me most!"

"…Right. Well, figure it out sooner rather than later."

He didn't seem that interested, and he didn't press the point. Tim turned and stalked away.

Watching him vanish into the crowd, Nanao murmured, "He seemed rather out of sorts."

"The lower league outcome stands to drive a great deal of votes one way or the other. Since Miligan and the Watch are in cahoots, and we're backing her, we're seen as being in their corner. We're part of this whether we like it or not."

Oliver nodded to himself. Tim's demeanor made it clear these new rules had rattled the Watch, which meant Oliver would have to confer with his cousins soon. He scanned the room once more.

"I'm curious what Godfrey's thinking. And what the other standouts in our year are—"

"Ah, were you looking for me?" a cheery voice interjected.

Oliver turned, looking through the crowds—and saw a tall boy with a friendly smile.

"Rossi," he said. "Yeah, I was curious about you, too."

"Bwa-ha-ha! Honored to be counted among the standouts. But seeing 'im with you, far less pleasing."

His voice dropped to a growl, and he glared at Yuri. Oliver was reminded that these two got along like oil and water.

He smoothly stepped between them. "I know you can't resist joining something like this," he told Rossi. "I'm with Nanao. What are your plans?"

"Hmm…so your third is yet unknown, eh? The idea of joining you does sound tempting."

"Betraying us already? You've got a lotta nerve."

A low growl echoed behind Rossi, and a large hand snagged his collar. He was hoisted onto his tiptoes, but that only made the Ytallian stick out his tongue.

"I jest, of course," he said with a grin. "Spare me the scowls, eh?"

Oliver's eyes locked on the intimidating form behind him.

"Mr. Albright—you're teaming up with Rossi?"

"Our options were limited. If we plan to *win*, that is."

His free hand was hoisting Rossi still higher, and the Ytallian's feet left the ground, swaying in the air.

"I would enjoy fighting by your side," Rossi told Oliver, "but that means I 'ave no chance of defeating *you*. I aim to settle things this time—no flukes or off days to excuse it."

"Yeah, I'm not counting that last time, either. And I'm happy to oblige."

Oliver nodded, accepting the challenge. But then he frowned. If the two of them were teaming up, how would that affect the election?

"…Not to change the subject, but how are you two voting?"

"I am apolitical, so I 'ave nothing to say. You?"

"Wish I had a choice." The big man shrugged. "But I'm the eldest Albright."

That told Oliver everything. Family connections and political positions could limit your options, even in a school election, regardless of personal feelings. If the heir to a major Gnostic Hunter clan voted for a demi-rights candidate, that alone could pour fuel on the fire. That meant Albright was forced to vote conservative—for one of the previous student council candidates.

At the same time, Oliver knew—in the first year, before he and Nanao had crossed wands, this boy would never have expressed dissatisfaction with those obligations, and certainly not made light of it. He nodded, rather touched.

"Yeah, sorry. I should have known."

"No worries. It's a trivial matter compared to our rematch. Right, leader?"

Grinning, Albright gazed over his shoulder. A new boy had joined them, and Oliver had to think fast

The long-haired boy was in their year, and his every gesture reflected good breeding. He'd fought Oliver far before the other two—on the first day of sword arts class. And they hadn't faced each other in some time.

"Mr. Andrews. You're their third member?"

"I am. I knew if it was a team match, I'd be asking these two to join me. For one purpose only—to defeat you two, Mr. Horn, Ms. Hibiya."

Richard Andrews was already issuing ultimatums. He had history with the pair—but then he spotted Yuri gaping at all this from the sidelines and frowned.

"…I assumed Michela would be your third. Not that you need to explain—"

"No, we haven't decided yet. I'm not hiding anything, just still considering our options, honestly."

Oliver left out Chela's issues, sticking to their perspective. He knew Andrews wasn't trying to pry; Andrews was simply hoping that Oliver and Nanao would be coming into this fight in peak condition. Two years had been enough to get the measure of this man.

Andrews nodded. Nanao had been watching intently by Oliver's side, but now she smiled.

"The fires are lit within you, Mr. Andrews. This battle will no doubt be a delight."

"If it looks that way to you, I can rest assured."

Andrews flashed a smile, then turned to leave. Rossi and Albright followed. Each knew well their own strength, and together, they had all the bearings of a powerhouse team.

"We'll face each other in the league somewhere," Andrews said. "Pick your third in light of that or live to regret it."

"Whoa, that means even *we* can jump in this league thing."

Throughout the Fellowship, it wasn't just third-years kicking up a fuss. Dean was reading over the newspaper's extra edition.

"Given how worked up the older students are, these rules are unorthodox," Peter Cornish said. Like Dean, he was a second-year student. "Dean, you seriously want to enter?"

"Hell yeah. I mean, we're at Kimberly; we *gotta* rack up some experience."

"I don't think Ms. Aalto would join your team," Rita muttered.

That made Dean do a spit take.

"*Cough, cough...* Wh-where'd that come from, Rita?!"

"Oh, uh, sorry. I just figured if she was in this, she'd be with Mr. Horn, Ms. Hibiya, or Guy."

This attempt at explaining herself just made Peter wince. He used a spell to clean the tea off the table.

"Just admit it," he said. "Everyone knows you've got a crush on Ms. Aalto, Dean."

"I do not! I—I just respect her! A lot!"

"True, I still can't believe she tamed that griffin in, like, six months. And that makes it even harder for you to get anywhere near her!"

"Stop making it weird! She helped me out a ton last year. Kept me safe and all that. And I wanna show how I've grown."

"...Yeah, *that* I get," Rita mumbled, picturing Guy's unguarded smile. She'd lost track of how many times he'd helped her out last year. Not to use a gardening metaphor, but she wanted to show all that watering had made her grow—that was a natural urge from any mentee.

She thought it over a minute, then smiled at Dean.

"Let's enter together, Dean. I feel like showing off a bit, myself."

"That's what I'm talkin' about, Rita!"

He threw up his hand, beaming, and Rita gave him a high five. Peter folded his arms, grunting.

"I wish I could join you, but fights just aren't my thing. I'd prefer to help you plan. If you just had another member..."

He glanced across the table to the friend who'd yet to say a word. Teresa was using a knife to cut some syrup-laden pancakes.

"...What?" she said, glaring back at him.

"Whaddaya mean, *'what'*?"

"Dean, don't start anything." Rita sighed. "Teresa, don't *you* have anyone to impress? This is your chance to show them what you can do."

Teresa's knife paused. It hadn't taken long for one face in particular to cross her mind.

*   *   *

Like the broomsports league before it, the combat league results would have a significant impact on the election. With that in mind, Oliver visited his cousins' workshop the evening after the rules were posted.

"We've got to ensure Godfrey's side wins. But if our actions are too coordinated, the faculty will be on to us."

Gwyn was standing by a cage in the corner, feeding the familiars inside. The election's balance hung by a thread—perhaps that was why his expression betrayed a rare glimpse of fatigue.

"It's a thorny field, but it's our job to plot our way between those two concerns. You're free to team with whoever you like and win your division fair and square. Or even stay out of the thing entirely. Just make your choice soon—it'll affect our approach."

"...I'm planning to enter," said Oliver. "It makes sense for me to wade on in, all self-assured. There's just a big difference between *winning fair and square* and *winning by any means necessary*. Are you sure the former will be enough?"

"Just give it your best shot—like an ordinary third-year would. We'll be moving behind the scenes, but you don't need to concern yourself with that here."

Oliver nodded. Act as a student, gunning for league victory—that alone would help Godfrey's side. That was the most natural course of action for him now.

Then came a nearby girl's voice:

"...What should I do?"

Oliver turned to look and found Teresa kneeling beside him. The rules allowed for her participation, so he gave the matter some thought.

"Why not invite your friends and join in?" he suggested. "The way the rules are written, teams will likely align along school years. My team will be all third-years, so there's no need to worry about backing us up."

With that, he glanced over at his cousin. Gwyn had finished feeding the familiars and was drying his hands.

"That work for you, Brother?" Oliver asked. "Teresa still hasn't exactly fit in at Kimberly. Proactively joining the league would probably help her mingle better."

"As you wish," Teresa said, not waiting for Gwyn's answer. She was trying to settle things before any objections could be raised.

Gwyn raised an eyebrow at her, then sighed.

"If you think it'll help, go for it. But, Noll, be extra careful in the labyrinth. You've already had people coming after Ms. Hibiya, but this time they'll be after *you*."

Oliver nodded, taking that to heart. He, Nanao, and Yuri had barely staved off that one ambush, saved only by the intervention of the late Clifton Morgan. The man's breathy laugh still echoed in his ears.

"For the duration, I'll ensure upper-form comrades are on the same layer as you whenever you're delving. Let me or Shannon know before you head in."

"Will do. Let's start that tonight."

Oliver stood up and took a step toward the exit—and someone tugged his sleeve. Shannon had been quietly sorting through magic tools in the corner, but now she was smiling up at him.

"...Sis?"

"I can join you. Partway. Teresa too."

She spoke as if they were out for a walk. But this was an offer Oliver had no means of turning down.

The second layer was ideal for an evening stroll. Lush green forests, open skies above, and a false sun burning in it. The more time he spent down here, the more Oliver came to realize that this layer served as a surrogate surface for upperclassmen too buried in their research to ever swing by the campus proper.

These thoughts ran through Oliver's mind as he walked with Shannon.

Teresa came running over. She was not in hiding today.

"Pepper weed," she said, holding up some grass she'd plucked from the ground nearby. "Can be boiled down to a good insect repellent. Eaten as is, it's extremely spicy."

"You know...a lot, Teresa. Good girl."

Shannon patted her on the head, and Teresa went darting off again. She roamed at a distance for a bit, but a minute later, she came running back to them. This time, she had a translucent caterpillar pinned between her fingers.

"A bleary moth larva. Edible, but the flavor is extremely unpleasant."

"...You've tried one?" Oliver asked.

"Yes. It turned my mouth purple, and it was some time before I could taste anything at all."

"Wow... Good to know."

"Would you like to sample it?"

"Maybe some other time."

Teresa tossed the caterpillar aside and dashed away again. She spent so much of her time concealed, not even allowing her breath to be detected—so Oliver wasn't quite sure what to make of this side of her.

"...Is she...excited?" he asked.

"Hee-hee. Adorable. Noll...when she's with you...she's always trying to impress."

Oh, Oliver thought. Excited she might be, but this was likely closer to the *real* Teresa, her usual reticence merely a by-product of her covert duties. The behavior she exhibited when those duties weren't required showed her true nature.

Catching the look in his eye, Shannon whispered, "Don't worry. Since she started classes...she's having fun. She does...talk about her friends. Often."

That was some small solace. He managed a nod.

Her little brother started walking again, and Shannon softly asked, "How are you...physically?"

"Completely back to normal. Movement feels natural—even better than before."

"...Oh."

"So you don't need to worry—"

"I do, though," she said, speaking over him.

Her head was down, and Oliver swallowed, halting his advance.

"I know…how much pain…it caused," Shannon said. "Not…all of it, perhaps. But…I was there."

"Sis…"

Unsure what else to say, he let her cup his cheek. Her eyes glistened, staring up at him. Her voice shook.

"I will never…stop worrying…about you, Noll."

Her tears wouldn't stop, and Oliver had no words to console her. Teresa was dancing from one foot to the other, unsure what to do or say—but then they sensed someone else approaching, and she did what covert ops do. As she vanished into the brush, Oliver pulled away from his cousin.

"Hmm?"

They turned to find a boy pushing his way out of the brush. Eyes gleaming with curiosity, he looked from Oliver to Shannon and back again.

"A new face!" he said. "I'm Yuri Leik. Rare to see you in different circles, Oliver."

"Hello. Shannon Sherwood. Seventh-year. You're…Noll's friend?"

She managed a forlorn smile. This brought an end to her dialogue with Oliver. For once, he welcomed Yuri's interruption, and he almost fled in his direction.

"…You're headed to the layer below, Leik? I'll join you."

Without waiting for an answer, Oliver headed deeper in. Yuri bobbed his head to Shannon and followed. She stood where she was long after they'd vanished from view, her eyes fastened on the spot where she'd lost track of her cousin.

Passing through the woods, Yuri spoke up.

"Sorry, I kinda barged in back there."

That was certainly a commendable gesture, but it earned him a frown.

"Since when have you ever not?" Oliver asked. "Why apologize this time?"

"Ha-ha, you got me there. But it's rare I see anyone looking that sad."

He must've been referring to Shannon's smile. Oliver's pace slowed, like he was carrying a lead weight. He felt an urge to turn and run back to her...and managed to trample that down.

"Something I didn't get the chance to ask about this morning—you mentioned you were investigating *two* cases. What's the Case of the Missing Bones?" he asked Yuri.

"Oh, right! Um, it's kind of a long story. Still interested?"

Oliver nodded and found a fallen tree to rest on.

"To be clear, this is just the name I've given it," Yuri began. "Pretty sure I'm the only person who's realized it's a mystery at all."

"? Only you know about it, then?"

"Mm, not quite. Everyone's heard about the events in question— they just don't think of it as a 'case.'"

These phrases were bewildering Oliver, so Yuri pressed on.

"And we know *who* did it: a seventh-year named Cyrus Rivermoore."

"——?!"

"You've met him? Sweet. I still haven't had the pleasure."

Yuri's eyes gleamed, but Oliver's expression clouded.

"...A few times, under less than auspicious circumstances. I'm sure you're aware, but he's a mage specializing in advance compound sorcery using bones as a conduit. Even in Kimberly, he's one of the biggest threats around."

"Yep! They call him the Scavenger. Anyway, Rivermoore's known for popping out and assaulting students in the labyrinth, right? I happened to find one of his victims right after the fact. A fifth-year named Pamela."

"Ms. Gorton? The Labyrinth Seller? I shop with her pretty frequently."

"Right? Her stall's often open on the first layer. Real handy when you just need to stock up quickly."

But as Yuri spoke, the implications were starting to sink in. Pamela Gorton provided a valuable service. She was someone you *wanted* to keep around. So why would Rivermoore go after her?

"You know the cave between the second and third layers? I found her lying there. I took care of her, listened to her story, and found out Rivermoore was behind it," Yuri said. "I only gave her a quick glance over—but one of her bones was missing. The second lumbar vertebra. And he'd nicely replaced it with a temporary synthetic bone. After a bit of rest, she was able to walk and made it back up to campus, but she was definitely not in great shape. Obviously, since the spine plays a major role in mana circulation."

"...He stole a bone."

Oliver folded his arms, thinking.

"So I got curious and hit the books," Yuri continued. "Pamela wasn't the only one. For the past three years, Rivermoore's hit up any number of students—and they all lost a bone. They were out of sorts for a bit, but proper treatment made them right as rain again. So the bulk of the students affected never even reported it to the Watch."

"...Then how'd you find out? About the unrecorded victims?"

"Nothing particularly outlandish. I just took a look over the Watch's records of labyrinth incidents and used that info to contact the victims and ask a few questions. I bet you've read through those records yourself."

Oliver nodded. That made sense, and he *had* made use of them on several occasions. Godfrey's long-term goal was the reduction of such incidents, so he would happily show the log to anyone who asked. The school papers regularly used those very records as the basis for articles about common labyrinth problems.

"Rivermoore's magic uses bones as a conduit, right? Everyone *knows* that, so nobody questions why he'd be going around stealing people's bones. They all just assume it'll be part of some ritual. But that didn't feel right to me."

Yuri was talking faster and faster. He pulled a notebook out of his robe—likely his notes on the investigation. Every page was filled to the margins. He flipped to one of them and showed it to Oliver.

"Look at this! Between the Watch's records and my personal inquiries, I wrote up this list of the bones Rivermoore has taken. Sixty-two in all! Likely not a full list—probably any number of incidents that never got out at all. But—"

Oliver's eyes ran down the list. Ribs, clavicles, radii, ulnae, tibiae, patellae—as he skimmed, a realization set in.

"You mean...?"

"Fascinating, right? Not a single overlap. There's, like, two hundred bones in the human body, and if you're grabbing sixty-plus at random, you're gonna get the same one eventually. If that hasn't happened, that makes it very likely Rivermoore is intentionally avoiding duplicate bones."

Yuri was grinning, but this was all leading Oliver to a sinister speculation.

"...He's gathering a complete human skeleton?"

"That's what *I* thought!" Yuri snapped his notes closed, his eyes brimming with curiosity. "That's the mystery I'm chasing. Why gather bones from students? What for? I just have to find out!"

"...Sounds like I can't talk you out of it. What's next on the agenda?"

"Good question. I've got data, and I formed a hypothesis—next up is dropping it on the man himself. The data say the bulk of Scavenger encounters are on the third layer and below, so I figure if I wander around down there, I'll meet him *eventually.*"

"And you fully understand the implications of that, right? You're trying to pry into the beating heart of that man's spell. And this is the Scavenger—running at him is tantamount to suicide."

Oliver was intentionally being harsh, but Yuri's face just lit up.

"You're actually worried about me? Awesome!"

"Don't act delighted! This is a perfectly standard response to your reckless behavior!"

His voice was getting a bit loud. Yet he knew all too well—mere words would never stop this boy. Yuri had already figured out what kind of mage he was. And the fear of death would never stop someone who had learned that about themselves.

Was there a way to prevent Yuri's suicide in light of that? Oliver fell silent, pondering the question. Eventually, he offered a suggestion.

"…You seemed interested in the combat league."

"Mm?"

"Peppering Rivermoore with questions within the labyrinth will just get you killed. But if you do the same thing on the surface…it's far less risky."

Yuri snapped his fingers. "Aha!" he said. "You figure Rivermoore's gonna join in?"

"I can't be sure of it. But given the insane money and prizes at stake, the odds are good. And it clearly allows for a more planned approach than your random labyrinth wanderings. Most importantly—if there are eyes on you, it's easier to stay alive."

A real shot, without the need to delve deeper. And Yuri was starting to nod.

"Achieve my purpose under cover of the festivities! I like it. But if that's the case, I'll have to join in the league myself." Then he exclaimed, "Oh no! Whatever shall I do? I have no teammates! Pray, do you know of two kindly people in my year who would be willing to join forces with me? True friends I can rely upon?!"

He ramped up the theatrics and kept shooting Oliver meaningful glances.

Oliver heaved the largest sigh he could muster—this was very much how he'd feared things would go.

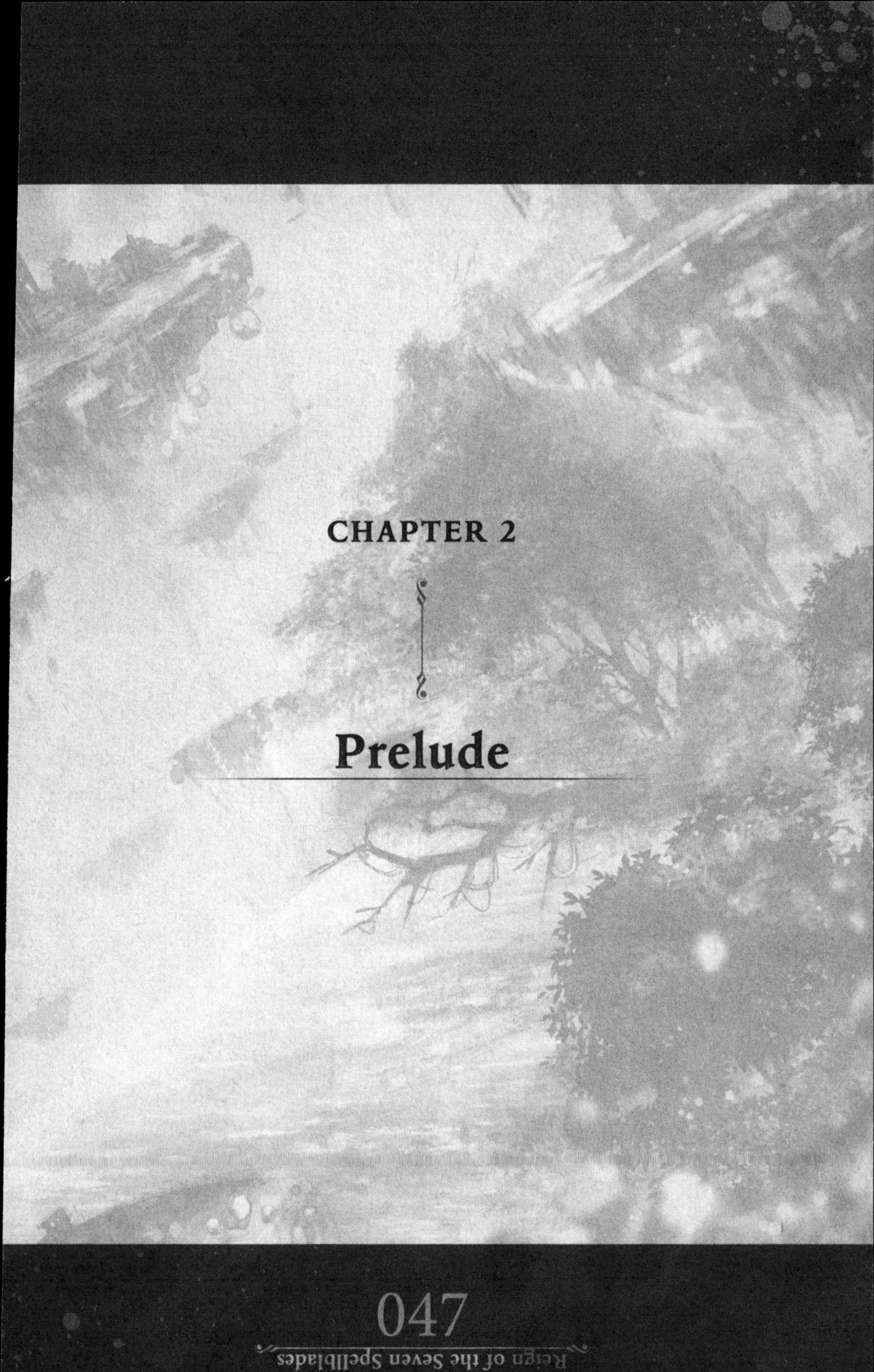

CHAPTER 2

Prelude

The combat league was a major attraction to begin with…and this time it took place right before an election, and the faculty had upped the money and prizes involved. The student body was positively foaming at the mouth.

The classrooms were converted to viewing chambers, with large projection crystals mounted in them, broadcasting in real time everything seen by the surveillance golems placed throughout the grounds. The lower-form prelim used the campus itself as the stage. In the halls outside the classrooms were long tables laden with snacks, and the audience could help themselves to food and drinks and freely roam the different viewing classrooms.

"Huh?! What's your problem?"

"You want some?!"

Fights were breaking out before the prelim even began. Watch members were stepping in if things got out of hand, but this was typical Kimberly pandemonium—fights themselves were tolerated as long as they *didn't* cross that line. Most students could heal their own wounds, so the school physician got called in only if someone seemed likely to die.

"Oh…my…myyy…"

The announcer's booth was in a third-floor lecture hall. Master Garland, the sword arts instructor, was seated with a female student who looked positively enraptured. The prelim was due to start at any moment, and the heat in the room was rising. Those taking part were falling into a tense silence. The air on everyone's skin crackled—this was gonna be *intense*.

"Aaah…be still. Stop the chatter; stop the brawling. Savor this hush."

She was starting off slow. Like Roger Forster with broomsports, Glenda Saunders was a combat fanatic, one of the best commentators the student body had. Her opening speech echoed over the passionate crowds and throughout the school building.

"Kimberly mages, do you like fighting? I *love* it. I love it more than three meals a day, more than waking up before dawn and going back to bed, more than the cherry pie my mama used to make. I love seeing mages throwing down more than anything else in the world. Oh, you know I fight, myself. I fought yesterday and this morning, and if I'm being honest—five minutes ago. But sadly, there is but one of me, and that is not *nearly* enough.

"So please. Lend me your bodies! Like a fish stuffed in a pot of salt, let the fights permeate me morning, noon, and night. In return, I shall *regale*. The exploits of the fighters, their exertions, their schemes, their cunning, their failures, their oversights, their blunders—and the infinite victories and losses that result from them. I shall talk you through it all even if I have to chew off my own tongue to do so! I can always heal it back into place, and I likely won't notice it's gone." She paused. "You know what this means. Even as I speak—the combat league is about to begiiiiiiin!"

With that, a cheer went up across the campus. The crystals in each classroom projected an image of the prelim start line with all the entrants stepping up to it. Glenda and Garland got right down to business.

"Okay, okay, okay! The second-years are off and running! They're trying to find the treasures hidden around the campus grounds. No longer freshmen, can these kids make the most of the ten minutes before the third-years join them?"

"Doing that requires the knowledge base and critical-thinking skills necessary to accurately interpret the clues provided," said Garland. "Students who thought the combat league was *all* about fighting will struggle here. Do they have a puzzle solver on their team?"

*   *   *

The prelim was a campus-wide treasure hunt. When the second-years set out, the first thing they encountered was a cluster of columns on the first floor, each covered in inscriptions.

The phrases on each inscription were different, but all were equally cryptic. Dean had his face up against one, scouring the contents. It read: *Appears with the morning mist, arms wreathed around the needle. The place where they most gather.*

"...Yo, Teresa! Any ideas?"

"At least *attempt* to think it over yourself before asking me."

"No amount of thinking would solve this! Mist? Needles? What is it?!"

He tilted his head so dramatically, his torso went with it. Beside him, Rita was running her fingers over the words.

"...I think I know," she said—softly, so the other teams wouldn't hear. "We learned about them in magical biology. The clocknoks."

Dean's eyes went wide. He glared at the inscription again, keeping his voice low, too.

"Oh, right! So this is all stuff we've learned in class?"

"Even Kimberly's not gonna put out riddles the students can't solve. The bigger the clock, the more clocknoks gather...and the biggest clock on campus is the one on the west side. Let's go, Teresa!"

Rita shouted that last part before running off. Teresa followed, genuinely glad they had her on the team. She didn't really bother listening to lectures and had been just as confused by the riddle as Dean.

Some teams were stuck on the riddles, but there were several that sped off right away. Garland grinned.

"Several teams already moving in the right direction. Putting their education to good use, I see."

"That's true! But allowing progression if you simply paid attention in class? How benevolent! That's hardly the Kimberly style! What's going on, Instructor Garland? Are you transferring to Featherston next year?!"

"Bit of a harsh turn you took there. Rest assured, this is the *combat* league. Solving a riddle won't get you anywhere if you don't have the strength to back it up."

They took the quickest route through the buildings, and less than three minutes after solving the riddle, Teresa's team was approaching their first objective: the clock tower on the east side of the building—which had both hands pointed in entirely wrong directions.

"Oh, is that it?" Dean said. "Is that where—?"

"Dean, don't!"

Rita grabbed the back of his robe, yanking him to a stop. He nearly fell over backward—and a massive beast landed right in front of his nose, wings flapping. It was more than twenty feet long, with an eagle's head and wings and the body of a lion.

"KYOOOOOOOOOOOOOOOOOOO!"

"Aughhh?!?!?!"

Dean's scream was nearly as loud as the beast's roar. Teresa slipped past him, eyes focused on the threat ahead.

"A griffin...," Rita said, stepping forward to defend Dean. She took a spot next to Teressa, athame drawn. Hawklike eyes glared down at the three of them from far above.

"And they've hit the first obstacle! Good Lord. A griffin's a bit much for second-years, Instructor Garland! Even I wouldn't wanna solo a fully grown one!"

"Nobody says that you have to beat it. The beasts used here have a dulling spell cast on them, so they are *just* obstacles. Students are free to get past them by any means they please. This tests their judgment and adaptability."

Garland never once took his eyes off the stream. This was a beast that could wipe a village off the face of the earth—how would inexperienced second-years handle the task? He couldn't wait to find out.

"Dean, keep it together! You can't afford to take your eyes off it!"

"Y-yeah! Right!"

Rita's warning helped, and Dean managed to get his athame drawn. All three of them, even Teresa, began by observing it from a safe distance. It stood between them and the clock tower. Teresa started edging toward the griffin one step at a time, and it screeched at her when she crossed the twenty-yard mark, ready to attack if she got any closer. Clearly, it was guarding their destination.

"...No way we can win if we fight this thing," Rita whispered, flummoxed. "So what *can* we do?"

Desperately charging in would get them wiped out, but if they just stood here looking at it, other students would overtake them. If they wanted to get through the prelim, they'd have to find a way past this griffin's defense and reach the clock tower.

"...I'll bait it."

"Huh?"

"Y-yo!"

Teresa moved out from between them, a step ahead. She swung her athame down, lightly slicing her thigh open. Blood began dripping onto the ground, and her teammates both gulped.

"Whoa?!"

"T-Teresa!"

"*Huff* –"

And with that, Teresa stepped into the griffin's range. The wound's influence, perhaps? She was nowhere near her usual sprightly self. Her gait unsteady, she left a trail of blood in her wake.

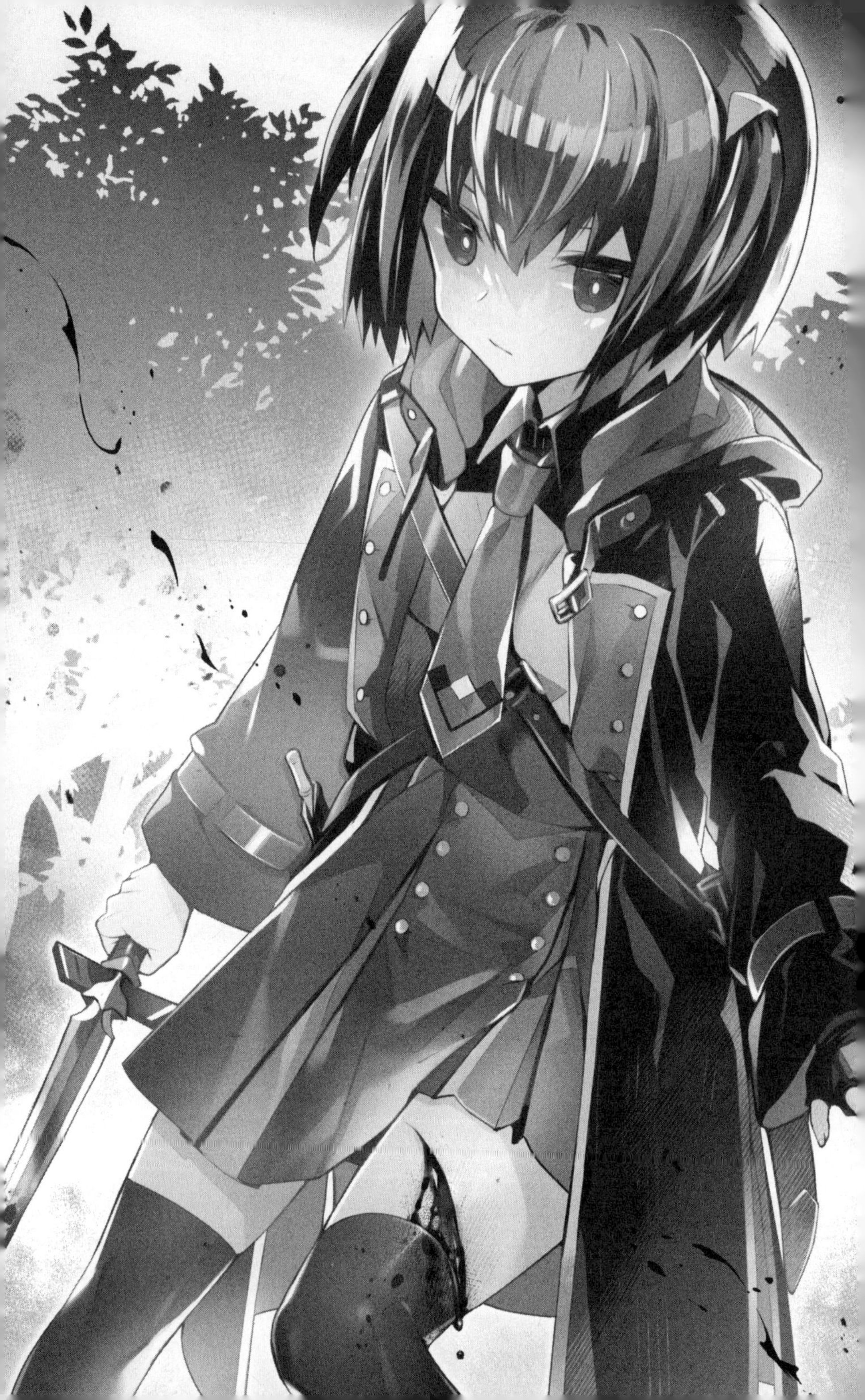

"...KYOO...?"

The griffin watched her for a few moments, then leaned forward, reaching a forelimb toward her. She dodged the swing by a hairbreadth.

"...Gotcha hooked," Teresa whispered.

"Ah. Nice moves," Garland murmured, sounding impressed.

"Wow, Ms. Carste cut herself open and is bleeding all over! Looks like the griffin's full attention is on her, too! What's going on here, Instructor?"

"The way she's moving speaks to a predator's instincts. With the smell of blood in the air, she's got its eyes locked on her. Like she's a wounded animal."

Glenda was well aware of all this, but it was her job to ensure the audience got it, too. Garland was here for just that, and he kept going.

"I suppose a good metaphor is a cat toy. Anyone who owns a cat knows *how* you move them makes a big difference in how interested the cat gets. What Ms. Carste is doing is an extension of that. The griffin can't help but go after her."

Still bleeding, Teresa was feebly limping away. She looked easy enough to catch—but despite that, she'd narrowly avoided the beast's claws every time. The longer they went, the more focused the griffin was— and the greater her control over it. The older students in the audience were suitably impressed by her sacrificial decoy.

"KYOOOOO!"

With an ear-piercing roar, the griffin slammed its talons into the ground. Teresa dodged the beast easily—while making it look like a close call.

"...What a hassle," she muttered.

With her true ability and the full range of her covert skills, she could easily slip past a single griffin. But right now, the whole school was watching every move she made, and she couldn't do anything outside the standard range for a second-year. The result of that dilemma was this cat-toy lure.

"…!"

Unaware of that, but very clear on what she was doing for them—Dean punched himself in the nose. Blood gushed out. The sight of his own blood was a trigger he used to calm himself down.

"…Rita, let's go. We can sneak by now."

"Dean? But—"

"If it reacts, I'll keep it on me. Not sure if the next clue will be anything I can get or remember, so you're the best person to scope it… D-don't worry—I'm an old hand with griffins."

His athame hand was shaking, and his grip was very tight. His history with griffins was more trauma than expertise, but he was pushing through his fears and standing his ground. And that was the push Rita needed.

She stared straight ahead and measured the distance. Just under thirty yards to their goal. If the hint was another inscription, she'd need five to ten seconds to read it. She could be in and out in twenty seconds flat.

"…Ready."

"Okay!"

Both kicked off the ground. Teresa had the griffin occupied, and they were clear on the way in. Dean put his back to the pillar, one eye on the griffin, while Rita quickly read the inscription.

"Twilight rainbow… Eight brushes… Got it!"

With that, she turned to leave—but then the griffin remembered its job. The manavian shook off Teresa's temptation and came charging at them. They both flinched.

"…!"

"Come at me, then!"

If they turned and ran, they'd be finished—so both cast burst spells.

The creature dodged one, but the second was aimed where it dodged. The burst of light robbed it of its sight.

"Go!"

Dean ran off. Rita followed, but her vision wasn't as tunneled, so she spotted the griffin's tail swinging down right where they were headed. It was seconds away from hitting Dean's head.

"Look out above!" she cried.

"Huh?!"

He saw it quick enough but too late to block or dodge. Rita was too far behind to cover him, and there wasn't time to cast a spell.

"…!"

The tail swung relentlessly down, demanding a split-second decision. Rita reached out her left arm—and something slithered out of her sleeve, wound itself around Dean's waist, and yanked him back. The griffin's tail sliced the air where he'd been standing. Rita's hands caught Dean's back, helping recover his balance, then she grabbed his hand, pulling him back into a run.

"…Uh, wow?"

"We're good now! Moving out, Teresa!"

Teresa left the griffin's rank, following her teammates wordlessly. It'd been close—but they had the second clue. The second-year team was on their way to the next destination.

"Um, was that some sort of whip up Ms. Appleton's sleeve?"

"Must have been a tool of some kind. The prelim has rules against familiars and golems, but tools are fine."

Garland was clearly deflecting the question, which bugged Glenda, but before she could press the point, he changed the subject.

"Either way, they're the first past the initial goal. They're a good team—certainly a little rough around the edges, but they're making use of their strengths and compensating for one another's weaknesses."

"Yes, that griffin battle showed some quick thinking! Can they keep their lead and run away with it?"

"That's another matter. We've almost hit the ten-minute mark—and the third-years will be hot on their heels."

At the signal, the third-years dashed off with the Andrews team at the fore.

"Our moment 'as arrived! 'Ow long I 'ave waited!"

"The last respite you'll get."

While Rossi and Albright traded jabs, Andrews had his eye on the finish line.

"We're aiming to be the top qualifiers—nothing lower than third place. Otherwise, what's the point of forming *this* team?"

This might just be the prelim, but he had no intention of taking it easy. In his mind, this was the first *real* fight he'd had at Kimberly.

The difficulty had been adjusted, but the basic flow was the same— solve a riddle, get to the treasure. When they reached the inscribed pillars, Chela snorted.

"They're serious about this? Stace, do you know the answer?"

"Of *course* I do! I'll solve this in no time!"

Stacy stepped up, reading the problem. Nothing here was beyond Chela, but she wasn't going to be taking point this time. Like Stacy's servant, Fay, the ringlet girl was standing back, smiling and watching her half sister work.

They had a ten-minute delay, plus more hints than the second-years— and those hints were much harder to solve. But a year made all the difference. Katie's team reached the clock tower not long after Teresa's team had left it.

"...A griffin on guard," said Pete. "Fully grown ones sure are imposing."

"Oh, that one's no problem. I'll go play with it; you two check the clue."

"You got it. Have fun!"

The boys went to look at the inscription, no doubts about the division of labor. Katie walked calmly toward the manavian, which looked rather unsure of itself—for the simple reason that Katie had already made contact with *every* griffin patrolling Kimberly.

"Ah-ha-ha-ha! Look, I'm riding it!"

"Oh, what a sight to behold!"

Led by a different clue to a clearing on the west side, Yuri was clinging to the back of a unicorn, the wind in his hair. Nanao was merrily running around after them. Like the griffin, this beast was *meant* to be a guard—but they were having *fun* with it instead. All on his own, Oliver glumly checked the inscription.

"You're hurting its feelings," he said with a sigh. "Okay, I've solved the clue! Let's move on."

Oblivious to the third-years' hot pursuit, Teresa's team had just gathered the third clue. They were running down the hall to the next destination.

"We're making good progress!" Dean yelled. "The treasure can't be far off!"

"Yep! No signs of other teams, either! We might be fir—"

But before Rita could finish, they heard footsteps behind. And by the time she turned to look—a tall boy had pulled up alongside. He glanced down at her stunned expression and grinned.

"'Sup, Rita! You're going *fast*."

"Greenwood?!"

"You must have taken the same hint! Getting past that griffin as second-years? You three are good!"

"Ms. A-Aalto…!"

Dean's eyes nearly popped out of his head. But the gap between them was already growing. They were left in the dust.

"Sorry, we're going ahead! If we meet in the main round, we won't go easy on you!"

"Don't push yourselves too hard," Pete said. "Survival over victory. First law of Kimberly."

And with that, they rounded the corner and were gone. The tables had turned so fast, it was a long time before any of the second-years spoke again.

The surveillance golems around campus all buzzed at once. On-screen, the remaining students slowed to a stop. Glenda's voice rang out, marking the end of the fight.

"That's all she wrote! Enough teams have claimed the treasure to fill the main roster, and the lower-form prelim is over. Sixteen teams made it through—so congrats! Extra accolades for the two second-year teams. Good fight!"

"Hmm…less balanced than I'd hoped," Garland muttered. "Maybe we should have made it a fifteen-minute lead."

Glenda started running down the list of qualifying teams, hyping them up for the main-league round in three days' time.

"We've still got the main act, but for now—"

"We all qualified!"

They'd gathered in a lounge after the prelim and were tapping flagons of cider. Once their throats were moistened, Katie let out a sigh of relief.

"I am *so* glad the prelim didn't have any direct combat. This sort of challenge is far more my speed."

"True," Guy groaned. "Not sure we'd have made the cut in a normal fight."

"Knowledge and observation skills are part of your power," Pete argued. "Those who neglect their studies in favor of fighting pay the price."

"Conundrums, creatures, and chases! A veritable smorgasbord!" There was no question that Nanao had thoroughly enjoyed herself.

Smiling at that, Chela steered the topic to other matters.

"The younger kids did very well. Two second-year teams qualified—and I recognized every name on one of them."

"Dean, Rita, and Teresa, right? They're amazing! They almost beat us to it!"

"Rita knows her stuff. Dedicated, hard-working, never gives up. I can't rest on my laurels."

Katie and Guy seized the opportunity to lavish praise on the younger students, although the former had one eye on a corner of the room. While everyone else was feeling festive, Chela's teammates, Stacy and Fay, were resting quietly.

"Hmm," Katie grumbled. "They could just come sit with us."

"I did ask them to. But…reticence is still winning out."

"Eh, they can suit themselves. We *are* rivals here. We might have to fight each other next time, so…distancing themselves ain't the worst idea."

Guy looked momentarily serious, and Katie flinched.

"…Urgh, now that I'm thinking about it—I might have to fight Oliver or Chela!"

"If it's a round robin, definitely," said Chela. "But I think that would be a bit too many fights. Each battle will last far longer than individual duels do, so I don't think we'll see a standard format until the finals."

"Well, either way, we'll solve that problem when we hit it. Oliver, give us a hint! How do we beat you?"

"Don't ask *me* that… But if you're taking this seriously, I promise not to hold back."

"*We* can hold back…if you agree to split the fifty million belc later."

"Guy! No cheating!"

Katie grabbed his cheek and pulled. Yuri spotted the uproar from the doorway and came running over.

"Sorry," he said. "You guys were nice enough to invite me, but here I manage to show up late! Any seats left?"

"You can grab one from another table—but, Chela, maybe it's time?"

Oliver glanced down the room, and Chela nodded, rising to her feet.

"Fair enough," she said. "You may take my chair, Mr. Leik. I'll head back to Stace's table. I did get permission to stop by, but she'll start sulking if I stay longer."

"Go have fun!"

"Tell them to have tea with us sometime!"

Guy and Katie waved her off, and Chela sailed over to her team with her conscience clear. She put great emphasis on friendship, and the others had learned it was best to give her a push at times like this. Chela was soon deep in conversation with Stacy, and Yuri took her vacated seat.

"How did it feel, Yuri? Teaming up with our best and brightest," said Guy.

"I just love solving puzzles! They can keep that stuff coming. No need to leave those in the prelims! Let's hope the main round is every bit as fun."

Yuri leaned back in his chair, basking in the afterglow, excited for what lay ahead. But Oliver had his chin in his hand.

"The three teams here, the second-year team we mentioned earlier, and Rossi's team—who naturally made it through the prelim. We know plenty about five of the sixteen teams. So we'll need to focus our efforts on the remaining eleven—"

But as he spoke, mouths opened on several walls and began talking. A message from Garland, speaking as the combat league administrator. His voice echoed through every room and corridor across the campus.

"Main-round teams, the format is now set. The first match will be Team Liebert, Team Mistral, Team Ames, and Team Horn. Details are

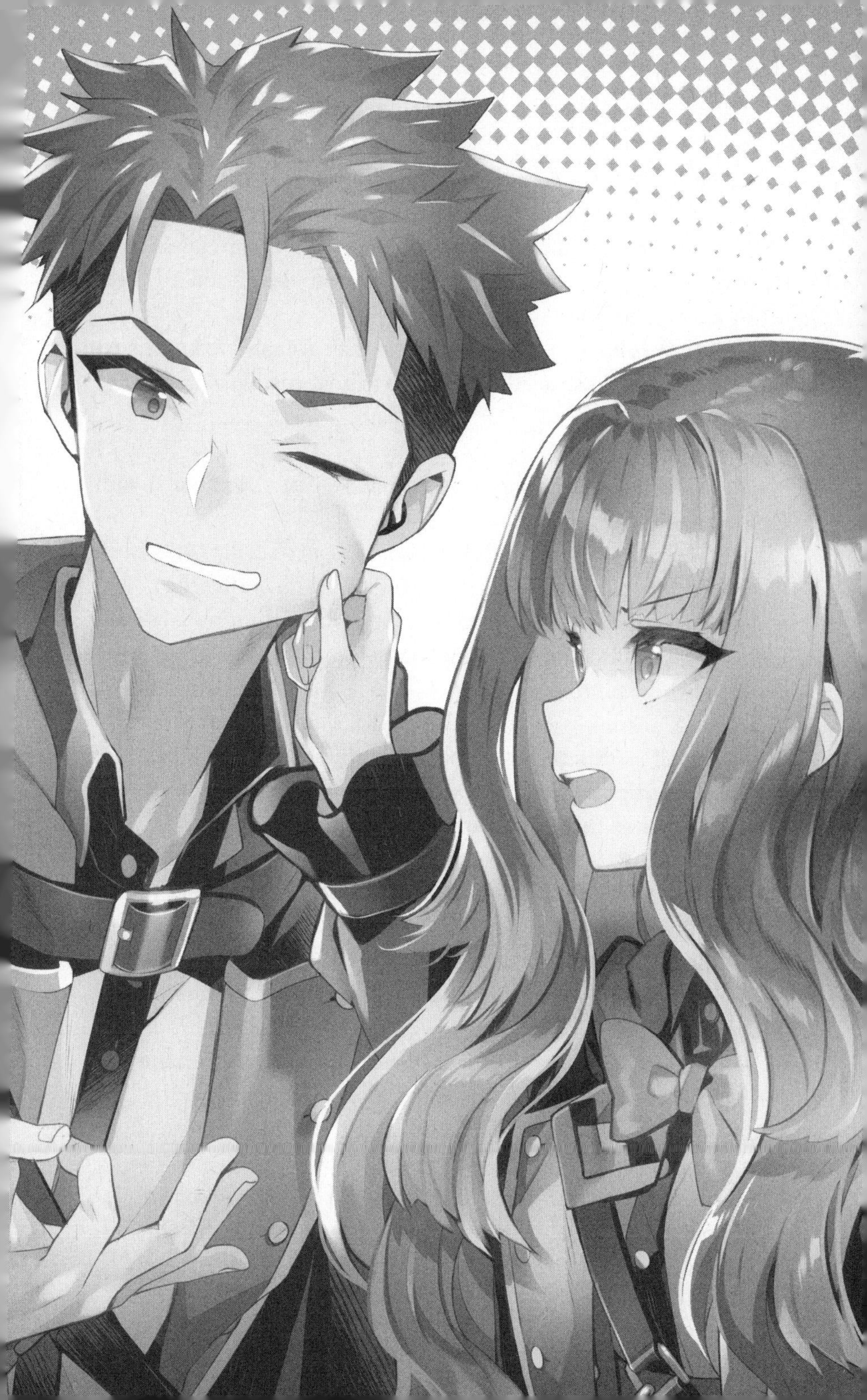

posted on the bulletin boards, so make sure you read up on them. I'll repeat. The first match will be—"

Oliver and his teammates were listening quietly, mildly relieved they weren't up against their friends—but that also meant all three teams were unknowns.

"As the words leave my mouth," he said with a sigh. "We know next to nothing about those teams. There's no telling what'll come at us..."

"That's the full list of lower-form prelim qualifiers, combined with their prior histories."

There was a bundle in front of everyone present. Full data on sixteen teams and forty-eight students less than half an hour after the prelim ended. Watch members gathered in their headquarters, quietly reading through the list. The first to break the silence was one of the president's aides, Lesedi Ingwe.

"Not bad. There some dumb luck in the prelim, but teams with true talent all made it through. That makes things easier to read."

"Yeah. Ms. Hibiya's team, Ms. McFarlane's team, and Mr. Andrews's team. At a glance, they're the three most viable candidates."

Tim Linton was dressed as an adorable girl but scowling down at the portfolios. The other members nodded at his prediction and turned their attention elsewhere.

"And of those three, who can't we count on?"

"No one on the Andrews team. Also rule out the transfer student, Mr. Leik."

"Andrews and Albright hail from hard-core conservative families. Given their positions, they're not able to swing our way."

"Let's look past them to the other teams. This is a free-for-all; no guarantee the top candidates will make it through."

"Five of them are clear Watch supporters, and four are old council. The remaining four aren't as obvious...so we gotta assume two or three are against us. Ain't no way Leoncio's side don't have their hands in that."

The Watch members had little time, so they were soon looking for concrete actions. Godfrey folded his arms, observing them as they worked.

"...If all the teams just fight fair and square, there's little we can do."

Footage of past fights was playing on-screen with Glenda's commentary. The celebration wrapped up early, and they dispersed, each team making final preparations for the main round in three days' time. Yuri was with Oliver and Nanao in a suitable classroom warming up—but stealing frequent glances at the hall.

"Still no signs of Rivermoore," Yuri observed.

"He *might* show up, but likely not until the upper-form leagues begin. No need to keep your eyes peeled—if he shows up, the buzz will reach us."

Oliver had an athame in one hand and was running through Lanoff stances. Half the reason he'd settled on this team was to prevent Yuri from making a suicide run, so he was certainly banking on Rivermoore showing his face. Even so—imagining the two of them together sent a chill down his spine. He swung his blade even harder, trying to shake that off.

"...Put that aside, and let's focus on the main round. Nanao and I have spent the last two years in the limelight, so our styles are relatively well-known. So people will have strategies ready for us. No matter what these battles hold, it won't be easy for us."

"Which is exciting!"

"My heart soars anew!"

His companions were like children before a holiday. He couldn't help but smile—and remember how much work they'd all put in already.

"First, we need to know your strengths." This had been Oliver's opener.

The newly minted team had gathered in a small room on the labyrinth's first layer.

Yuri was smiling brightly, but he offered no response. He didn't seem to realize that statement was meant for him.

"Mm? Wait, whose?"

"Leik, please. *Yours.* We can't strategize if we don't know what our team can do. If you're with us, we need to have a thorough grasp of your strengths and weaknesses."

Oliver had been moving closer and closer, leaning in, and Yuri threw up both hands to hold him back.

"I'm happy to answer, but…how? I mean, we've run the labyrinth together. Haven't you basically seen everything I'm capable of?"

"Obviously I've analyzed what you showed me there. Your magic output is high across the board, you excel at snap decisions and adaptability, yet your body and blade are astonishingly free of any conventions. At the same time, you aren't intentionally ignoring the foundations like Rossi was. I have no idea what training could make a mage like you, but if I had to put a name to my impression—you're a *feral* mage."

"Ah-ha-ha-ha! Okay, yeah, that works for me."

"My impression is much the same. You smell of the deep woods, Yuri. I know not where you hail from, but I sense you spent your tender years at one with the mountains."

Nanao's take drew a quiet smile out of Yuri.

"…It was a peaceful upbringing. My parents were village mages in the countryside. I don't remember them ever teaching me things—not, like, knowledge or technique. Like Nanao says, the hills I ran through were likely my real teachers," Yuri explained. "I was just having fun, but in hindsight, it was really dangerous. All kinds of magical creatures live out there, and I imagine I nearly died several times on any given day. But y'know—I was never once scared. I wonder why not?"

Yuri looked puzzled. Oliver was already analyzing the transfer student's past as if he was deciphering a tome written in an unknown tongue.

"Minimal knowledge passed through written or oral sources, training with the land itself as a mentor. Not entirely unheard of, but…probably more of an Azian concept, really."

"I have tried wilderness survival training myself. 'Tis well suited to honing the heart and mind."

Nanao had her arms folded, nodding. Rather than train to a purpose, placing yourself at the mercy of the environment might well cultivate body and soul. If this was indeed Yuri's background, Oliver now had a hazy image of it—but since they were teammates, he required clarity.

"We've discussed this before, but let's try one more time. When we were ambushed on the second layer, there were unseen enemies hidden in the brush, and you said, *'I asked.'* Who—or *what*—did you ask?"

"Hmm, that's hard to explain. How can I get it across?"

Yuri closed his eyes, thinking. After a long silence, he pointed at nothing in particular.

"For example…let's say there's a tree growing there and someone lurking in the shadows behind it. Naturally, I can't see them. But the *tree* knows there's someone hiding behind it. Then I come along and ask if there's anyone back there—and I get a hazy answer back. Or feel like I do."

"So…you're communing with plants? Or some sort of elemental harbored within them?"

"Um, am I? Neither of those seems quite right."

Yuri had his head buried in his hands, clearly trying to put the inexplicable into words.

Oliver changed tactics. "So how does it work in man-made environments? Do you still get answers?"

"Depends on the thing. Sometimes it comes right back; other times they're stubbornly silent. But—if mages have directly worked on an object, it'll most likely ignore my questions. I wonder why?"

Yet more questions, but before Yuri could ponder further, Oliver put up a hand to stop him. No use making his head spin.

"That's enough thinking for now. I've got a few hypotheses, but they're difficult to verify here. Let's call that good enough—and sorry to make this an interrogation, Leik."

"? What's there to be sorry for? If you've got a mystery before you, prodding it is only natural. I'm kinda thrilled to be a mystery myself for a change!"

Back to his usual smile, Yuri clapped Oliver on the shoulder.

"Let's move on," Oliver said, wincing. "Sword arts and spellology classes don't pair us up with the same partners all that often—but that's really the fastest way to get to know your strengths."

With that, he drew his athame. Yuri got it right away and nodded.

"So we duel? Me and you or me and Nanao?"

"Six rounds with each. For rules, let's go spells and blades..."

The training that followed steadily turned the three mages into an actual *team*. It was hardly a flawless outcome, but Oliver knew they'd done what they could in the time allotted. They were not going into the day lacking. Which was why—

"That's how you two *should* be."

Oliver smiled approvingly. It was only right that his teammates approach the free-for-all expectant and excited. Teaming with promising pals, preparing yourselves appropriately—all that was left was to have *fun*. No matter what other motives swirled in the background the league was about testing your skills. *Not* risking your lives.

As Oliver got his mind on the right track, Nanao turned toward him, looking proud.

"How can my heart not sing? Every team in this has made ready, just as we have. What schemes will they bring? What techniques and spells will they unveil? And how will we respond to it all? How could such speculation ever cease to thrill?"

A towering foe brought equally lofty joy. Nanao Hibiya was a dyed-in-the-wool warrior by nature, something that felt like the sun scorching Oliver's brow. He might not ever be like her—but at the least, he would strive to be worthy of standing at her side.

And indeed, they were not the only team getting ready. To ensure their victory in the main round, combat league participants did everything they could. And to teams deemed ahead of time to be at a disadvantage, that process was all the more urgent.

In a remote section of the labyrinth's first layer—the quiet, wandering path—a male student stood, back to a stone wall lit by the dim glow of crystalline lanterns. By his tie, he was a third-year—with his upturned nose and hair dyed partly purple, he cut a distinctive figure.

"...Ah, you've arrived."

Hearing wings flap in front of him, the boy tore his eyes off the ground. Two bats flitted out of the night, followed by several silent figures: three to the right, three to the left. The bats were the boy's familiars, and they landed on his outstretched index fingers.

"A real *thrill* to have you. Please relax—if you can. We *are* enemies here."

"If you're aware, then don't mince words. State your business, Mistral."

There came a low growl from the leader of the pack on the right, a boy hidden below a hood. He was unusually large, with a composure like he had one foot in the upper forms—but his tie, too, was a third-year's.

Mistral shrugged at the larger boy's glare. "So eager, Mr. Liebert. You know full well what I intend. You've seen the brackets for the main round."

With that, he crossed his legs and plopped himself down on the ground. His eyes raked across the half dozen shadows before him.

"Be honest," he said. "Can *you* win? Against any of us?"

The questions were thrown like daggers. One figure cast back their hood: a girl, her eyes hidden behind long bangs. She spoke in a murmur.

"If the flow goes our way…we might…have a chance."

"Correct, Ms. Ames," Mistral replied, his lips curling in a sardonic smirk. "And shall I define the word *flow* for us all? You intend to wait until Ms. Hibiya's team has been exhausted by your opposition. When they are most tired, you seize your chance to dive in and cast your nets. The particulars may vary, but that's the gist, I'm sure."

He received only silence in response.

"I *agree*," Mistral spat. "Every one of us is planning the *same thing*. But where will that get us? Not one of us intends to fight them for real. There'll be no *combat*, just short straws drawn, worn down by attrition, a sight to shame us all. The anticipation makes me weep."

"…Your point being, Mistral?" Growing tired of this spite, Liebert cut to the chase. But as he did—a voice came from *behind*.

"If all roads lead to shame—"

"—then let us *embrace* disgrace."

Mistral excepted, all present spun around. Five spread out, athame drawn—and one did not hesitate, drawing into a lunge, her blade stopping just before the skin of the intruder's throat.

"Oh? Oh! Quite the reflexes, Ms. Ames."

"Scary stuff! *Someone* was hiding their skills. You've not shown *that* in class!"

The figure cackled even with her blade to their jugular—and the *exact same voice* echoed from the figure staring down Liebert's sights. Six pairs of eyes widened in surprise. Before them stood two identical figures—each with the same face as the boy they'd been speaking to.

"Hackles down. Sorry for the shock, but I've *kept* my word. I came here *alone*."

The seated Mistral cackled.

Liebert compared those words with the contradiction before him, examining each in turn.

"A transformation…? No, this is—"

"More of a splinter, I imagine," Ames whispered. "But at an exceedingly high level. So much so, I can hardly be sure."

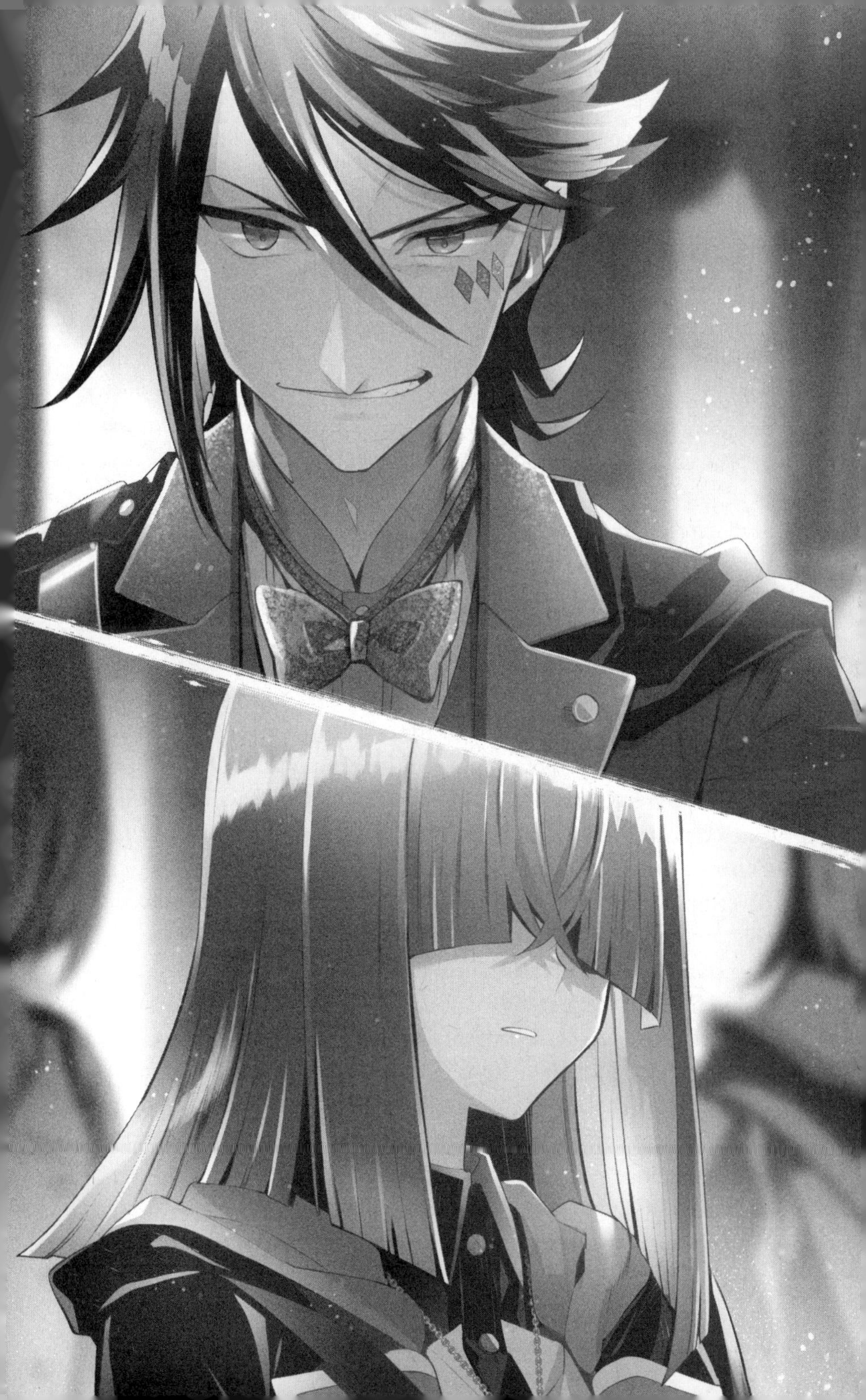

As their minds caught up, the standing Mistrals spoke in turn.

"Since I'm suggesting this strat, I figured I oughtta show my cards."

"These ain't too shabby, are they? A little family *secret*."

Ames had yet to lower her athame. Each Mistral looked identical. Each *sounded* identical. Like a haunting dream during a troubled sleep. Liebert furrowed his brow, but the issue at stake was not the spookiness of the skill but the simple fact that he was observing them from point-blank range yet could not begin to tell which Mistral was real. The darkness around them likely helped, but even so—this was downright *uncanny*.

"I'm sure each of you has a trick or two up your sleeve. Keep what you must, but share what you can."

"We can't very well work together if we don't know what we each can do."

At that phrase, Ames finally retracted her blade. She took a few steps toward her companions.

"The three of us join forces and throw everything at Ms. Hibiya's team," she said. "That's your suggestion—or the essence of it."

"Battin' down the stars is the advantage of a free-for-all. We know her team's a powerhouse, and that alone forces the match into one pattern—a deeply sad game of hide-and-seek."

"So why waste that time? What use is us yanking the rugs out from under one another? This is *not* a team we can defeat on *those* terms!"

The standing Mistrals were speaking in turn again, and the one by the wall finished the speech.

"First, we swear an oath. Until Ms. Hibiya's team is eliminated, none of us attacks one another. Nothing gained in refusing that—unless you don't *want* to win."

His voice grew extra harsh on that last phrase, and it drew a long, studied silence.

After some thought, Liebert was the first to speak.

"An informal alliance, then. If we were all on board, the match would begin as three-on-one. And the plan would be obvious to all. Will it earn us Master Garland's enmity?"

"Holding back or throwing a match assuredly would. But look at it this way—our plan is the exact opposite."

"This format is all about gunning for the favored team. We're simply making that the crux of our plan."

"Fighting all out, with every tactic we can. What is there to decry?"

The Mistrals sounded sure of themselves. Another silence followed.

"…Allow me to clarify," Ames said. "The moment Ms. Hibiya's team is out of the running, we become foes once more. Am I correct in that assumption?"

"You got it in one, Ms. Ames."

"From that point on, we fight one another."

"Anything goes! Feel free to team up once more and eliminate *my* team next."

All three Mistrals laughed aloud.

Liebert snorted. "No promises post our initial goal. Fair enough. But our interests do align until that point."

Only then did he sheath his athame. His eyes flicked to each of his teammates and got a brief nod in return.

"I'm a classical golem dispatcher. What I can do varies by the terrain and ground type. Assume I do a lot of delegating."

Once on board, he wasted no time in describing his style. When he glanced toward Ames, she nodded and said her piece.

"…I've been put through the paces of both Lanoff and Rizett. If the terrain is sufficiently cluttered…no matter who I'm fighting, I… should be able to manage effective hit-and-away tactics."

"Dive on in and get out quick, mm? Against Ms. Hibiya and Mr. Horn?"

"I make no promises. But…there is little I *can't* do. If you need someone filling in the gaps in a strategy, I can make myself useful."

A bolder offer than he'd expected—Liebert certainly seemed surprised.

With that, the three teams were allied—and the three Mistrals grinned.

"Now that—"

"—is more like it."

"Bring it on!"

Their discussion began in earnest with them concocting a plan to take down the biggest prey.

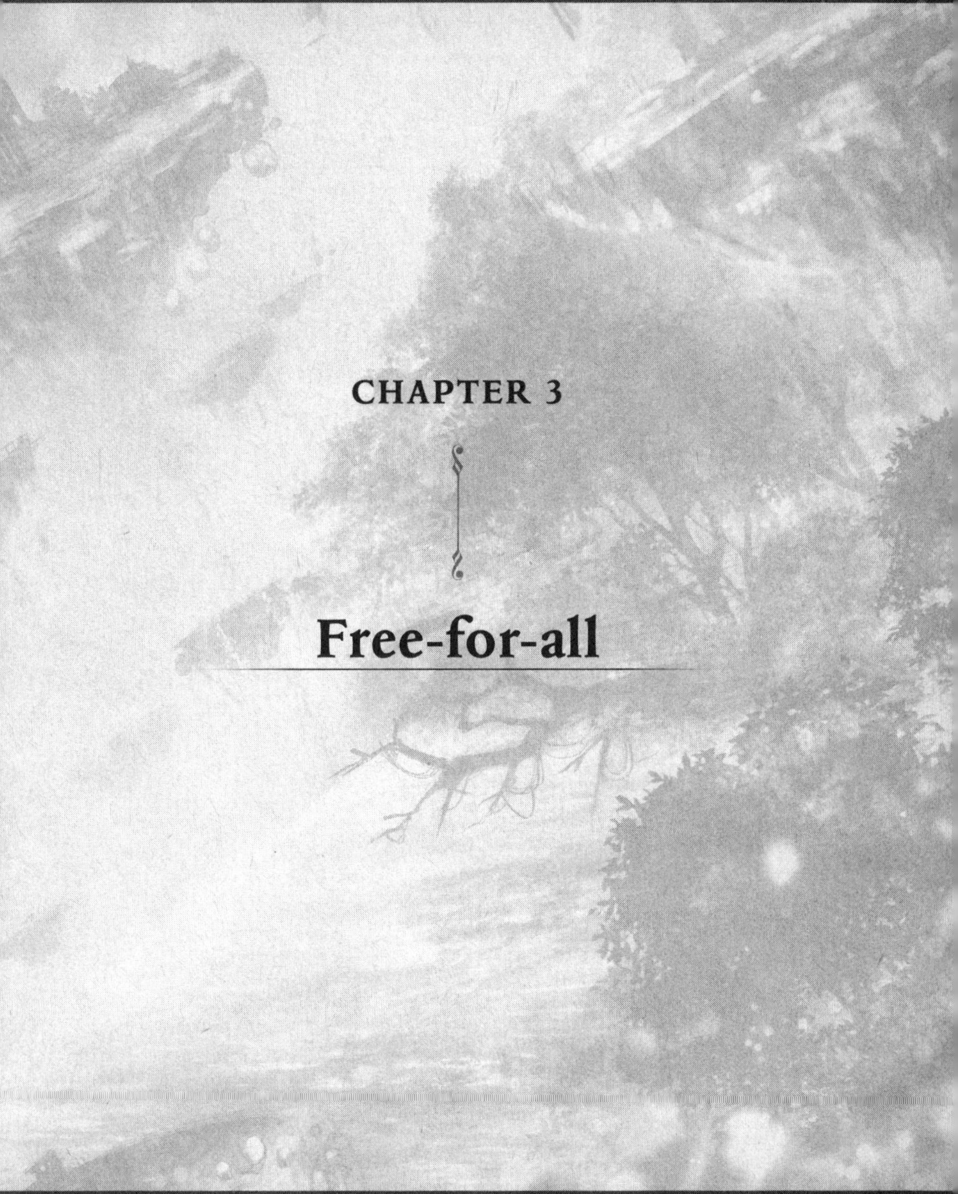

CHAPTER 3

Free-for-all

Where would the current of battle flow on its path to the end? Far too many potentials existed, and no one could begin to predict them all. With multiple teams in a free-for-all, that was exponentially worse; a minor coincidence in the opening moments could prove decisive in the finale.

"Oh, wait, Nanao," warned Yuri. "Dragon breath's in effect there."

"Hrm."

Three days had passed since the prelim. The main act lay before them, yet in the first-floor waiting room, Oliver's teammates were absorbed in a game, showing no hints of nerves.

"......"

Oliver himself knew there was no use fretting over things. He'd drilled a set of basic expectations and countermeasures into their heads, and now all they had left to do was stay flexible and take the match as it came. Perhaps relaxing was the best thing they could be doing. Certainly far better than stressing out. Still...

"Hmm, the golems are in a line. I believe I can combine them now!"

"Oh, nice, Nanao. Lemme check the rules. Um...once earth golems fuse, their resistance and attack..."

"...Increase eightfold, in that variation," Oliver said, unable to stand by while they dug through a very thick rule book.

He glanced over the board stuffed with minis of all shapes and sizes, looking appalled.

"The match is upon us, yet you're enjoying this chaotic mess of a game."

"The turmoil is the fun! Have you not played Magic Chess Dynamic?"

"...I started with the fifteenth edition, Coolish, and kept up until the twenty-eighth, Invisible. But there I learned my lesson. Rules update every month, each completely overturning the fundamentals of the previous edition. Ordinary chess is far more polished and preferable."

Even as he spoke, Oliver winced, hearing himself sound exactly like his father. The memories were coming back to him already. His mother, the undefeated champion—his father, reeling from another loss and wailing, *"Noll, play me again!"* But no matter which of them was seated across the board, he was always at his wit's end.

"Five minutes till start. Take your places."

An upperclassman's voice dragged him from his reverie. Nanao and Yuri abandoned their game.

"Oh, it's time!"

"Verily."

They stood up, and Oliver joined them.

A voice echoed from the ceiling.

"Before our match begins, let me run over the rules again."

As ten AM drew near, Garland kicked off the commentary. The feed from the surveillance golems showed the twelve students about to do battle.

"This is a four-team free-for-all. All teams will hit the field at the match's start. Spells and blades allowed. You earn a point for each member of the opposing teams you take out, and teams that survive till the end of the match earn two additional points. The team with the highest total score is considered the victor." Garland continued: "As per the previously announced terms, familiars and golems *are* allowed. Entrants wishing to make use of these but without any ready may borrow thoroughly average units from the league administration. Feel free to ask."

These loaners were primarily to assist the second-year teams. Third-year students were expected to have familiars on hand for scouting and messaging, but it was hardly reasonable to expect younger students to match that. But since the competition about to start was entirely third-year teams, this was hardly a serious concern.

"This is the lower-form league, so naturally, dulling spells have been applied. Contracts are in place to ensure spell lethality is limited to noncritical damage, and the field itself has dulling spells applied to ensure no unfortunate accidents from, say, bad falls. In other words, league combat requires a means of determining *injured* and *eliminated* beyond the entrants' actual physical condition. These are the rings you see around the entrants' wrists, ankles, and necks."

"These right here!" Glenda leaped to her feet, showing off the rings she herself wore.

"These rings detect extreme heat, cold, and impacts," Garland went on. "In other words, *offensive interference with the flesh*. When the values registered cross a certain threshold, the spell activates—applying a local paralysis to the area around the ring. So if a spell scrapes by the ring on the left wrist, you'll lose some feeling in your entire left arm—but if you soak that hit directly, you'll lose the use of that arm entirely. Blows to the head or torso are registered by the ring around the neck, causing not paralysis but unconsciousness—in other words, eliminating you from the match. Even if the neck ring itself is intact, if all four limbs are down, you're taken out."

At this point, he paused and glanced at Glenda. She caught the signal and drew her athame, holding it in her dominant right hand. The screen zoomed in.

"The key point to understand here is that the loss of one's dominant hand does *not* result in immediate elimination. Unlike a regular duel, this is a *team* battle. Without that hand, fighters may not be casting spells or swinging swords—but as long as they're running around, they can still help their team win. With that in mind, we're expecting everyone to scramble like crazy."

As a general rule, mages could wield wands only with their dominant hand. In light of that, standard duel rules held that a cut to the dominant hand—incapable of casting or swinging—was a loss. But in a group event, this might not be true. There was still plenty that could be done: Mages could serve as decoys, soak blows for the others, or even focus on controlling familiars.

"We have several fields prepared, and these will be chosen at random for each match. The time limit is one hour. You are free to fight however you like within the parameters of the rules, but if you lurk or flee or avoid combat for too long, you'll be declared unwilling to fight, and your rings will activate and eliminate you. Take care that does not happen."

Fight—and survive. As primal a theme as any.

Garland wasn't quite done yet.

"Forbidden actions—first and foremost, any and all dangerous behaviors that could lead to death or lasting damage. That includes all curses. Even if it doesn't fall under those parameters, inflicting unnecessary or excessive pain is obviously forbidden. Anyone spotted engaging in such behavior will receive a warning or a penalty, and if deemed dire enough, they may be immediately disqualified. To that end, there are upperclassmen placed around the field to act as referees. Remember, their eyes—and mine—are always on you."

"So don't be an asshole!" Glenda roared. A succinct interpretation.

Garland nodded, and Glenda turned to the two other students seated at the commentators' table.

"For this match, it won't just be Instructor Garland and me! We've also called in two candidates for the next student body president. Ms. Miligan, Mr. Whalley, can we get a word from each of you before the match begins?"

"Vera Miligan, presidential candidate. It's an honor to be offered a seat at this table. Can't say I love the company, though."

"Percival Whalley, presidential candidate. I'll ignore the inscrutable squawking next to me and simply say that I can endure *any* hardship for the future of Kimberly."

They were already trading barbs.

"Yikes! Tensions are clearly *high*." Glenda chuckled. But her eyes were on the clock before her. "Whoa! Two minutes till the match begins. Let's welcome our fighters to the field!"

"Okay, it's time. Get out there!" the upperclassman administrator barked.

The cloth covering one side of the room fell away, revealing a painting of sheer rock faces. They knew at once—this was the entrance to the battlefield.

Nanao and Yuri were clearly raring to go, so Oliver issued his first instruction.

"Hoods up. You ready for this?"

"You bet!"

"I can hardly wait!"

Enthusiastic faces vanished beneath their hoods. The pair's anticipation clearly outweighed any anxiety. There was no need for Oliver to encourage them further. All three stepped forward as one and leaped into the painting.

For a few seconds, they plunged through darkness—then they were thrown out into an open space. Landing silently, they swiftly checked their surroundings.

"...The painting told no lies."

Steep terrain, boulders bathed in orangish light. Few signs of life, but even with their eyes closed, any mage worth their salt could sense *power* emanating from beneath the ground. Even without a proper investigation, Oliver knew exactly what type of field this was.

"The first match will take place on the beldite reserves! Applying the labyrinth's magitech, our battlefields reproduce real-world terrain in a limited locale! Both our guests have experience in team combat, so what do you make of this field?"

Glenda was already getting her guests involved.

The Snake-Eyed Witch smirked. "A mineral-rich zone? Certainly a field type that'll rattle a newcomer. The first test will be accurately reading the properties of the terrain, and the second how they incorporate that into their strategy. A chance for our adorable juniors to display their skills."

It would be faster to show them. With that in mind, Oliver applied a little mana to the ground at his feet. A rock pillar rose from it, growing to waist height in the blink of an eye.

"Oh!"

"Whoa."

Nanao and Yuri both looked fascinated. It was a standard foothold alteration in the Lanoff school's earth stance, but under ordinary conditions, you could hardly get an effect this dramatic without casting. Which just showed how extraordinary this terrain was.

"As you can see, the terrain here is primarily beldite—a spellstone with a high mana capacity. Magic that alters the ground will get a major boost. Even something like Clypeus. On the other hand, oppositional-element spells will be absorbed by the ground and their power diminished. Be prepared for that."

Even as he explained it, Oliver felt like this was a pretty tricky field. His personal style made great use of the earth stance, so it had a big impact, and there was no telling what effects it would have on their opposition—whom they already knew far too little about. Before they entered combat, they'd have to adapt to the terrain itself.

"You can cause big changes with a tiny amount of mana, but if you forget that, you'll end up shocking yourself with the power of your own spells. Or the lack thereof. You've been warned."

As for the minimal necessary precautions, he deliberately explained no further. A verbal breakdown would be less useful for these two than acquiring an innate grasp. He quickly moved to other subjects.

"How's it going for you, Leik?"

"Uh…not the best. The voices are quite soft… I can barely hear 'em."

Yuri had his hand on a rock nearby, shaking his head. His quirk was still a mystery, but the voices of nature he heard were not going to help much here. This was far from a natural environment—the field itself had been made by the combat league administrators.

"Then we'll do this legit." Oliver nodded. He swung his athame. **"Satus sursum."**

At his incantation, three shadows flew out of his robe, each headed in a different direction. Little golems, modeled after birds. They made a quick circuit of the airspace above the field, sharing their visual intel with Oliver.

"...Ngh..."

Processing four fields of view at once left him mildly "drunk," but he adjusted after a few seconds. He closed his eyes and focused on the terrain observations.

"...I've got golems scouting," he said. "They're getting a big picture of the field itself and locating the other teams if possible."

"Everyone starts by hiding and probing, huh?"

"Naturally, if we're attacked, we'll handle it, but nobody's going to be running around without any information. Relative positions are going to be a major factor in the outcome here. If multiple teams surround you, you're instantly in trouble."

He held his athame out between Nanao and Yuri. Catching his drift, they placed theirs on his, and the map he'd drawn in his mind was shared with them. This approach required knowledge of the methodology and some practice, but mages could link minds this way.

"Sending the image. See it? I've set provisional directions, but we're on the southeast side of the map. No enemies for around two hundred yards. The outskirts have some greens, but the elevation increases as you reach the center, leading up to a towering peak. Keep it stealthy, but let's head there at top speed."

"Mm-hmm, got it."

"Position ourselves on higher ground. A military fundamental."

All nodded, and they dashed off toward their first destination. Yuri glanced up from behind a rock—there were several small golems flitting around. The admin's surveillance golems and the scouts of opposing teams.

Like Oliver's team, the others were on the move.

"Spellstone reserves? It's our lucky day."

Jürgen Liebert, leader of one third-year team, was examining a stone in hand. The students flanking him nodded. The girl with hawk-like eyes was Camilla Asmus, and the boy with fair, messy hair was Thomas Chatwin—the other members of Team Liebert.

"Then let's get started."

"Gonna be a real showstopper, boss?"

"Yeah. High-quality beldite... The build's gonna be *ideal*."

Liebert drew his athame and pointed it at his feet. His first spell flattened the ground around them. Then light flowed from the tip, drawing on the ground. As he worked, he issued orders.

"Blueprint A-3. It's in your heads?"

"Yep."

"Not forgetting it anytime soon, not after all that practice."

Both set about their respective tasks, treating the ground as a canvas and covering it in letters and diagrams to sketch out a giant, ornate magic circle.

"Horn to the southeast, Ames to the northwest, Mistral to the southwest—all three teams on the move. Everyone's running straight to the peak at the center! They all started at roughly the same distance from it, so who will get there first?!"

Surveillance golems had every inch of the action covered, and the audience was fully aware of what each team was up to. Watching the three teams converge on the high ground, Miligan put her hand to her chin.

"Yes...Horn's team *is* noticeably fleeter of foot. Oliver and Nanao I expected, but I'm rather shocked Mr. Leik can keep up with them. He transferred in last year and hasn't really made a name for himself—so perhaps we just *didn't know*."

"Hmph, speed alone will get you nowhere. Under these conditions, gaining the sole high ground means you must be prepared to be the target of all other teams. Have they given thought to what lies at the end of this race?"

Sensing that his political rival was backing Oliver, Whalley immediately moved to disagree. Her guests locked horns, and Glenda shot them a sidelong smirk—it was her job to keep the hype going.

"But the three-way race is not the only attraction! Look to the northeast, to the Liebert team! They haven't taken a step outside their starting location!"

"Avoiding the race to high ground is one strategy, although I'm not sure what they stand to gain from staying put. I can see they're sketching something…but do they plan to *camp* there?"

Whalley folded his arms, puzzled. To avoid affecting the battle, the surveillance golems were keeping their distance—and no one could work out just *what* was being drawn. Miligan looked equally lost.

"Even if they're going full defensive and waiting for the other teams to crush one another, they're still too far from the main action. They might be deemed unwilling and find themselves disqualified. So what *is* their plan?"

Eight minutes after the match started—the last chunk of which involved running up a very steep slope—Oliver's team reached the top.

"Well, that was easy," said Yuri.

"Stay on guard. No ambushes, but odds are the enemy's close," Oliver cautioned. "**Clypeus**."

He cast a spell to adjust the terrain and swept his eyes over their surroundings. He had scout golems patrolling, too, but he had to keep them high up or they'd be shot down, and the functionality of golem eyes was a far cry from those of a mage. Placing himself on high ground gave him far more detailed intelligence, which made it easier to guard their vicinity and freed up the golems to cover a broader area.

"First, we've gotta find the enemy. Once that's done, we hit whoever is a close run downslope. Our goal is always swift strikes to take one team at a time, not to defend this location."

The increased elevation helped locate enemies, but Oliver had no intention of camping here. The advantage it offered was not worth getting surrounded. Yet it would be tricky if their opponents occupied it, so as they scouted, all three of them were planting spells in the ground and placing magic traps. Only a third of them would actually trigger, and the rest were fakes, but just knowing there were traps around would make a foe hesitate. The mineral deposits strengthening earth magic really helped here.

"…? There's a team to the northeast, but they aren't approaching. They're drawing something on the ground, but I can't tell what. They don't seem like an immediate threat…"

It bothered him, so he left a single golem wheeling in the sky above. Nanao and Yuri were checking other directions, so he glanced their way.

"Hmm, not finding anything."

"Nor am I. They excel at hiding."

Oliver nodded, unperturbed. Unless you were specialized in stealth like Teresa, moving unnoticed was a real challenge in these conditions. If the enemy was escaping detection, they were either moving extremely slowly or not at all. Most likely hiding behind rocks and waiting for an opening. Inspecting the surroundings in light of that and their potential locations was limited.

Perhaps it was time to flush them out. As Oliver considered that, a vibration came from underfoot. All three saw rock fragments skittering down the slope.

"Mm, the field's shaking," said Nanao.

"An earthquake?" Yuri wondered aloud.

The pair exchanged frowns. But the cause was no mystery—the golem Oliver had monitoring the northeast was watching the ground rise at prodigious speeds.

"——?!"

"Build complete," Liebert said as the spell finished deploying. He wiped the sweat from his brow. He and his teammates were in rather different surroundings now.

A tower had rapidly grown from the ground, carrying them up. The top of it was now *taller* than the mountain peak, looming over the entire field. But it was no mere pile of rocks. There was space inside, windows coating the exteriors, and a defensive wall surrounding the level ground at the base. A literal fortress born from sheer rock.

"Nice."

"Whew, glad that didn't collapse halfway."

Long white wands in hand, Camilla and Thomas had their eyes trained on the sights below. As they stepped forward, Liebert sat down heavily, his job done.

"…I'll rest a moment. It should be tall enough. Can you aim?"

"'Course."

"I've spotted them. On top of that little *hill*."

They each took aim—at what had once been the field's highest point. Their wands targeting the prey in position there, their chants rang out.

"Flamma!"

"Tonitrus!"

"Clypeus!"

Flames and lightning shot out of the tower's tip, and Oliver quickly threw up a barrier. The wall creaked from the force of the spells, and hot electrified winds billowed around the sides. Still scrambling to catch up with these changes, he barked an order.

"Spell snipers to the northeast! Don't return fire! Stay low!"

Repairing his spell's defenses, he urged Nanao and Yuri to defensive positions. He would've loved to shoot back himself—but the enemy was much too far away. At this distance, they'd be lucky if their spells even traveled that far. And they had other teams to worry about—defense was their only option.

"Wow, that's really something. A whole new tower!"

"Indeed! That was not how I expected to lose the height advantage."

Their cries were astonished and delighted, and Oliver couldn't help but laugh, all the while analyzing what these latest developments meant.

"...Pretty sure it's a golem fortification. Never seen one *that* size before."

"Wowzers!" Glenda cried. "Team Liebert went for some crazy construction! They made a whole new tower and claimed the highest point with brute force! Or I suppose incredible skill. And the moment it was done, they started sniping Team Horn!"

"A golem fortification!" Garland added. "Well done, Mr. Liebert. An advance application of classical golem techniques."

You'd expect him to elaborate, but the sword arts instructor broke off there, his gaze turning to their guests. Catching his drift, Miligan and Whalley spoke up.

"Allow me to explain. Modern mainstream golems prize careful construction, from materials to schematics, while classical golem practices merely prepare a core formula and use materials at hand to complete the build. The primary advantage is that you need merely carry a small core with you but can create large-scale golems."

"The disadvantage is that the size and quality of the golems vary wildly by the materials at your location. Common dirt will just make cheap mudmen—the quality of the ground may make construction entirely impossible. But naturally—that can work the other way around, as it has here. A field of high-capacity spellstones is the *ideal* environment for golem work. Under ordinary conditions, three lower-form students would never have enough mana to build a structure that size. But here, if the caster is skilled enough, it becomes possible. Though clearly it took a lot out of him."

Like Whalley said, Liebert himself was leaving the fighting to his team and recuperating. *Perfectly understandable after a feat like that*, Miligan thought.

"The bigger a golem is, the more mana it requires to move," the Snake-Eyed Witch said. "But there has long been a view that you simply need not move them at all. In essence, golems are *containers*, so they do not technically require arms and legs. This golem fortification is clearly based on that principle. Essentially a mage's pop-up fort."

Garland nodded approvingly.

"Solid exposition, both of you. If I have anything to add—it's that a build this large is hardly a matter of burying a core and chanting a single spell. You need thorough knowledge of the earth's composition and the support of appropriate magic circles to ensure nothing gets unbalanced during the build itself. That alone is difficult enough, but Team Liebert pulled it off without a hitch less than ten minutes into the match. Mr. Liebert's skills on main construction are commendable, but this proves the entire team came well prepared." He then added, "Effectively, this flips the terrain advantage that Team Horn's speed gained. They're in trouble already—and if they make the wrong judgment call here, they'll be swiftly cornered."

Meanwhile, at the base of the rocky mountain Oliver's team had occupied, another team was getting ready to act.

"There goes Team Liebert. What a sport."

The three-man team led by Rosé Mistral. Like Oliver assumed, they'd been hiding behind rocks, waiting for a chance to attack. And that opportunity had just presented itself.

"Time we do our part. **Effingo frable.**"

He closed his eyes, beginning an incantation. An amorphous fluid born from his wand steadily took form, the outline growing clear—and in time, two more Rosé Mistrals stood before him.

"Clypeus! Down the hill! This is no longer the highest point, so no use staying put!" Oliver barked, strengthening the barrier against the powerful spells raining down from the northeast.

Yuri turned in the opposite direction.

"Mm, if we want to avoid the snipers, we'd need to head west…," he said, peeking down the slope. A lightning spell hit the rocks nearby, and the shower of sparks made him duck back under cover. "But, uh, it's occupied. We're pinned down above and below."

"I see full teams to the northwest and southwest. We're punching through the latter."

The results of his scouting informed Oliver's decision. Using the mountain itself as cover against the snipers, they'd head southwest and use the momentum of the downslope to push past the team stationed there—or even take them out. The terrain switch up had been a surprise, but the general plan hadn't changed: one team at a time, as hard as they could.

With their new goal confirmed, the team set out—but then Yuri stopped in his tracks.

"? What's wrong, Leik? If we don't move now, we'll be a punching bag."

"…Mm…but still…"

Yuri tapped his forehead, falling silent.

"This your thing?" Oliver asked.

"…I think so? It's faint, but something's speaking to me. Hmm…"

Yuri started cocking his head. Feeling like this was a bad sign, Oliver took another look around. The scouting he'd done had given him a good idea what their opponents were up to. Given their current positions, southwest was the safest move to make. But was he missing something?

As the wheels in his mind churned, more sniper spells came in, and Nanao's spell strengthened the rock wall. Feeling the heat of the wind gushing past that barrier on her skin, the Azian girl murmured, "Most impressive. Spells of this force from so great a distance."

She meant little by it; she was simply voicing her admiration. But it tugged at Oliver's mind in a way he could not ignore.

"...No, that makes no sense."

"Mm?"

"It's downright unnatural. One team to the east, two to the west, but the teams on the west side are much, much closer to us. Yet the attacks from the east are *clearly* far stronger."

This was feeling more and more wrong by the second. From their opponents' perspective, this was a prime chance for all three teams to focus fire on Team Horn. There was no point in anybody holding back—and to keep the tower team's line of sight, they'd actually *want* to push Oliver's team to the east side of the mountain. Which would mean they'd *up* the pressure from the west. Yet the spells coming from that side were clearly far and few between.

There must have been a *reason* why the teams couldn't hit them harder. At this point, Oliver had one of his scout golems look toward the peak upon which he and his teammates stood. There, he saw three figures plastered against the barrier wall, hiding among the snipers' flash and noise.

"——! Behind you, Nanao!"

The Azian girl swung around just as one of the figures leaped over the barrier, lunging straight at her. Nanao braced her katana—but as the figure reached her, so did a pair of lightning bolts.

"Hrm—!"

Cover spells timed perfectly with the assault. Three blows at once—and Nanao *knew* she couldn't block them all. She made her choice and stepped hard to the left, dodging the right bolt, parrying the thrust to her chest and taking a swing to force her foe back. Inevitably, the bolt she had *chosen* to soak struck her left elbow.

"Bold and decisive. You live up to your reputation."

"**Tonitrus!**"

"**Impetus!**"

Oliver and Yuri soon had spells flying in, but the figure danced around them and flitted back up on the rock. As the figure fell back down beyond, the wind caught their hood—revealing distinctive long bangs.

"But we took an arm. Next time—it'll be your head."

"Ms. Ames...!"

And with that, Ames was lost between the boulders to the east. With the sniper fire raining down, they couldn't exactly give chase. Oliver had a scout golem follow, and he ran to Nanao's side. The hit had resulted in her left arm dangling limply.

"I'm afraid my left arm is done for. I could not well afford to lose my right or chest."

"Not your fault. I'm the one who failed to spot them in time. I was sure I'd found all our foes, and they took advantage of that. Those three must have circled around the south—which means half the foes I spotted are *fakes*."

Oliver was as impressed as he was frustrated. It all made sense in hindsight. The western offense had lacked ferocity because there was only *one* team over there. The fakes had simply made it appear there were two. And before that perception error could be corrected, Ames's team had slipped through the sniper fire, closing in from the south—then retreated to the east, preventing their pursuit. Hit-and-run, no injuries to their side.

There were several reasons why Oliver had failed to see it coming—chief among them being just how impressive the fakes were. Splinters and illusions ordinarily couldn't move like the real thing, but nothing he'd seen through golem eyes had seemed remotely out of place. Was he controlling them expertly, so they appeared natural? Or had they been given an unusual degree of autonomy? Either way, the splinters were a major threat.

The second factor was the sniper barrage from the northeast. Alone, it was tricky—but it had also served a *function*, covering Team Ames's approach. With the fakes tricking them into believing they knew where their foes were, none of them had been checking the south slope. If Yuri hadn't sensed something amiss, their damages would have been far worse than Nanao's arm.

"Worst of all, this means our foes are working together," said Oliver. "You can't pull off a strategy like this without prior planning. From the get-go, they were teamed up to take us out."

"Three against one? A standard enough practice when one team is clearly stronger, but they're not making any bones about it."

Miligan was frowning, reassessing the match flow.

"Not a fan?" Whalley sneered. "I'm inclined to praise them. They're doing what they need to *win*. That is how a Kimberly student ought to be. It goes against no match rules, yes, Master Garland?"

He glanced behind him, and their sword arts instructor answered with a silent smile. Encouraged, Whalley lambasted his political rival.

"To avoid this outcome, Team Horn should have made overtures themselves. If they'd managed to ally with just one of these teams, we'd be seeing a very different match. Their indolence is a sign of their conceit. Or can you refute that, Miligan?"

He shot her a challenge, but the Snake-Eyed Witch pointedly ignored it. Fixation on victory was one thing—but mages had pride and style, too. And that must be proven not by her—but by the underclassmen fighting before them.

"...Message from Team Ames. Surprise attack successful; Ms. Hibiya lost her left arm."

A signal via mana frequency from a scout golem above, sent to Team Mistral in the rocky foothills to the west. The teammate who received the message relayed it to their leader.

"Then she can't use that two-handed Flow Cut," Rosé Mistral said, laughing aloud. "The wind's blowing our way!"

"Hate to burst your bubble, but they'll be coming right at us. And they're onto the splinters," the third team member added.

Mistral cracked his neck. "Bring it," he said. "I ain't shown even a tenth of the Mistral bag o' tricks!"

At the same time, with three teams breathing down their necks, Team Horn had to make a choice.

"...They're positioned well," Oliver muttered, his mind's eye tapped into the view of his scout golems. "No matter where we go, we'll have eyes on us from at least two directions."

With the height advantage gone, they gained nothing by staying on this peak. The only question was how to get down. The eastern slope was bathed in sniper fire and had to be avoided, but going west would leave them fighting the other two teams at once. Now that they knew their foes were in cahoots, it was all the more important they target one at a time.

Oliver made his choice in light of that, turning to his companions.

"Let's try and surprise *them*. We'll take a big leap that way." He glanced to the northwest. "You both up for some acrobatics?"

Nanao and Yuri caught his drift and nodded in response. They all lined up in a row, facing the same direction. Athames in hand, the trio aimed for their feet and chanted in unison:

"""""Clypeus!"""""

Oliver's fine control pulled the three spells together. The spellstone ground gave them a boost—the rocks shot up, lifting them all. That lift hit their feet and propelled them into a bound, sending them hurtling across the sky toward the northwest.

"Whoa, this feels amazing!"

"Most exhilarating!"

"Enjoy it all you like, but be ready to land. **Elletardus!**"

Their flight was all too brief. The ground was coming up fast, and their last-second deceleration spell applied the brakes just before touchdown. They intentionally left plenty of momentum so they'd land running pell-mell.

"C'mon!" Oliver roared, at the fore. "Straight at Team Mistral and take 'em down!"

"Gladly!"

"Before Team Ames gets here!"

With everyone on board, they rushed through a patch of boulders toward their target team. Positionally speaking, things weren't at all bad. They'd landed to the south of Mistral's team, so if their foes tried to run for it, they'd have to go north. But since Team Ames was on the southwest end of the field, going north would *add* to the distance between them. Oliver's goal was to *isolate*. And with terrain this uneven, from the northeast, Team Liebert had no line of sight.

"…Hmm, they're not running," Oliver muttered.

Clearly, his enemies knew flight would be pointless. His golems could see Team Mistral holding their ground, ready for battle. Another few seconds of sprinting and they could see them with the naked eye.

"Did *not* see that flight coming. So hasty, Mr. Horn!"

"Mr. Mistral—"

Oliver's team ground to a halt. Before them lay a cluster of stone columns and three hooded figures among them. But then the hoods went down—and three identical faces appeared. Three more opponents emerged from the pillars on either side, and now there were *six* Rosé Mistrals facing them.

"We've got your welcome wagon ready. Let's party!"

All six sprang into action. Nanao raised her katana one-handed, and Yuri blinked furiously.

"Wow! They've all got the same face! Sextuplets?"

"Splinters and transformations mixed together!" Oliver yelled. "Don't be fooled—the splinters can't use magic!"

That was his best guess at the trick here. He knew this foe could use exceedingly impressive fakes—so of the six, half were splinters, and the real foes were Mistral and two transformed teammates.

"Going in!"

"Frigus!"

A spell interrupted Oliver's thoughts, and he blocked with the oppositional. Figuring the caster must be real, he aimed for them—but they quickly slipped behind a column. Another foe joined them, and then each stepped out from different sides. Oliver scowled.

"...Okay, if they shuffle often enough, it'll be hard to track who's real."

"Then we gotta down 'em as we spot 'em!" Yuri yelled.

He and Nanao plunged into the fray, and Oliver backed their strategy. It might have *seemed* reckless, but showing no fear was the right move. Splitting strength into the splinters reduced their enemy's output—going all out would overwhelm them.

"Gladio!"

Nanao's severing spell knocked down a stone column. If the obstructions allowed the real foes and splinters to trade places, then best to clear those away. Naturally, if possible, she planned to cut an opponent *and* the column.

While she kept the enemy on their toes, Yuri made his own aggressive move.

"Those footsteps sound off," he said. "If those are fake—then you're real!"

The moment his observations detected a discrepancy, he made a beeline for his target. Oliver and Nanao each shot a spell to back him and keep the other foes from stepping in. In the blink of an eye, Yuri was right on his foe—

"Huh?"

But as his athame swung in, he froze—in a very awkward stance. The Mistral before him smirked.

"Keh-keh-keh! Wrong answer!"

The laughing foe's body glowed white—and exploded, scattering fireworks. Yuri instinctively leaped back from the blast radius but couldn't avoid the light itself; he was left blind. The enemy pressed that advantage, firing a spell at his unguarded flank.

"Flamma!"

Oliver's spell barely managed to stifle it in midair. He and Nanao quickly moved in, shoulder to shoulder, clearing out the volley of spells.

"Tonitrus! You okay, Leik?"

"I'm fine! That was close, though."

It took only seconds for his vision to recover, and then Yuri was back in the fight. Certain he was uninjured, Oliver went back to analyzing—armed with new knowledge of their opponent's formidability.

"...Self-destruct magic embedded in the splinters. A nice trick, Mr. Mistral."

"Such praise! I'm touched."

"We accept tips."

"But which of us is *real*?"

Five foes taunted Oliver around five columns. If the fakes exploded, it was harder for Oliver's team to cut their way in. Their foes lacked offensive options, too, but Mistral's goal was to buy enough time for Team Ames to arrive—so he didn't really care.

The gist of the strategy was clear by this point. In light of that, Oliver turned to their next plan—but Yuri was frowning, mulling over his misstep.

"Man, it doesn't make any sense. I was *sure* I could tell them apart."

"His goal was to make you think that. I imagine—"

But midsentence, Oliver did a sudden about-face.

"Fragor!"

The spell he launched raced through the air—and a figure shot out from behind the pillar where it landed. A *seventh* foe, on the exact opposite side of the battle from the previous Mistrals.

"That one's real, Nanao!" Oliver yelled.

The Azian girl was already rocketing forward. With Oliver's team between the seventh foe and the rest of the Mistrals, the latter could offer no aid to their newest comrade. Realizing he would have to fight his own way out, the seventh foe drew his athame. Nanao's course never wavered.

"*Tonitrus!*"

"*Tenebris!*"

The bolt of lightning was blinding, so Nanao produced a blackout; the spells clashed, canceling each other out. The enemy tried to cast again, leaping back—

"Gah!"

—and a blade pierced his neck. Still in her casting stance, Nanao had thrust her way *right through* the clashing spells.

"Ms. Hibiya's strike goes through the throat! The first fighter down!"

"He misjudged the distance. Likely assumed without her two-handed Flow Cut, his spell would actually hit her."

Garland broke off again, glancing at the guest commentators.

Miligan quickly took over.

"Darkness against lightning. A beautiful use of an oppositional counter. For the benefit of the first-years, I'll explain—you *can* shoot down spells even without the use of the oppositional element. Push back a fire spell with fire of your own. But if you take that approach, both your spells will linger, clashing in the air, and as long as they're fighting for dominance, neither caster can step through that space. It leads to both parties keeping their distance and firing more spells. Since Team Horn needs to swiftly take teams down one at a time, Nanao wanted to avoid that outcome."

A clear explanation of the techniques and a demonstration of her ability to lead the younger students. Whalley was not about to let Miligan score all the points, and he rather forcefully interrupted.

"But if you *do* employ an oppositional element, the spells cancel each other out and quickly fade away. If there is little discrepancy between the power of the spells, you can *chase* your spell and close in fast. You

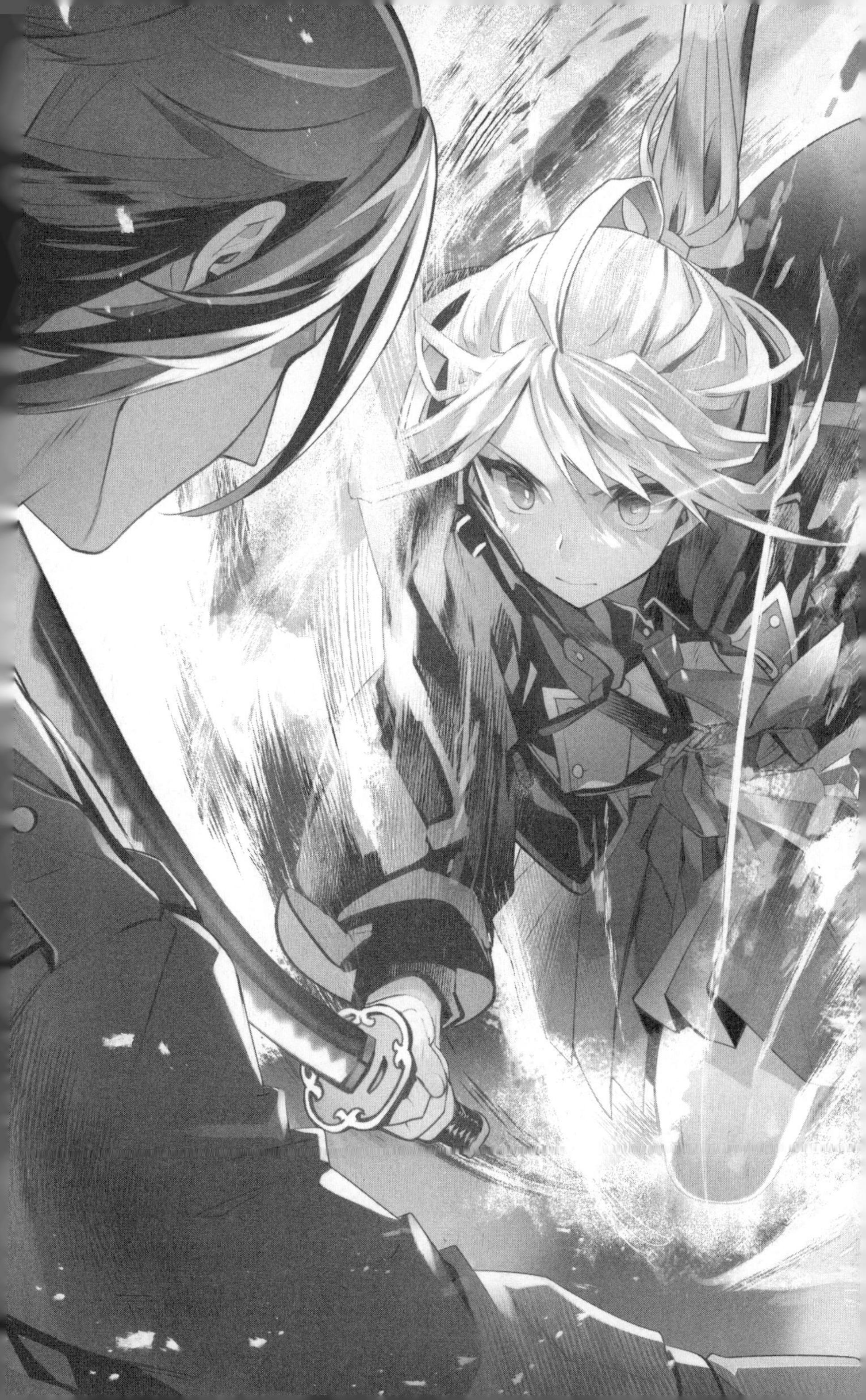

first have to identify the element your foe has used—so the closer you are, the harder it is. But if you pull it off, you'll be on top of your enemy a moment after casting. Whether that was the right judgment call in this situation aside, her decisiveness and gumption are certainly commendable. I would have gone for a more orthodox castoff myself."

Whalley wrapped things up with a trace of sour grapes, and Miligan smirked at him. She knew full well that whatever he might *say*, he was far too rational to underestimate the feat Nanao had just achieved.

Thrusting through an oppositional cancel was a choice she ordinarily would not have *needed*. Nanao Hibiya's primary style would simply employ her two-handed Flow Cut to deflect her opponent's spell and cut her way in. What was truly remarkable here was how effortlessly she'd pulled off an approach she ordinarily had no use for. A purely situational technique—one she'd nonetheless clearly honed till she could wield it on instinct.

And Percival Whalley was not one to diminish that type of slow and steady self-improvement. Which was why Miligan seized this chance to boast.

"Ha-ha! It's all too easy to be blinded by her uncommon skills, but Nanao has clearly mastered her magic-duel fundamentals, too. Oliver would hardly let her remain remiss on that front."

"But the match is still anyone's to win. The lost teammate was *not* Mr. Mistral himself," Whalley said with a frown. On-screen, the situation was in rapid flux.

The instant Nanao took out one Team Mistral member, two of the remaining foes disappeared into thin air.

"Fewer splinters," Oliver observed. "I'm starting to see the trick here."

Oliver stepped in—and Team Mistral turned on their heels, running. But he knew perfectly well there were no other teams ahead, and he swiftly gave chase.

"After them!"

"Sure," Yuri said, keeping pace. "But can I get a briefing as we run? My head's spinning!"

Oliver made sure Nanao was on their heels and started explaining.

"There were two types of splinters. The detailed corporeal models with the self-destruct and shadow splinters that were easier to detect. The former were likely under Mistral's own control, while the latter were operated from hiding by the opponent we just eliminated."

He was keeping it simple. When the fight started, they'd been facing Mistral himself, a student disguised as Mistral, a student hiding behind a rock, two corporeal splinters, and two shadow splinters for a total of seven. Since one type of splinter was more tangible than the other, they had assumed those were real—a trap that exploited the way the mind worked.

"Hmm, okay. So the one I thought was real was just a corporeal splinter. But how'd you know there was someone hiding nearby?"

"It's a classic strat. Flashy stunts and actions to distract you from the real threat. A technique common in magical comedy—your basic misdirection. That's why I had a scout golem wheeling overhead and keeping an eye on what it saw, which helped me spot the foe sneaking around."

Camouflage spells used while hiding were easier to spot on the move. Assuming there would be someone lurking nearby, he had intentionally left his back turned, making his foe *think* he was exposed. And when that lurker started moving, he'd spotted them through the golem and fired a quick spell to flush them out, sending Nanao in for the kill.

But there had been surprises, too—Oliver had assumed the foe in hiding was controlling the *corporeal* splinters, yet they'd actually been in charge of the shadows. That meant they still had to deal with one that could blow itself up—one that was that much worse. And of course, there was still Mistral himself.

"If they start working with any other teams, it'll be tricky. Finish them here!"

"Gladly!"

Nanao caught up with them, and they gave chase. Oliver's team had the speed advantage, so the gap was steadily closing. Oliver drew his athame, certain they had them—

"___?!"

Sensing a surge above, he leaped back. Nanao and Yuri did the same—and the ground before them exploded.

"Don'tcha go thinking you'll escape my sniping that easy," Camilla Asmus muttered.

She stood atop the northeast tower, white wand drawn. Naturally, she couldn't see Oliver's team at all from this vantage point. They were too far—and the steep rock formations themselves blocked her line of sight. No amount of squinting would help.

But that applied only to her *own* eyes. The eyes she was using were *above* her prey.

"Magnus Fragor!"

A second spell, fired at a high angle. It flew in an arc, cresting, before falling directly toward Oliver's team on the other side of the obstruction.

"There it is!" Thomas Chatwin cried, glancing up at his teammate's spell. "Angling her shots through golem spotters. Sure is something else."

He was busy building a slight distance from the tower. The moment Team Horn had ditched the peak and headed west, he'd stopped sniping and headed to ground level. He wasn't a half-bad sniper himself but definitely couldn't manage what Camilla was doing.

"No time to watch in awe. Gotta get my own job done. Argh, so much to do!"

Grumbling, he cast toward the ground, generating a wall. While the battle raged on elsewhere, he had time to prepare for what lay ahead.

*   *   *

A second burst spell dropped down ahead of Oliver's team. Not a miss at all—if they'd taken the shortest route after Team Mistral, they'd have been right under it.

"They can aim without any line of sight…!" Oliver shuddered.

And the tower was a considerable distance from here—few could even make the shot aiming *normally*.

There were three barriers to long-range spell sniping. First, getting the spell there. Second, hitting your target. And third, predicting where your target would be. The first barrier required high magical output and a honed mental image. The second required practiced technique and stable casting. And the third—well, reading the battle was a mix of sheer experience and an innate knack for it. Three towering obstacles, and their foe had added a fourth—aiming over a *literal* obstacle. They must be making indirect shots using scout golems stationed overhead, but that was clearly not something just any mage could do.

"We can't get too close to each other!" Oliver yelled.

Nanao and Yuri spread out. That at least should avoid them getting taken out together, but they'd need a much better plan, and fast. As Oliver racked his brain for one, Yuri raised a hand.

"I'll stave off the sniping," he said. "That'll keep me out of combat, but you can handle three-on-two, right?"

"…Go for it!" Oliver called, nodding. If they had one of them focused on the skies, the other two need spend far less of their attention on the snipers. This cost them a big chuck of their offense, but Team Mistral was already down one member—though they did have the remaining splinters. But Oliver and Nanao alone were enough to handle them.

They were back on the chase now. Yuri lagged slightly behind, eyes above, but they were steadily closing in.

Sensing that, one of the four Mistrals yelled, "They're on our heels! What do we do? Turn and fight? Spread out and hope for the best?"

"Hya-ha! Don't panic."

The real Mistral cackled. The perfect time to spring a trap was when your foes thought they had you.

"Turn and fight? Spread out? Don't be daft! We do what we do—*trick* 'em!"

He was already putting that into practice. Spotting a good-sized boulder up ahead, two Mistrals went on either side of it, shuffling the splinters and real team members. The new pairs ran off in opposite directions, but Oliver's side was prepared for that.

"Nanao, right! Leik, you're with her!"

"Consider it done!"

"Roger that!"

They broke away, and Oliver himself *acted* like he was chasing the pair on the left. But as he passed the boulder they'd used to shuffle their members—

"Tonitrus!"

—he fired off a spell without even looking, his arm alone pointing directly to one side. The ensuing bolt lit up the rock's surface, and a figure shot out of the damaged camouflage spell.

"...Dammit...!" the figure swore, grimacing.

Team Mistral had made it look like they'd split in two—but they'd actually added a splinter, leaving one behind the rock as an ambush. When Oliver had seen through the ruse, the lurker hadn't dodged in time—and was now down on one knee.

There was a trace of the oppositional element on his athame, so this was no splinter. His injured foe couldn't run, but Oliver approached with caution.

"That's the second time you've pulled that trick. You're the real one, Mr. Mistral!"

The moment he was in one-step, one-spell range, he lunged forward. With a leg lost, his foe stood no chance. Oliver knew he had him—but in that instant, lightning shot toward *his* side.

"____?!"

He quickly leaped back and fired off a spell at Mistral to keep him in place. As his foe dealt with that, Oliver quickly scanned his surroundings. On a rock to the rear left stood a short girl with bangs over her eyes.

"I barely made it in time," Jasmine Ames whispered, faintly out of breath, athame in hand. Very conscious of her, Oliver leaped behind a boulder, plotting his next move. She'd caught up faster than anticipated, and he couldn't afford to take risks here.

Keeping rocks between him and their spells, Oliver ran north. Once she was certain he was moving away, Ames sighed and lowered her blade.

"A swift retreat. That gentleman never overestimates himself. Most admirable."

"Ha-ha…you saved my ass for sure."

Mistral wiped the sweat from his brow. Ames quickly moved over.

"I'm unable to provide assistance to your compatriot," she said. "The odds of your team emerging victorious are slim—but may I ask one more favor of you, Mr. Mistral?"

Her tone cold, she had her athame's tip pointed his way. It was an order phrased as a question—and Mistral had no choice but to agree.

With one crisis over, it fell to the announcers to sum things up. Miligan was smiling, arms folded.

"A fight well worth watching. We simply must lavish praise on Team Horn's adaptability. Don't you agree, Mr. Whalley?"

She took a jab at her political rival, which earned her a frown. Garland stepped in instead.

"Two types of splinters, of very different natures. Mixed in with transformed teammates, creating confusion, and using hidden companions to attack from their blind spot. Team Mistral's strategies were plenty viable in their own right. The fact that Team Horn handled that on sight is, as Ms. Miligan said, well worth praising."

That went straight to the Snake-Eyed Witch's head, and she jumped at the chance.

"Oliver's the one making the calls here. Nanao may find her route to victory through pure instinct, but that's not him. He must be bringing in a wealth of projections—a genuinely dizzying number—and incorporating those into their combat on the fly. The instant he realized their opponents were using splinters, he was already prepared for a trap like that."

Sensing that this would never end if he allowed it, Whalley cut in.

"…He can make such accurate calls based on prior conjecture alone? How exactly has this boy trained?"

"Curious?" Miligan said, leaning in. "Want me to teach you the secret art of flawless judgment? Mm?"

Meanwhile, Guy was watching them from the stands.

"…She's got nerves of steel. Already making it sound like this is *her* doing."

"Well…um…she *is* teaching us stuff…," Katie said, looking highly ambivalent.

Miligan was definitely providing Katie with firsthand instruction, but she wasn't exactly teaching Nanao or Oliver on a day-to-day basis. But since they were rooting for her in the election, pointing that out seemed unwise.

In the booth, the two rivals were still bickering. Whalley had started edging away from Miligan.

"We have praised Team Horn enough!" he declared. "Ms. Ames's movements were equally commendable. No normal run would have reached Team Mistral in time, so she closed the difference in a bound, using the same convergence magic as Team Horn. Leaving her team behind extended the length of the flight. A decision that paid off big-time."

"Very true," Miligan said readily. "I thought from the start that her movements were head and shoulders above her teammates. You'd think a girl of her abilities would have made a name for herself by now, and I'm downright baffled that this is the first I've heard of her. Was she intentionally hiding what she can do?"

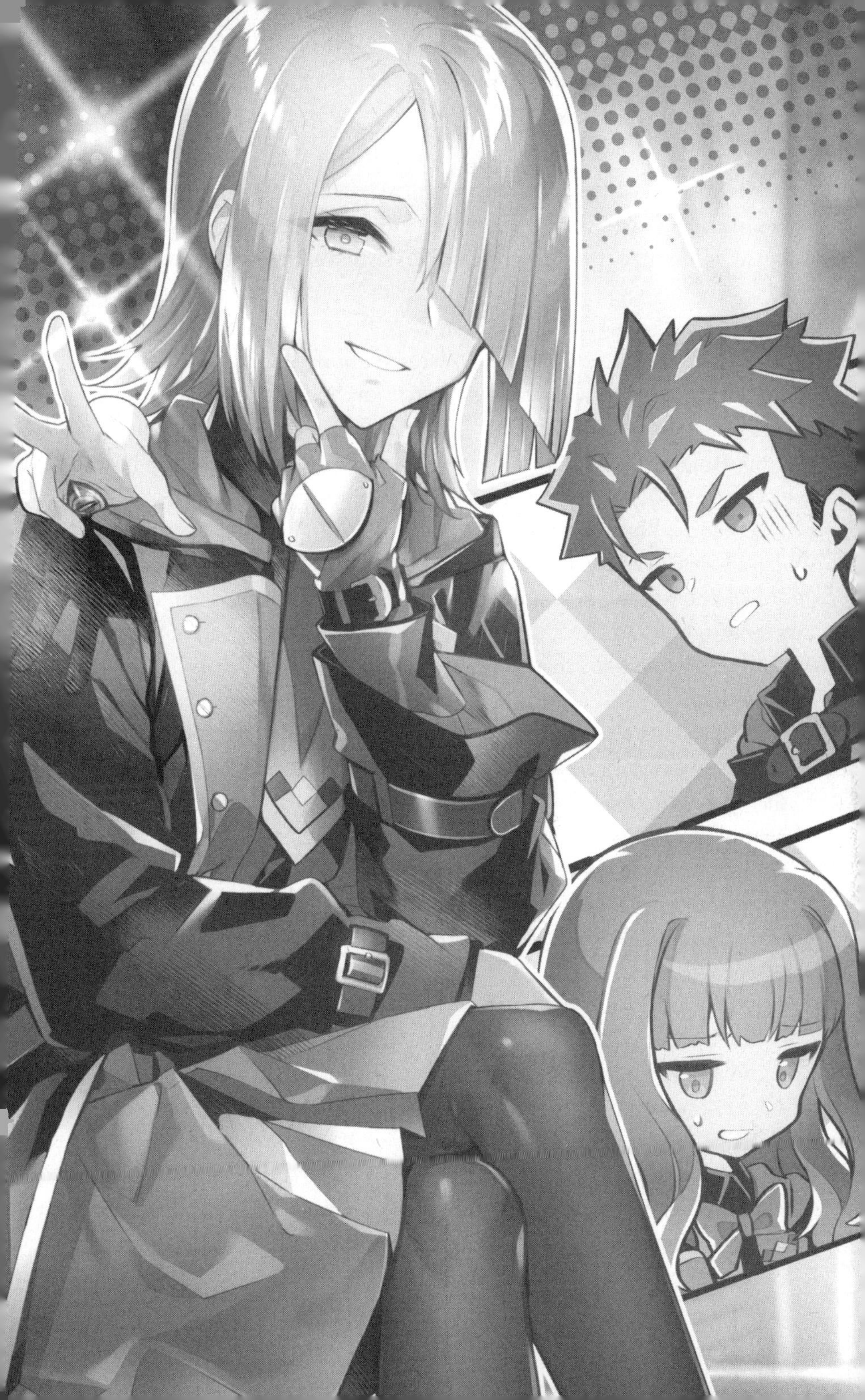

"Oh!" Glenda cried. "Ms. Hibiya has caught the remaining Team Mistral member! With their leader down a leg, Team Horn has made a big comeback from a clear disadvantage! What will each team do next?"

Team Mistral had made several miscalculations, but their biggest was just how much the loss of an arm *didn't* slow Nanao Hibiya down.

"*Flamma!*"

Spotting her behind him, the last Team Mistral member must have decided escape was not an option. He cast a spell to intercept her.

Nanao's athame was a two-hander—it was natural to assume the loss of an arm would be a disadvantage. Loss of blade pressure during sword art exchanges, and the reduction of swing speed when using it as a wand, would work against her in a casting duel. And naturally, both of those applied to her.

"*Frigus!*"

So she had to *compensate*. Avoid getting bogged down trading spells. Use the minimal necessary strength to cancel unavoidable spells on the approach and redirect any magic conserved by that to her legs, helping her close the distance faster. The precision was astonishing. The moment she heard the first syllable of her opponent's chant, she knew the oppositional and was already chanting a spell of her own. Once fired, she didn't wait for the spells to dissipate but charged straight through the space as they clashed. Such a move required snap judgment and steady nerves.

"*Tonitrus…!*"

The Mistral member desperately chanted another spell, thinking, *It wasn't supposed to be like this!*

Generally speaking, oppositional elements were primarily used by those with low magic output. After all—in a basic one-on-one duel, whoever was more powerful didn't *need* to pick and choose what they cast. No matter what spell they used, they could power through—freeing them up to focus on aim and speed.

But at a power disadvantage, that was not an option. They were forced to make up for their lack of might. Use of oppositional elements was a key part of that, and even if they couldn't entirely cancel the spell, they could deflect it, improving their own evasion. With directly opposed elements, the clash effects were simple and easy to predict—if other elements clashed, it was far harder to tell how the spells would react. Mages might find themselves soaking the brunt of a surprise flare, and fear of that tended to make their footsteps falter.

The astounding thing here was that Nanao Hibiya in peak condition had *no* such concerns. Her magic output was at the top of her class and was expected to get even better as she grew. It was rare for her to encounter situations that forced her to make careful use of oppositionals, and her infamous two-handed Flow Cut made short work of it if she did. She never *needed* this kind of precision casting. Training for it would be low priority—at least, that's what everyone assumed. Mistral's team had.

So their error came from neglecting what effect having Oliver Horn around would provide. Missing the fact that his coaching ensured that Nanao Hibiya had a thorough grounding in *all* things a mage could require.

"Gah... **Clypeus!**"

In range of her blade, the Team Mistral member would wind up like his companion before him. Desperate to avoid that fate, he went for a blockade spell. The spellstones in the ground strengthened it, giving him a sturdy rock shield—

"Gladio!"

—yet her spell cut right through it *and* hit him hard across the torso. "Kah...!"

Detecting a fatal blow, the ring around his neck activated—and in the instant before his consciousness faded, the Mistral member knew why he'd lost. Barriers made with blockade magic could defend against most spells, but there was a delay between the cast and the wall fully sprouting from the ground. He was well aware of that weakness, and that had led him to emphasize the speed at which the wall had formed. And that haste had undermined his image of the spell, creating a barrier too flimsy to stand up to her severing spell.

"...Shit..."

With a curse on his lips, he toppled over. When she was sure he was down, Nanao silently lowered her blade.

"Oh, you got him already? Quick work, Nanao!" Yuri cried, catching up. The scout golems above signaled them to remain on standby, so neither moved. Less than two minutes later, Oliver appeared from the west. He'd seen the whole thing through his golems' eyes.

"I took out the left side. A corporeal and a shadow splinter. The latter vanished quick."

"Hrm? Then what of the last member?"

"Hid behind the boulder while they pretended to split up. I spotted that and took out his leg, but Ms. Ames interfered before I could finish him."

As he spoke, he took a good look at the face of the boy Nanao had downed. With the loss of consciousness, the transformation had faded, revealing his true form. Having confirmed that, Oliver looked up.

"This isn't Mistral, either. That means the one I fought must be. He still has his corporeal splinters available, so watch out for them as we fight the other teams."

"Sure, but he can't move that fast himself. Think he can keep making corporeal splinters?" Yuri asked.

Oliver considered it a moment.

"Splinters of that detail must burn through mana like crazy. He didn't seem like he had an unusual capacity, so if he can make more, it'll be two at best. Shadow splinters are another matter, but those are only sustainable near the caster."

At most, they had to worry about only two more self-destructs. Aware that was functionally the last gasp of Team Mistral, Oliver focused his mind on the scout golems. He had one to the west, but it was showing the boulder, now deserted.

"...Team Ames has scattered and gone into hiding. We could go search for them, but it'll take time to flush them out of cover. And there's every chance Mistral's splinters will waste even more of our time. Plus, if Team Liebert moves to the center of the map while we're at it, they'll be a problem. For safety's sake, we should go the other way around."

"Whoever acts first prevails," Nanao agreed.

Oliver nodded and looked east.

"If we run at speed, Team Ames can't keep up. Head for that tower."

All three broke into a run, but once they were up to speed, Oliver spoke softly.

"One more thing as we run. Something I noticed while my golems were doing a full map scan. This field might well—"

Meanwhile, up the top of that distant tower, they'd already spotted Team Horn coming. Team Liebert's sniper, Camilla, had long been biding her time, and she muttered, "Two down on Team Mistral— they're coming for us."

"I figured as much," Thomas said, shrugging. "Rough luck they didn't get at least one."

He had only just returned from his groundwork outside. He glanced over his shoulder, where their team leader sat—Jürgen Liebert.

"Boss, you recovered yet?"

Liebert opened his eyes and got to his feet.

"...I'm good to go. We'll just shoot 'em down."

His voice never wavered. His teammates both nodded.

"*Lutuom limus!*"

Oliver's spell hit a rock dead ahead, melting it. His team was picking routes with comparatively even ground, but obstacles like this kept blocking their path. This struck Yuri as odd.

"All these walls in our way, slowing us down. Another team's plan?"

"**Lutuom limus!** Yeah, while we were fighting across the map, they altered the terrain, knowing we'd be coming for them."

"Makes sense. Whoops, up above. **Frigus!**"

Yuri's spell intercepted another spell flying in. It was fired from the tower straight ahead, so not that tricky to handle, but focusing his mind and mana on defending did tend to slow him down. And that frustrated him.

"Hmm, this path is right in their line of fire, and there's all these walls. Maybe we should just circle 'round the mountain to our right?"

"No, this is the correct route. We'll just *pretend* we're circling 'round."

Oliver curved to the right, and Nanao and Yuri followed his lead. Not long after, two lights flashed at the top of the tower—spells activating.

"Now! Back to the left!"

All three made a sharp swerve onto their original route. A few seconds later, both spells hit the right-hand slope—and a large swath of it began to slide. A gray flow of rocks and sand.

"A landslide?!" Nanao cried.

"Yikes, glad we didn't go there!" Yuri said, eyes wide.

"They loosened the soil there and then hit it with a burst spell. If I were in their position, I'd have expected approaching foes to use that mountain as cover. That would be the first place I'd leave a trap."

He'd predicted their opponents' response to the situation at hand, and that was some small measure of comfort. Oliver's gaze shifted back to the tower above.

"For the same reasons, I'm intentionally not avoiding the blockades in our path. Odds are high they're trying to tempt us into using the less obstructed route nearby. They do slow us down, but traps we can't see are a bigger problem than walls we can."

"Hmm. Hmm... Hmmmmmm."

Yuri had pulled up alongside Oliver and was now staring intently at his profile.

Puzzled, Oliver asked, "Leik, is there something on my face? Focus on the path ahead."

"Ah-ha-ha, sorry, my bad. Just—suddenly real glad I'm on the same team as you."

"Uh, thanks? But frankly, you're getting the short end of the stick here. They came after *us*, and you're caught in the crossfire."

This was accurate enough; Oliver's and Nanao's reputations had encouraged the other teams to join forces. Yuri might have had better odds if he'd found another team.

"He speaks not of outcomes," Nanao said, smiling from ear to ear. "Do you, Yuri?"

Yuri flashed her a grin, one as bright and clear as any little kid's.

"I dunno how to phrase it," he began. "It just feels like I see the world clearer when I'm around you, Oliver. Maybe 'cause you're so good at explaining? Anyway, it's super fun."

The unexpected compliment left Oliver speechless. He turned his head away, cleared his throat, and changed the subject.

"…The tower's not far off. Once we arrive, it'll be full-on combat. Keep your wits about you."

"Yep!"

"Always!"

Good answers from both, and Oliver realized something. It was buried beneath the tension and need to concentrate, but…he, too, was really enjoying this match.

Back up at the tower, Thomas was spell sniping from the roof with Camilla, frustrated by their plans gone awry.

"Why aren't they taking the bait?! So not fair!"

"Horn's in charge. I expected nothing less," Liebert said. "Quit griping and slow 'em down."

Their leader was the kind of guy who never crossed a stone bridge without knocking it down and building a steel one in its place. He'd never bank on his enemy's mistakes. To his mind, this was proof things were going smoothly. Logical, accurate—it was easy for him to guess how Oliver thought.

"Shoot a few more, then head down. Be extra careful not to get detected."

"Sure thing."

"Got it."

Neither teammate looked concerned. Their faith in their leader was every bit as strong as Team Horn's.

"Hmm, the base is in sight."

Spotting a change up ahead, Nanao drew to a halt, and Oliver checked the view through his scout golems. The random dents and protrusions gave way to a smooth decline into a rounded crater, at the base of which were the tower foundations, encircled by a ten-foot-tall wall. He shared that view through his teammates' athames.

"That wall goes all the way around," Yuri said. "Any sign of our opponents?"

"No, none." Oliver shook his head. "Not since they left the roof."

He'd been watching carefully with two scout golems but had seen nothing at the base or the windows on the side. He *could* try sending one inside, but these golems specialized for conducting reconnaissance and, if discovered, could be easily taken down. If Team Liebert was their last target, that might be worth it, but Team Ames was still in full health, and he couldn't risk losing his scouts.

Oliver thought a few seconds longer, then picked a plan.

"…First, let's get over that wall and in on the first floor. If the enemy comes down to fight, we'll meet them there, but expect them to hole up elsewhere. In that case, we'll use convergence magic to collapse the tower from the base."

"A bold strategy!"

"Sounds like fun but a bit of a shame."

With both on board, Oliver lowered his voice.

"Enter as one from three directions. Leik on the left, me in the center, Nanao on the right. Don't just watch for enemy fire—expect traps."

Splitting up prevented the enemy from focusing their attacks. Once each companion had hit their start point, Oliver chanted a spell at the wall before him.

"**Lutuom limus—?!**"

But as he was about to gouge an opening, a bullet of wind came through the wall. Oliver twisted his body, dodging. The hole it made was barely the size of a fingertip, and the sight of that made him shudder. Wind this focused meant the caster was aiming directly at him.

"Whoa?!"

"Hng!"

Shouts went up from either side of Oliver. Yuri and Nanao had met similar fates. Natural reflexes and instincts allowed them both to dodge—

—and a flat voice drifted through the wall.

"You've come a long way—and this next part'll be longer. **Impetus.**"

"**"Impetus!"**"

All three leaped back as the foes across the wall fired more spells, aimed directly at their vital points. To avoid this, they began running, circling the defenses.

"Sniping through the wall…?! Nanao, Leik! Block their view above! **Covell!**"

He soon unfurled a curtain of darkness overhead, and his team followed suit. The first attack had been a shock, but he'd fired spells through walls himself in the fight with Miligan. Their opponents clearly didn't have a direct line of sight—which meant the blackout spell would shut down any scout golems and—

"——?!"

But his read was quickly overturned by two spells that skimmed past, one in front, one behind.

"The accuracy's not letting up…?! They're not watching from above, then. But how?"

Oliver's eyes darted around, searching for an answer. When he looked down, he found it. The ground was *too* flat. Even a golem fortification had no need to make the surface this smooth—all it did was make things *easier* on encroachers. And the lack of magic traps around the base was downright unnatural. If there was meaning in that—

"You're kidding?! The ground's—!"

Across the wall, Team Horn was in trouble. The three members of Team Liebert couldn't see them but knew right where they were. Magical maps of their base were installed on the floor here and there, displaying three moving dots.

"**Impetus!** How do you like dancing in the palms of our hands?!"

"**Impetus!** Don't get cocky. They'll figure it out soon enough," Liebert growled. He fired a spell through the wall, and it *almost* hit.

"…The ground's part of the golem! We're on the enemy's skin!" Oliver yelled, dodging spellfire as he raced along the wall's length. But the conclusion he'd reached provoked looks of surprise.

"Um—you mean the ground can sense us? Like we can see bugs walking across our skin? The tower knows where we are?"

"Accurate enough! They can pinpoint our positions!"

Even as Oliver answered, his mind was racing. The ground's flatness and the lack of magical traps were both choices made to improve the feedback precision. That suggested the tower's detection was likely using pressure, heat, or mana, but figuring out which and preparing countermeasures would take time. Team Ames was closing in from the west, likely less than five minutes out—time was a luxury they could not afford.

"Should we just shoot back?" Yuri suggested. "If these walls are a circle around the tower, then they're in the center, right? Random shots should hit!"

Oliver shook his head. "I considered it, but the inner and outer sides of this wall handle attacks differently. Our spells won't penetrate as easily as theirs are. A shootout through the wall leaves us at a disadvantage."

They could arc their spells over the wall, but that meant their spells had to travel farther than their opponents'. He'd rather punch a hole in the wall itself, but that would require focusing a spell on the same spot for several seconds running, and the ceaseless barrage prevented that. He even considered running up the wall and vaulting over, but the enemy must be watching for that—the moment their faces came into view, they'd be hit by focused fire and downed.

They had to get past the wall, but aggressive measures would backfire. With that in mind, he thought, was there a way to overcome this impasse?

"But what part?" Nanao asked, running some distance from him. Oliver and Yuri looked her way, throwing feints into their runs to throw off their foes' aim. "If this ground is skin, what part of the body? The tops of the feet, the palms, the brow? Perhaps the chest or stomach?"

"? Uh, that was a metaphor—"

"Ah, I see." She frowned. "Taken literally, I imagined the sensitivity of it might vary by location."

A simple notion, but it caught Oliver's ear.

"…That actually makes sense."

"Impetus! See, see? You're helpless!"

Team Liebert alone was on the offensive here. But a moment later— their assault died down. This strategy relied upon the magic maps on the floor, but the three dots had stopped flitting around the surface—and vanished completely.

"…?"

"Yo, boss! It ain't showing their positions!"

Suspecting something amiss, Camilla and Thomas turned toward the caster. But Liebert himself was scowling at the wall.

"…Well played."

Across the wall, Oliver's team was still on the move—just not on the ground. All three were using Wall Walk, their feet planted on the side of the wall itself.

"Big drop in shot accuracy! Sensors *were* only on the ground!"

Spells were still coming but well away from any of them—proving this was the correct solution.

"Ohhh," Yuri said, looking very impressed. "If the ground won't work, try the wall! Good idea, Nanao!"

"I solved nothing myself, but if we have our answer, I welcome it."

They were speaking softly lest their voices reveal their locations, running lightly around the walls. Even more certain his theory was right, Oliver focused his attention on the other side of the barrier.

"They're on the wall…!"

Footsteps echoed in their ears, clearly coming through the wall itself. Thomas's eye twitched.

Watching the other direction, Camilla asked, "Can't tell where on the wall? Ain't that part of the golem?"

"…Afraid not. There's no sensors on the wall itself. Adding them would have to start with the schematic."

Liebert was clearly not happy. He'd certainly anticipated they might try running up the wall, but he assumed his team could handle that based on where the run began. He hadn't expected them to turn the wall's surface into their main footing. And having them perpendicular to the ground meant they were much smaller targets. Sniping them like this was unreasonably harder, and Thomas let out a wail.

"I need height…! Can I move to the top of the wall?"

"Absolutely not," Liebert snapped. "You'll be cut down before you get there."

From above, they might have a clear view of their foe, but Team Horn would hardly stand by and *let* them reposition. Relentless spell-fire from all three of them was the only thing staving off incursion; if the barrage died down at all, their opponents would hit back hard and make short work of them.

"Don't *panic*," Camilla sneered. "We've got *more* walls, and they'll have to punch a hole—and that'll give us a target."

That brought Thomas back to earth. With mana diverted to their feet, it was tough for any third-year to doublecant while Wall Walking. If Team Horn wanted to punch a hole in the wall, they'd have to converge and repeatedly cast single-incantation spells. And the hole itself would give away their location. Their aim would be approximate, covering the general area, but they could make up for that in size and quantity of projectiles.

With the plan in mind, they bided their time. And they weren't wrong—soon enough, magic turned a chunk of the northwest wall from gray to dark brown. Camilla turned her wand to it.

"See? **Magnus Fragor!**"

"**"Magnus Fragor!"**"

It wasn't just the one. Two, three doublecant spells from the interior. Oliver's team watched them fly from their positions on the wall, well away from that location—and their run resumed.

"Three doublecants! Get through now!"

The enemies themselves had destroyed the wall, and they stepped on through, flinging themselves to the interior. Opening any hole would allow for telltale signs on the far side; they'd been well aware this would leave them exposed. The liquefying spell had merely primed the pump; they'd backed off quickly once their foes reacted, making Team Liebert open a hole for them. Unable to determine Team Horn's actual locations, they were forced to up the attack size, using doublecants to blow away a big chunk of wall.

But getting through one wall didn't exactly mean they were able to directly engage. The second they stepped inside—a *second* wall rose up from the ground before them. Yuri blinked, surprised.

"What? Another wall?!"

"They have spares?!"

"Don't worry—the same plan'll work. Pick our moment and get through!"

Oliver led the way. He'd never for a second believed there'd be only one line of defense. If once wasn't enough, they'd just have to try twice or three times. He, Nanao, and Yuri started running along the second wall.

Team Liebert had prepared three walls for their tower defenses. Since getting through the first wall meant they'd have figured out there were sensors in the ground, the area before the second wall was covered in magic traps. But these were not designed for foes running on the wall itself. Team Horn had simply jumped from the first wall's interior to the second wall's exterior, never once setting foot on the ground and giving the traps no chance to activate.

And the fact that their own spells had allowed this intrusion made Team Liebert hesitate. Sensing that, Oliver's team quickly opened a hole themselves and were through the second wall. The final wall rose maybe ten yards from the tower itself.

"Dammit!" Thomas yelled, feeling their foes breathing down their necks. "That's the last one! Hit, please, let me hit! Impetus—gah!"

He was starting to fire frantically, so Camilla kicked him in the back. He fell flat on his face, then gaped up at her.

"Cool your head," the sniper snarled, her wand trained on the wall. "If you start praying for a hit, you're done. Better off not shooting at all."

There was a quiet fury behind her voice, fueled by the countless hours she'd put into her craft. That time had given her a sniper's pride.

"Don't pray. *Aim*. No matter if they're too far, too fast, or outta sight. As long as they *exist*, they've got a *tell*."

Words her mentor had left with her. Teachings direct from the Supreme Witch of a Thousand Years echoing in her heart, Camilla Asmus focused all senses she had. The situation was tense, but from another perspective—not all that bad. With the walls this much closer, it was easier to detect their foes. The ears were more viable than the eyes—the sound of footsteps on the walls was all she needed.

"———"

With her mind focused on sounds alone, she could tell someone on Team Horn was running diagonally up the wall in front of her. It wasn't enough to take proper aim, but she could tell generally where they were headed. That made it possible to place a pebble in their way.

"Fragor!"

Camilla's wand released a burst spell, her image leaning hard toward penetration, set to detonate just after it passed through. Since the bulk of the mana was devoted to just piercing the wall, the blast itself was not that strong, but no opponent could ignore an explosion in their path. Especially during a Wall Walk—they'd have to change direction or slow down, either of which would make it tough to maintain the technique. The result—they could no longer fool gravity, and it caught them—dragged them down.

A dot blinked on the magic map at her feet. In that instant, she knew right where her foe was through the thick wall.

"Fortis Impetus!"

Her aim locked on, a gale shot from her wand. Its range of damage spread wide to each side. This shot was closer to her target than any shot before, and they'd just landed and were off-balance. They stood no chance of dodging. She *had* them. The spell carved an ellipse in the wall like a cookie cutter.

"...Did you get 'em?"

The footsteps had ceased. Keeping one eye on his surroundings, Thomas peered into the hole, expecting to find a fallen foe—but Camilla had the answer first.

"Hah..."

It was Nanao Hibiya. On one knee, the katana in her right hand thrust to the fore, the strength in her eyes diminished not one iota. That sight alone told Camilla the fate of her spell.

"...Nice," she said, unconscious praise escaping her lips. Objectively, her shot had been nigh flawless. The speed and force of the spell had been on point, timed to maximize the difficulty of evasion or blocking. If there was any chance of failure, it lay in one thing—a foe who *expected* to be hit on a landing and was already chanting an oppositional doublecant as their feet left the wall.

"*"Fragor!"*"

An instant later, two figures leaped through the hole Camilla had dug. As they passed through that final barrier, Oliver and Yuri cast to make Team Liebert flinch. Then they split up, closing in from both sides. Nanao herself came down the center.

Seeing their defense about to collapse, Camilla yelled, "Go, boss!"

"Obliged! **Clypeus!**"

Leaving a small barrier as some modest support, Liebert turned and fled. Three-on-three at this range, they could not win—and they were way past the point of escape. Liebert still had a part to play, and the others would be his shield. Their roles here were designated well in advance.

Camilla simply raised her wand, and Thomas stepped up next to her. All traces of his earlier consternation had since vanished—he was almost eerily calm. The failed attempt to snipe Nanao had blown aside all unnecessary emotions.

"Sorry. My head's level now."

"Good. Then overlap with me."

Oliver and Yuri were trying to flank them, but the tower's pillars and the barriers Liebert had left were momentarily shielding them. Sparing no thought to what would happen once those fell, they aimed their wands for Nanao Hibiya alone. Their mage's instincts told them so—even down an arm, she *had* to be their primary target.

"Flamma!"

"Frigus!"

As she closed in, Thomas and Camilla fired polar-opposite spells that overlapped. Even if Nanao used an oppositional to cancel the first, the other element would hit. She was running full tilt toward them and could not dodge to either side. On her own, she could never block this attack—

"Flamma!"

—but Oliver spotted it, and his spell shot in, canceling his foe's second spell. Nanao canceled the first with the oppositional as Yuri's lightning hit Thomas in the chest. Camilla switched from her sniper's wand to her athame, but by then Nanao was on her, piercing her chest before she could even raise the blade.

"Magnificent shooting," the Azian girl said.

"Thanks."

A brief exchange in passing. Then the spell on the rings activated. Thomas and Camilla went down, and Team Horn never even looked back, charging in after the final foe.

"——!"

Oliver's eyes went wide. Liebert was ignoring them completely, his athame pointed at his feet. He was standing dead center on the first floor, in the middle of the tower's foundation. A prediction—no, a conviction—sent a shiver down Oliver's spine.

"Delclts!"

And the incantation that followed put truth to his fear. The floor caved in beneath Liebert, swallowing him—and cracks ran out, up the pillars across the ceiling. The waves of destruction rose higher and higher, collapsing the golem fortification less than an hour after it was built.

The ground was covered in the tower's rubble, kicking up a cloud of dust so thick, visibility was measured in yards. One boy was left looking around.

"They knocked it down themselves?! Hope everyone's okay," Yuri Leik said.

It might be a golem, but that fortification was still a *building*. It had taken a fair amount of time to completely collapse—enough for the people inside to get out before the rubble buried them. But each had fled in a different direction, and Yuri hadn't been able to confirm his companions' well-being. Much as he'd love to shout, Team Ames was likely on top of them, making that ill-advised.

"Send a mana frequency to the golems above... No, bad idea. With no visibility below, he'll have them spread out, and that just means our opponents' golems would pick up my frequency. Hmm, now what?"

"Over here, Leik."

As he pondered how to locate his teammates, a voice came from shockingly close at hand. Yuri spun around and saw a pile of rubble towering high—and his friend's voice came from within.

"My arm's stuck...in the rubble..."

"Oliver?! Just you wait—I'll get you out!"

Yuri hustled over to him. He wanted to start casting, but without knowing exactly how Oliver was buried, he had to check that first. He bent over, trying to see between the gaps.

"Huh?"

Then he heard something that made his body leap back faster than thought. The rubble exploded from within, a blade thrust out directly at his throat. Yuri barely got his own athame up in time to deflect it.

"Yikes?!"

"…You blocked that?"

The figure took a step back, facing him at one-step, one-spell range. A girl with bangs over her eyes—Jasmine Ames. Yuri's brain finally caught up.

"Ms. Ames…you mimicked his voice? Fascinating!"

He seemed to take it in good cheer. Ames inched ever closer.

"You are an enigma, but I am lacking in time. I need you out, Mr. Leik."

"Cool—let's do this!"

He nodded, delighted to go toe to toe with a powerful foe—

"Leik, where are you? Answer me!"

"Yuri! Reveal yourself!"

Oliver, too, was searching for his team in the dust. He'd found Nanao and no longer needed to keep quiet—Yuri must have been close, so they prioritized locating him and started yelling. Then their ears caught a hint: shoes treading on loose rocks. They ran that way…

"Whoa—"

…and that's where they saw Yuri's eyes gleaming with curiosity—a marked contrast with the view below: Ames's athame was stabbing him directly in the chest.

"Yuri!"

"…!"

Both Nanao and Oliver had their blades up at once, but as the ring knocked Yuri out, Ames used his body as a shield. When they halted their attacks, she shoved him their way and fled. They tried to pursue, but two lightning bolts shot over Ames's shoulders.

"A close call, but at least we've downed one… There's hope for us yet."

Ames left a murmur in her wake, and Oliver caught a glimpse of two more figures in the swirling dust. Once more, she'd sent the most mobile member out ahead, her teammates bringing up the rear before she picked Yuri off when he was isolated.

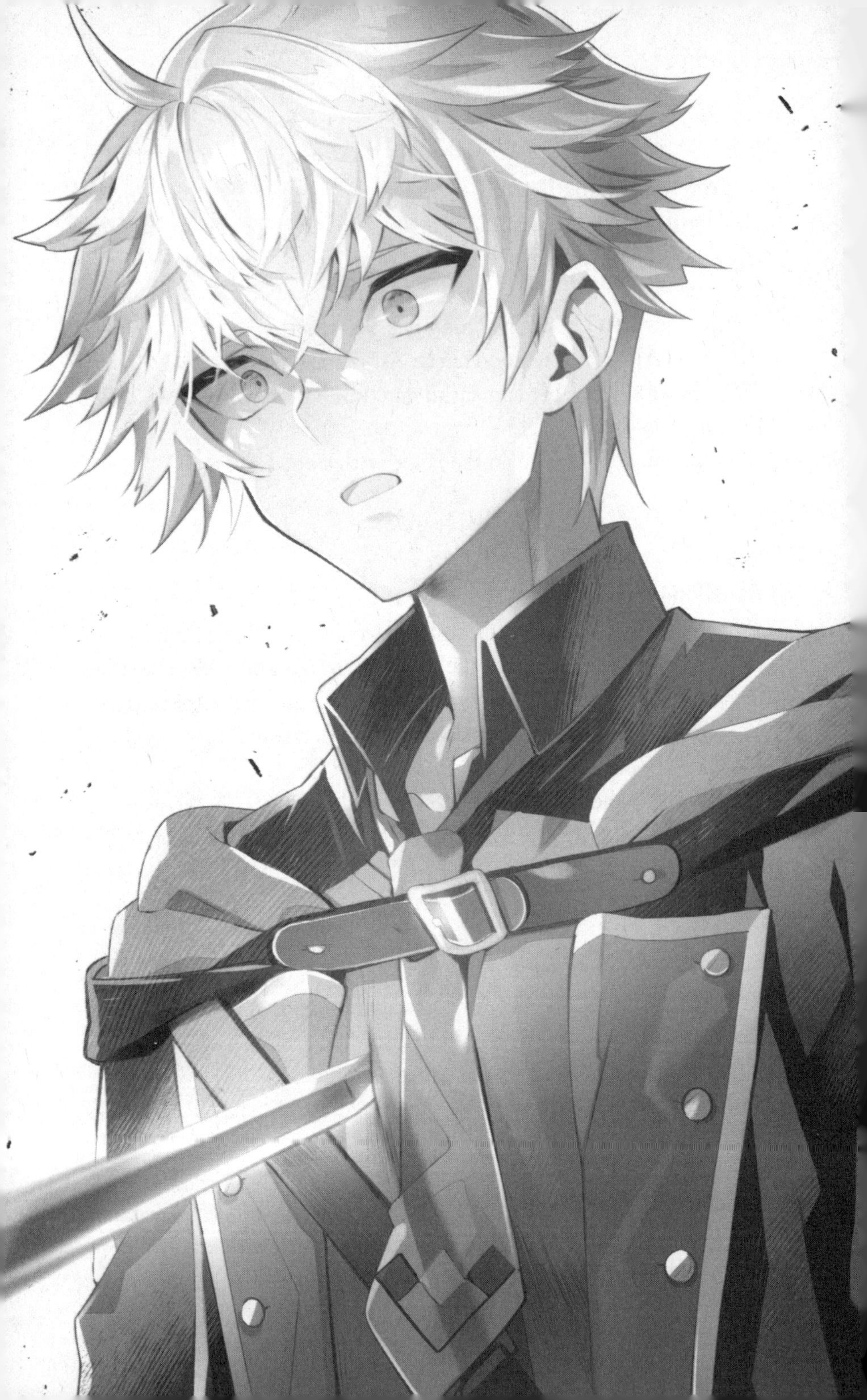

Oliver braced for more. Once she was a safe distance from him and Nanao, Ames glanced up at the fallen tower.

"Team Liebert was prepared for anything, yet you took them down in no time. An impressive feat."

"...All part of your grand plan? Including the part where you didn't make it here in time?"

There was a trace of spite in his query; Oliver was mostly trying to buy time for the dust to settle.

But a smile played on Ames's lips—then she sighed softly.

"Would that I could claim it was, but you give me too much credit. You remaining while the other teams drop out is the opposite of our intent."

Seeing no reason to conceal this, Ames allowed herself a moment of self-deprecation. They were not yet in any state to snatch victory from the embers. They had not delayed their rescue of Team Liebert—they had simply arrived too late. Ames had been moving out ahead and arrived as the tower fell, with no opportunity to interfere in the battle that came before.

"That said, Mr. Leik is out, and Ms. Hibiya has lost her left arm. Far from what we'd hoped, but not yet worth lamenting. Still, this is no time for idle chatter. As promised, I'm here for your head."

With that bit of bravado, Team Ames moved forward. As the dust thinned, Oliver and Nanao stood ready.

"*Clypeus!*"

"*Gladio!*"

Team Horn acted first. As the battle began, Oliver threw up a wall before them. Nanao leaped behind it, her severing spell aimed through the wall at their foes in a surprise attack based on the same principle that had allowed Team Liebert to torment them. Ames and one team mate heard the incantation and dodged, but the third member's thigh was gouged by the magic blade.

"Guh...!"

"*Haaah!*"

The ring on her ankle activated, numbing her right leg as badly as any real injury. Slowed by this, Nanao stepped in close. Ames jumped in and barely parried; Oliver had cast a spell at the same target, and the remaining teammate narrowly managed to cancel that. This at last got them off the ropes, and all members of Team Ames backed off.

"Sorry, Jaz…!"

"Fine," Ames whispered. "As I feared, three against two is still not enough."

A single exchange had been enough to prove their disadvantage. Oliver and Nanao were guarding each other's backs while realizing their full potential, but Ames had to cover for her teammates, which meant her own attacks lacked bite. With one down a leg, this would only get worse.

If the two teams kept fighting, her side would not last long. With that calm assessment, Ames switched plans—and laid the foundation for her next tactic.

"Then if you'd be so kind, Mr. Mistral—launch the final firework."

"Keh-heh…," Mistral laughed.

Behind a rock on the west end of the field, far from the flow of battle—with his leg gone, he couldn't reach the others if he tried. But that didn't mean he couldn't *fight*.

"Outta mana anyway. Might as well dump it all!"

The yell helped psych himself up. He squeezed the last power out of his brain to process the view—from the two splinters who'd just reached the collapsed tower.

Two figures flew out from behind a mound of rubble. Oliver and Nanao immediately sensed their approach from the south.

"Hrm—!"

"…Thought so!"

They weren't hard to spot. This was the only timing for the splinters to join in, and since constructing the collapse tower had absorbed all the spellstones in the area, the view was excellent. They'd been careful not to let Team Ames draw them into more obstructive terrain, watching for an attack from all directions. As long as they kept the upper hand in battle, this was a simple task.

"I'll watch the splinters! You keep pressing Team Ames!"

"Gladly!"

They were already moving. Both were far faster than the splinters, and it seemed safe to assume their sole means of attack was exploding in proximity. They could not easily approach while the two of them were forcing Team Ames to fight defensively, and if they tried anything while Team Ames was on the retreat, it was easy to swing back and take them out. And the situation afforded no opportunities for Mistral's tricks.

"Keh-heh!"

"Or so you'd think!"

The Mistral splinters smiled cryptically—and the game changed. Leaving their leader on the spot, Ames's backup duo turned and ran south. Oliver frowned at that.

"Splitting up? Joining forces with the splinters?"

They'd been struggling with all three, so dividing themselves still further didn't seem like a viable idea. His side could just pick them off, and even if they did join with the splinters, they were unlikely to work well together. And even getting that far seemed like a long shot. Without Ames nearby to back them up, Oliver's team could make short work of them both.

""It's fun time!""

Deeming it the natural choice, he and Nanao had turned toward Ames's backups. But out of the corner of their eyes, they saw both Mistral splinters explode. Oliver hadn't expected them to self-destruct here, but when he noticed how much smoke billowed out, he changed his mind.

"Smoke orbs…!"

Mistral had given the splinters magic tools, triggered by the self-destruct, and the winds of the blast spread the smoke far and wide. The Ames duo plunged right into the thick of it. Oliver quickly changed his mind. They *could* still catch them, but by then they'd be inside the smoke.

"Going into that's a bad idea. Start with Ames!"

"Indeed!"

He and Nanao swung back north, running toward Ames. The worst-case scenario here would be chasing the others into the smoke and exposing their backs to Ames's blade. In which case, they'd just have to take her out first. He'd yet to gauge the measure of her skills, but with Nanao by his side, he could not imagine they'd fail.

Nanao had been leading the charge to the south, so the moment they'd turned toward Ames, their positions were temporarily reversed. That left Nanao at Oliver's back, not all *that* far behind.

Ordinarily, this would have been no big deal—but a moment later, the ground shot up between the two of them.

"Wha—?!"

"Oliver!"

A wall, before Nanao's very eyes, right on Oliver's heels—no warning whatsoever. Unsure what to make of it, both stopped—and Ames didn't miss a beat. She lunged at Oliver, and their athame guards clashed.

She yelled at her distant companions: "Now's your chance!"

"*"Fortis Flamma!"*"

The Ames duo had turned back and had spells ready. Two doublecants—and Nanao was up against the wall. Even she had no choice but to dodge. Leaving the wall put even more distance between her and Oliver, and he gritted his teeth as he forced Ames's blade away.

"…Liebert's doing…?"

"You don't miss much."

A reluctant compliment.

Oliver himself was more impressed than shocked. Their opponents had devised all manner of schemes to take his team down.

*   *   *

"...He'll know what that means," Liebert muttered, lowering his wand.

He was in a crypt-like space underground, not far below the clashing duelers.

"And that's the last of my mana. Finish him, Ames."

His eyes were on the wall in front of him—on a magic map, like the ones they'd used during the fight with Team Horn. This time, however, it wasn't displaying the defenses around the fallen tower but a location to the east—exactly where they were fighting now. It had taken all three teams working together to lure Oliver's group to the site of this final battleground.

Team Liebert had readied several contingencies in case their tower was taken. The tower's self-destruct was the first of these—naturally, it was designed to take out their opponents with it. Second was this underground bunker—an escape route available only to the caster who knocked the tower down. That was how Liebert had wound up inside.

And the third contingency—a golem fortification sensor zone some distance from the tower and a magic map to display the targets within that range. This allowed him to follow the battle from down below. He wasn't buried that deep, and the spellstones in the ground were boosting certain types of magic, allowing him to cast down here and affect the surface. And the magic map to pinpoint the positions of the other teams. Liebert had spent several minutes watching the dots, figuring out which dots were which team and how the battle was flowing.

He wasn't sure what difference splitting up Team Horn would have on the battle's outcome. But however the chips fell, he'd done his part. That spell had taken the last of his mana, and he was no longer even capable of digging his way back to the surface. He would have to hope for Team Ames's victory and wait for the league staff to rescue him. With that thought in mind, he leaned back against the wall—

"...Um...?!"

Liebert felt a powerful vibration from below—and found himself floating.

* * *

The ground glowed and began shaking—and their bodies were pulled toward the ceiling. Oliver and Ames both acted swiftly.

"Hah—!"

"Tsk—!"

Their athames had been guard-locked, but they pushed against each other, using that force to open the gap between them—and start casting.

"Flamma—impetus—tonitrus!"

"Frigus—prohibere—tenebris!"

Freed from all contact with the ground, combat was no different from trading spells at a standstill. Spell after spell clashed in the air, canceling each other out. All the while, they fell toward the ceiling above. Even as they cast, both were flipping themselves upside down for the landing to come.

""Elletardus!""

Deceleration spells cast moments before landing. Each went immediately into a sideways roll to lessen the impact and were back on their feet, athame trained on their opponent. Boulders that had fallen in tandem landed like a meteor shower all around them. They faced each other once more, their respective handling of the situation so identical, it was like a mirror held up between them.

"Magnificent," Ames said. "I take it you were aware that was coming?"

"Yeah...thanks to all the sniping, I was forced to take a broad view of the field."

As he answered, Oliver kept an eye on their surroundings. After all that time on even rocks, this ceiling was almost entirely flat, a gently sloped dome. The result of large-scale reversal magic cast on the majority of the map.

The moment had arrived without warning, but not without any prior indications. If one understood that Kimberly loved this kind of big gimmick, careful observation of the map did provide some clues—chief among them being the distribution of the spellstones. It was well camouflaged, so you'd never see it from ground level, but viewed from above, the map's rocky outcroppings formed lines, and those lines formed a pattern. Specifically—a massive magic circle.

"I figured it would activate as the match drew to a close," said Ames. "But…probably because Mr. Liebert used so many spellstones to create that tower, a chunk of the circle was rendered inactive. I did not expect us to be divided by polarities."

"Oliver!"

"Jaz!"

Shouts from above, where Nanao and Ames's teammates still stood. The reversal spell had caught Oliver and Ames, but the others had been closer to the tower, and in the nonfunctional section of the circle. When the spell activated, they were left behind—yet Oliver could not afford to glance their way.

Eyes on his opponent, he called out, "Don't step into the reversal zone! You'll be picked off as you fall!"

"I require no assistance! The two of you keep Ms. Hibiya occupied!"

This way, everyone could focus on their own fights. Then—mixed in with the falling rocks, a student fell behind them: Liebert, yanked to the ceiling, shelter and all. The blow of the fall had activated his rings, and he was unconscious.

"Mr. Liebert," Oliver muttered, confirming that in his peripherals. "Not surprised he was out of mana—the wall that split us up must have used the last of it."

"It seems it did. He and Mr. Mistral both fought till they could fight no more."

Ames's praise made Oliver wonder about the latter opponent. Mistral had used a lot of mana on those splinters and was likely unconscious somewhere on the west end of the ceiling. Even if he'd avoided an outright knockout, Oliver was sure he wouldn't be rejoining the fray.

"And I must live up to their efforts. While my girls are holding fast, allow me to finish you off."

Ames changed her stance. Her edge grew far sharper, and Oliver felt a tingle on his skin. The four teams had fought their way down to the

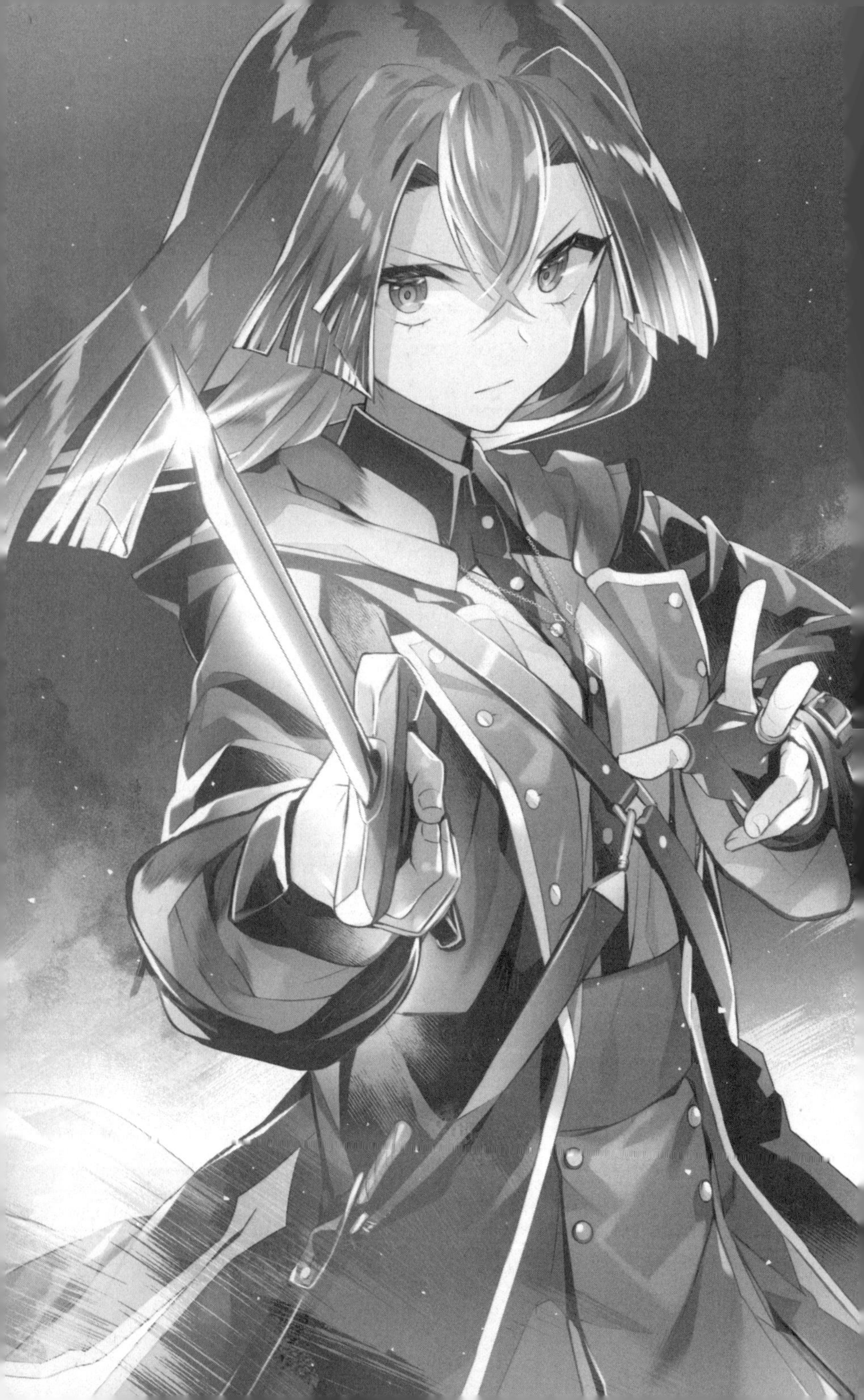

simplest of outcomes—whichever of them fell, the other would return to the surface and claim victory.

She looked ready to pounce, so Oliver adjusted his own center, shifting it forward.

"You've turned this into a proper duel. You've got the skills for it, then."

"They would have served me poorly against Ms. Hibiya. Fortunately, I am facing *you*."

A confident smile played on Ames's lips. Her manner suggested she believed he was beneath Nanao, but Oliver felt no anger. In fact, he smirked.

"Spare me the taunts, Ms. Ames. That's not your style."

His attitude sent a message—Nanao would never once consider buying time, waiting for the outcome above. Nor would he flee the duel, whether Ames resorted to words she never meant or not. When she caught his intent, the smile on her lips fell away.

"...Forgive the indiscretion. Pray forget I spoke at all."

As she said those words, a gust of wind caught her bangs. Her eyes contained the light of madness—and her lips curled into an uncanny arc.

"...!"

"In return, allow me to demonstrate—the Ames Spellblade."

The thin veneer of pretense gone, what stood before Oliver now was something he'd seen so many times in this hellscape. An arrogance that never once doubted her victory. The smile of a true mage.

"Gosh, the field's gimmick is live! A reversal spell on the whole field pulling our contestants to the ceiling! Chaos reigns over the finale!"

Glenda was at peak hype in the commentator's booth. But in the guest seat beside her, Whalley frowned at the view before him.

"That, I welcome, but the dust is rather intense. The fighters on the ceiling are completely obscured."

He spoke for the entire audience there. The feed provided by the surveillance golems showed nothing but the dust kicked up by the reversal spell's activation. The cloud covered every inch of the ceiling where Oliver and Ames were dueling. A chorus of boos went up from the stands, and Garland awkwardly scratched his head.

"That's on me," he admitted. "The reversal spell shouldn't have made line of sight this bad, but because Mr. Liebert drew ground from all around him, there was that much more rubble and loose earth than I anticipated. And it disabled a chunk of the circle, so…room for improvement."

As the sword arts instructor chalked it up to a planning failure, Miligan was scowling at the dirt cloud.

"Shame we can't see it. I imagine this duel will be over before the dust clears."

First—this would be no spellblade. As he faced Ames down, that was the first thought on Oliver's mind.

The reason for this was simple—if it *was*, he could not win. Fighting it with a spellblade of his own was naturally out of the question. That had to be saved for when there were no eyes on him and used on foes he had decided *must* be slain. This duel met neither condition.

His second thought—this was no mere bluff, either. The basis for that was none other than the fact that she *had* felled Yuri. That boy was made of instinct and inspiration, yet her blade had hit home—no matter what technique was employed, that was a formidable feat. Oliver himself had experienced it firsthand as they trained—Yuri could dodge moves he'd never seen like he was *meant* to. Even if caught entirely by surprise, his body would react via means the boy himself did not fully understand.

That wasn't flawless, of course. Oliver and Nanao had each landed hits several times during practice. But most of these were the result of a lengthy duel that wore him out, and it was very rare that either managed it in short order at the start of a fight. As long as Yuri's body could keep up with his mystery instincts, even an upperclassman would be astounded by how hard he was to put down. Yet Ames had managed it in the blink of an eye.

Oliver hadn't witnessed the entire fight. But the information he had proved it had been exceedingly brief. He found them together not long after the tower's collapse, without ever hearing a spell cast or the clash of blades. The fight had been over on the first hit—or at most a few extra swings. That was his best read on their encounter.

She had a way to take out Yuri in a handful of moves. Even if that was no spellblade, it was worthy of the utmost caution. In light of that, Oliver now had to consider the potential nature of her move.

"............"

"_____"

In the moments before either stepped in, he made observations. Ames was in the Rizett mid-stance, Lightning. A form he'd often seen close at hand, as Chela regularly employed it. Given the outcome of her match with Yuri, several points added up.

When he'd arrived, Yuri had been stabbed from the fore in the chest. In other words, she'd thrust her blade right at him, yet he'd been unable to parry or dodge. What stances would make that possible? The Rizett school was all about sharp thrusts and quick lunges, and Lightning stance was one of the fastest such moves. Whatever form she'd used to take Yuri out, it was only natural to assume speed had been a factor. From what he'd seen of her fighting style so far, Ames employed a mix of Lanoff and Rizett techniques, so this was consistent.

The logical conclusion was that his opponent's finisher was a snap thrust. There were hard limits on speeds that could be practically achieved, so it was likely a thrust that followed a series of high-level feints. Oliver knew the second spellblade by reputation alone, and *that* likely required no such thing—but in this case, he had decided to ignore that possibility from the get-go.

"...Whew..."

Lanoff style's mid-stance was all about balance and would not allow him to land a first strike against Lightning. Could he appropriately respond to the attack he was expecting? The accuracy of that reaction would determine his fate.

He had to parry the thrust in time, yet not get baited by the feints before it. Observe his opponent's breathing, center of gravity, even the direction of her gaze—every move she made. Miss no signs of the attack to come, read them all accurately—and then land a counter. A tightrope act with no margin for error, but his sole path to victory.

"...Ngh..."

Easy to say. But in actual practice, the daunting difficulty of it left him nauseous. He hated having only two eyes. No matter how wide he opened them, it hardly seemed enough to catch movements this skilled.

"See, that's a bad habit."

He focused so hard that his ears rang—and the echo of her voice came back to him. His chest tightened. It almost made him cry.

"Aw, don't look so sad. It's okay. We all have habits. You can't fix 'em that easy, and if you think you have, that's the most dangerous moment. Ed's still a disaster. Let's take our time here."

He remembered this. He wanted to do what she could, but he couldn't. And that was so frustrating, so depressing—he'd cried about it back then. The memories were so vivid now. Her hand mussing his hair, the warmth of her palm.

"But, Noll, remember this for me. When mages are really in trouble, it isn't their eyes they rely on but their own personal world."

His mother's voice gave him a push. His tension unspooled. He unstuck his eyes from what he could see and simply *felt* the world that was his, letting himself expand out into it.

He felt no fear. And thus, he could leave his eyes open yet put his vision out of mind.

"Ah—"

In his expanded self, he felt something hard and sharp on the move. It was not his eyes that caught it, nor the other four senses. He needed no sensory organs to know what happened *within*. What a mage called their "self" was the entirety of the space in their domain.

"So *slow.*"

His error was clear at once. He moved to that feeling. His left hand touched her wrist and deflected the blade; his right leg moved him to her side—and raked her throat. It required no real speed. Just slightly more than she had.

The vision he'd pushed aside told him Ames was just now beginning her thrust. A chill ran down his spine. If he'd still had his eyes peeled, he'd have been staring right at that as her blade pierced his chest.

"...Magnificent..."

Her voice was a whisper right beside him; her body went limp and crumpled to the ground. Only then did his vision correct itself and show Oliver the girl he'd cut down.

"A terrifying art," he said solemnly. "This is a victory I'm proud of, Ms. Ames."

He held respect for her craft and gratitude for allowing him to hear his mother's voice again.

With Ames down, Oliver rejoined Nanao on the surface, and the battle from there proceeded without incident. Minus their leader, the girls had no means of resisting Team Horn, and they were both eliminated less than two minutes later. Mistral was left barely alive on the west side of the ceiling, but he held his wand backward and put up his hands, indicating surrender.

"The match is over! Three out of four teams eliminated, so the victory belongs to the survivors—Team Horn! Unfortunately, a big part of the climax was impossible to see, but we know all entrants fought hard! Truly a match worthy of launching the combat league!"

In high spirits, Glenda brought the event to a close.

"Indeed," Miligan chimed in. "Team Horn spent the entire battle thwarting their foes' plans, but that in no way diminished the plans themselves. Team Liebert's golem fortification upended the very lay of the land. Team Ames excelled at disruptive assaults and Team Mistral at use of splinters and transformations to delay. Including the early loss of Nanao's arm, we can say the flow of the match itself was consistently on their side."

"And yet Team Horn never succumbed to it," Garland said, folding his arms. "Largely because their precision responses and constant movement prevented the other teams from grouping up. Had the fight with Team Mistral or the shoot-out with Team Liebert been prolonged by even a minute, Team Ames would have joined the fray, and they'd have been in real trouble."

He glanced toward the guest seat, forcing Whalley to break his sullen silence.

"I'll acknowledge Team Horn's apt responses. But I can't shake the impression they regularly made things harder for themselves. Rather than walk a tightrope in a three-on-one, make a deal yourself to ensure it's at least two-on-two. I must insist it was conceit for them to neglect that."

"Hmm, I'm not sure I'd push for off-field scheming that hard," the Snake-Eyed Witch said from beside him. "The league is a festive occasion, and these things are allowed to slide, but if every league match was that obvious about it, they'd crack down hard. Striving to win is admirable, but let's not forget the true purpose of this contest is to compare your techniques in a spirit of sportsmanlike rivalry."

Whalley started to argue but then decided better of it. He realized anything he said here would sound like sour grapes. Miligan, well aware of this, fixed him with her best smile. She'd personally trained with the team that had weathered a tough battle and emerged triumphant—this outcome clearly bolstered her candidacy.

Rescue of the downed students proceeded apace, and thirty minutes after the match ended, all participants were back in the school building. As the campus buzzed with hot takes, Yuri awoke on a bed in the break room.

"...Mm? Where am I?"

"You have awakened, Yuri!"

He squinted at the ceiling, then turned to find his teammates awaiting his return to consciousness. Realizing what had happened, Yuri bolted upright.

"Oliver, Nanao, how'd it end?!"

"The other teams all wiped out, and we won. It was a tough fight the whole way."

Oliver heaved a long sigh. Yuri hoisted himself up on the bed, turning to face him.

"Oh, so you did win? Then, uh, did you see that thing Ms. Ames does? That's so neat! You can see her not moving, but she actually *is* moving, just really slowly!"

"You saw through her technique?"

"I am confounded."

Nanao blinked at them both, but Oliver's jaw was hanging open. Yuri had just blabbed the entire secret to Ames's finisher.

In simple terms, it was essentially an illusion. Show an enemy something not real to make them react wrong—classic stuff. But the artifice involved was something else.

Specifically, using spatial magic (sans incantation) wouldn't normally allow such detailed illusions. Even the shadow splinters Team Mistral employed required a singlecant, and if those appeared before you, the lack of detail would instantly prove them fake. Everyone knew that fooling your enemy with an illusion was incredibly complex, and thus it was almost never employed in the rapid-fire exchanges of sword arts combat. But Ames's finisher completely flipped that assumption. How did she do it?

Simple: She *didn't* create an illusion different from reality. She merely slowed the reality her opponent's eyes perceived, overriding the truth. More specifically, she slowed the speed of light evenly across the range of her own spatial magic. This left Ames's opponent piercing her movement on a one-second delay, and in that time she *slowly* moved forward to stab them. If she moved too fast, nonvisual senses would kick in—they'd hear her footsteps or the wind and figure out what she was actually doing. When Oliver said, *"So slow,"* he meant it literally.

Nanao was pressing for an explanation, so Oliver summed this much up for her. She listened avidly, eyes sparkling, then hit the key concern.

"Fascinating, fascinating. How were *you* able to see through it, Oliver? From what you've told us, your eyes were fooled and saw not her true actions."

"Yeah, but I wasn't relying on my eyes. Every mage has a world of their own—an innate grasp of everything within the range of their spatial magic. I tracked her movements with that alone. Without the aid of your sense, you can just *know* those things. I'm sure you've both done it."

Oliver reached out his hands, indicating the range. This had come up before, but a mage's concept of self differed from that of an ordinary human. The most striking aspect is the personal "space" each of them possesses. This is equivalent to the range in which spatial magic can be used, and to a mage, everything within that range is a part of them.

Naturally, everyone is aware of what happens inside themselves. Carried to the logical extreme, you don't need any of your senses to tell you what happens in that range. The accuracy of this knowledge is somewhat dependent on the individual but can be improved with training; at the highest levels, you can count the raindrops falling behind you, like Oliver's mother could.

"The clever part of Ames's technique wasn't just the surprise factor in delaying light but that her stance and actions leading into it are suggestive, tricking her opponents into sharpening their eyes. If you see the Lightning stance, you expect a high-speed stab—and any mage will likely hyperfocus, trying to catch a tell before it comes. And that's the trap. Since her magic is slowing light itself, no matter how hard you *look*, you'll never actually see her move. By the time you notice, she's run you through."

And that concluded the lecture. Nanao grew all the more excited. She clearly wanted to pepper him with further questions about Ames and the fight, but he held up a hand, discouraging it.

"One moment, Nanao. Let's go back a bit," said Oliver. "It makes no sense, Leik. If you knew how Ms. Ames's move worked, why were you downed by it?"

"Uh, so…I was just so excited to find out what would happen that I totally forgot to dodge. Sorry!"

"You *forgot*?! And you think *'sorry'* will cut it?! Do you have any idea how hard we had it without you?!"

Oliver was ready to give Yuri a piece of his mind, but someone burst through the door of the break room. Chela saw the three of them in the corner, and her face lit up.

"Nanao! Oliver! Mr. Leik! A brilliant victory!"

"Oh, Chela!"

"Whoa—"

Before they could even finish responding, Chela had them both in an embrace. She was even more enthusiastic than usual, and Yuri looked very jealous.

"Lucky! Chela, don't I get a hug?"

"Perhaps in two years I'll consider it," she replied, rubbing her cheeks with the friends within her clutches. It was nearly a minute before she was satisfied, and once she let go, she turned to Yuri. "That said, you did quite well. You've got my attention. What training lets you move like that?"

"Um, a few things, but…you know, eat well, play hard, lots of sleep!" Yuri shot her a thumbs-up.

"I'm not asking the secret to good health." Chela sighed.

It was impossible to tell if he was playing dumb or actually was dumb. Either way, she abandoned the idea of getting answers, turning back to her friends.

"If you're uninjured, let us return to the stands. The next match is about to begin."

"Yeah—Katie's team is in it, right?"

Oliver nodded. His match might be over, but their friends' was just beginning.

"...I-I'm getting nervous."

The time was ticking closer. In the waiting room, Katie had her hands clutched in front of her.

Guy patted her shoulders. "Loosen up! Let's just have fun. Like, *everyone's* stronger than us anyway."

"I'm not convinced," Pete snapped. He was looking over his magic tools. "Mages, teams, free-for-all—the kind of strength we're comparing isn't *that* simplistic."

"...Ha-ha, you've sure changed."

Guy started mussing his hair, and Pete pushed him away. Then the upperclassman by the door called out, waving them to the field.

The trio exchanged looks.

"Right," said Katie. "Time to go."

"Yep."

"All right! Let's kick some ass!"

They tapped their athames together and dove into the painting at the back of the room. A few seconds of darkness, then their feet landed on soft soil. They could smell moisture in the air, and all three opened their eyes, soaking in the sights. The ground was covered in tall shrubs and surrounded by water.

"It's..."

"Pretty pastoral!" Guy said.

But Katie ran straight to the water's edge, kneeling by it. Waves lapped gently. The water was clear and quite deep. She took a scoop of water and tasted it.

"…Fresh water."

"All teams are in the field, and it's time for the second match! This go-around, we've got the lake zone! They'll be fighting on a cluster of islands floating on a big body of water! As always, we've got Instructor Garland here to offer commentary. And our new guests are Ms. Ingwe and Ms. Albschuch!"

Where Miligan and Whalley had been during the first match sat two upperclassmen. Lesedi Ingwe narrowed her eyes, scowling at the field on the feed.

"…I dunno about *this* map. Second-years won't know Lake Walk yet; they're at a big disadvantage."

"Try not to furrow your brow, Lesedi. It undermines your dashing features."

This purr came from the seventh-year elf Khiirgi Albschuch, but all it earned her was a vise grip to the jaw.

"Silence. Do *not* speak again. Quit breathing and blinking, and don't even let your heart beat."

"We actually *do* want our guests talking!" Glenda wailed.

Lesedi snorted and removed her hand from Khiirgi's face. Garland chose to respond to the original claim.

"Ms. Ingwe's concern is a valid one but one we're aware of. We've provided something that should even the gap between the years."

With that, he waved his white wand, and his voice echoed across the battlefield.

"This is Garland coming to you from the commentator's booth. Can you hear me, contestants?"

Katie's team lent an ear to the voice from the sky. Garland paused a beat, then continued.

"As you can see, this is a lake-district stage. A huge advantage for third-year students—they've mastered Lake Walk and can move around on the surface of the water here. So how are we making up for that?" Garland answered his own question. "The waters around you are filled with magical creatures. They come in all shapes and sizes, and some varieties are inclined to attack people. But these dangerous beasts are, without exception, trained to attack *only* third-year students. They pose no threat to second-years."

Pete made a noise, stroking his chin. That was a pretty big handicap. It allowed the younger students to focus on fighting alone, while forcing the older students to constantly be on guard against rampaging fauna.

"Like every fighter here, the beasts have been enchanted with a dulling spell. But their training will be the only handicap in this match. Teams, bear that in mind as you determine your best path to victory. That's all from me; may the fights be glorious."

Garland's voice petered out, and silence settled over the field.

Swiftly hiding himself in the nearby underbrush, Guy whispered, "And we're off, huh? This sure is nothing like what Oliver's team dealt with."

"First, we've gotta know the lay of the land."

A classic opening action—Pete drew scout golems from his robe and released them into the sky above. Where Oliver's had resembled birds, Pete's looked more like locusts. They flew off, exploring the entire zone in mere minutes; Pete sketched a simple map in the air with his wand, giving his team an oral rundown.

"...We're on the northwest end. One of six islands on this lake. There's some mist, but not enough to limit our field of view. No signs of any opponents."

"If there's no one close, then there's no rush to move. Pete, can you look around *in* the water?" Katie asked, her eyes locked on the surface.

Pete grinned. "You know mine are amphibious!"

And at his command, two of the three scout golems changed trajectory, plunging into the water. As they did, they transformed, their wings replaced with fins, slicing through the water as fast as any fish. A specialized configuration Pete had developed as part of his magineering studies.

They couldn't see as well as in the air, but the water was clear and visibility was not half bad. As they explored, Pete held his white wand out to the girl beside him.

"Touch wands, Katie. I'll send you what they see."

"Okay."

She put her wand on his and let the two golems' sights flow into her. The multiple perspectives briefly made her head spin, but she'd been training for this. Katie briefly closed her eyes, focusing on the two new points of view.

"...Two-humped frog eggs...a school of spearfish...a forest of thorned kelp...and a six-eyed water snake within. Okay, okay, I'm seeing the pattern here..."

As she observed the ecosystem, Katie started nodding. Twenty seconds later, she opened her eyes and voiced her conclusion.

"...This is definitely Instructor Vanessa's handiwork. The whole design fits her tastes."

"Huh. You can tell that much?" Guy asked.

"We've been butting heads for two whole years now," Katie said, making a face. Then a beat later, that gave way to a cocky grin. "But it's paying off here. Let me tell you how this field'll work for *us*."

"Whoa...!"

While his teammates watched, Dean gingerly stepped onto the surface—and his feet sank right in, water splashing everywhere. He quickly retreated to land.

"...Enough," Teresa said. "I get the picture."

"W-wait! One more try—"

"Give it up, Dean. Not like I can do it, either," Rita said.

The vast majority of second-years had not yet mastered Lake Walking, and on this team, only Teresa could stay afloat. They wouldn't be able to move around like the older teams.

Rita folded her arms, thinking this through.

"If we can't walk on water, that makes this harder. Worse comes to worst, we can just have Teresa go off on her own..."

"That's fine with me. But you'll get taken out immediately if I do," Teresa told Dean with a snort.

This left Dean grimly staring at his soaking wet shoes, but a few seconds later, he spun around and dove back in.

"Dean?" Rita asked, blinking at him.

He surfaced again, in a cloud of bubbles, only his head above the water.

"If we can't walk on it, then we'll just have to swim. I know how to do *that*!"

Teresa and Rita exchanged glances. He had a point. That *was* one way to do things.

Meanwhile, Andrews, Rossi, and Albright had finished their survey and were already on the move.

"Clear 'em out clockwise. Any arguments?" Andrews said.

The simplest-possible plan. And his teammates both shrugged.

"Suit yourself. Either way's the same."

"I must object! Counterclockwise is inherently superior, no?"

Andrews led the way, ignoring Rossi's bullshit. Both teammates followed as if they were taking a stroll on a sunny day.

"No need for gimmicks," Andrews intoned. "Find them, beat them, done."

Seeing Team Andrews move out a bit ahead of the others, a stir ran through the audience.

"Whoa! Team Andrews is already on the move! The only team here that isn't in hiding. A bold tactic!"

"They're well aware they're the most powerful team on this field. With fighters like that, you expect a confident attitude."

"True! What do our guests make of it?" Glenda asked, turning their way.

Lesedi had her arms folded. "Agree with the master here. Only surprise is that Mr. Andrews is the team leader. I'd have thought that role would go to Mr. Albright."

"Ha-ha. Not so fast," Khiirgi breathed. "I like the look on his face today. Makes me want to lick his throat."

Barely resisting the urge to elbow the elf in the face, Lesedi settled for silently scooting her chair farther away.

A clockwise advance, taking out opponents as they found them—Team Andrews's bold approach did not go unnoticed by the other teams.

"...Yo, look at that."

The first team to make contact had this misfortune of starting closest to them—a third-year team led by one Marcus Bowles. He'd had scout golems out watching them advance, but spotting them with the naked eye really drove it home.

"Damn, Team Andrews already..."

"No need to hide, huh? Talk about cocky."

All three were hiding in the brush by the water's edge. Team Andrews passed by a hundred yards out, and they began to follow.

"Stay hidden and on their tails. When they start fighting the next team, we start slinging spells."

"Real painful ones. I wanna hear 'em scream."

"Don't be a dipshit. Before we waste time on that, we've gotta align elements or the oppo—"

But as Bowles scoffed at his teammate's cretinous behavior—Andrews drew his athame.

"*Impetus.*"

He never even turned around, just fired the spell backhanded. A wind projectile with explosive force swiftly covered the hundred-yard gap, scoring a direct hit on the shrubs hiding Team Bowles.

"Gah—!"

"Huh?"

"No, wait…!"

It was all too easy. The sheer impact knocked the wind out of one team member—and he fell over, unconscious. While the other two were still gaping at that, a barrage of burst spells followed it up. The ground at their feet detonated, and their brains at last caught up with reality.

"Th-they spotted us!"

"Crap, run for it!"

"Whoa, what a fast match! Mr. Andrews's spell has already taken out Team Bowles's Mr. Quark! Looks like he didn't realize his team had been spotted, and he failed to dodge in time!"

"Mr. Andrews did a good job acting natural until the spell went off, but the real deal here is Mr. Albright's scouting," Garland said. "I hadn't seen that familiar before, but it's a doozy."

To illustrate his point, the footage of the spells chasing Team Bowles froze and zoomed in—on a tiny insect. A stir went up from the stands.

"Bees…and rather small ones."

"Lovely!" Khiirgi said. "They blend right in with the field's ecosystem. You can have two or three buzzing around you and never even notice."

"The smaller the familiar, the harder it is to spot," Garland added. "But at this size, the functionality of the sensors on board drops. Each of these little bees is gathering far less intel than the scout golems the other teams are using. Mr. Albright compensates for that by having dozens—hundreds—in flight at once, then collating all those data to locate his opposition."

"That is some *transcendent* scouting! He's not from a family of famous

Gnostic Hunters for nothing! Sounds like the other teams will have a tough time hiding!"

The sound of Andrews's magic downing an opponent soon reached the ears of Katie's team. Pete was in charge of scouting, and when their eyes turned to him, he said, "That would be Mr. Andrews's team. They're strolling across the northeast island now."

"Like, out in the open? That's an opportunity. We should sneak in close."

"Don't you move!"

Guy had been about to push through the brush, but Katie's hiss stopped him. She had her eyes locked on the air in front of her.

"I just saw a bee fly from their direction. I might be overthinking things..."

"A bee?"

"Not native to this field, I take it?"

"Bees that small don't usually fly at that height. And look at what's growing around us—do you see any flowers they'd be gathering nectar from?"

Pete and Guy eyed their surroundings—and there definitely weren't many flowers. But they noticed that only because she'd pointed it out; left to their own devices, they'd never have noticed the bees at all. Based purely on his faith in Katie's ecosystem analysis, Pete put his mind to what these bees could be.

"Honeybee-size familiars are tricky to use—but I wouldn't put it past Albright. I know for a fact he's used a stinger bee before."

"Buuuut...we can't exactly hide forever, yeah? How do we move?"

"Bees don't have great vision, so we just have to move when they're not right on us. Be very cautious of your surroundings, and keep your mana in check."

All three nodded and began making careful movements. The whole time, Pete's scout golems were keeping tabs on the other teams, and he was relaying what they saw.

"...Team Andrews is across the island. Still fully exposed. Looks like they're making a clockwise circuit and planning to crush anyone they come across—sounds like them."

"Well, they can bring it on! We'll be ready."

"Don't let them bait you, Guy," Katie cautioned. "We need to ambush them. And from an advantageous position."

With all the elements at play, Katie considered their plan. Their own skills, their opposition, the lay of the land, the ecosystem—the world only she saw led to ideas only she could have.

"...Okay, I think I've got it. Listen up, boys."

Approximately five minutes later, Team Andrews stepped out onto the water, headed for the next island—and saw three figures waiting for them.

"Hmm."

They were still a long way out, but this trio was easily recognizable. Katie, Guy, and Pete—all clearly ready for a fight.

"Oh my!" Rossi whistled. "I 'ad expected them to 'ide."

"Hmph. Judging from the looks on their faces, this'll be a better fight than those nobodies."

Albright grinned. Chants rang out on the far cliff, and a moment later, the water beneath him burst.

Naturally, the commentator booth didn't miss the outbreak of hostilities.

"Team Aalto hits Team Andrews as they cross the water! What are their chances?"

"Not too shabby. The timing here is excellent; Team Andrews has to keep a portion of their mana diverted to Lake Walking. But since Team Aalto is onshore, they've got the firepower advantage. Team

Andrews will be wanting to get back on land quickly, but Team Aalto knows that and is firing burst spells into the water nearby. The resulting waves make Lake Walking that much harder, both slowing them down and siphoning away their mana."

Garland was focusing on the basis for this attack—when fighting a superior opponent, it was crucial to start the fight on your own terms, with every advantage you could find.

"And once they're slowed, Team Aalto keeps the burst spells flying. They can try to use the oppositional, but with your foothold rocking, precision aiming is rough. And if they just dodge, then the water gets even choppier. Even Team Andrews won't easily escape this one."

"Team Aalto really used the terrain to their advantage! Perhaps Team Andrews's frontal assault *was* ill-advised!"

But despite the turbulent waters, Team Andrews was taking the barrage in stride.

"Going right."

"Then I will take the left!"

With that alone, they went their separate ways. Clumped together, the waves affected them all, so splitting up was the obvious choice. Naturally, Katie's team had predicted this.

"Three-way split!" Katie cried. "Albright went left; Rossi's coming onshore to the right!"

"Yeah, that's what I figured."

Guy grinned and started chanting. His spells struck two spots on the island—places where, given the landforms, their opposition was likely to come ashore. From those locations, trees grew—toolplants he'd placed there ahead of time, ready to quickly grow when the time came. Rossi and Albright found their advance blocked by thorny brambles.

"…Hrm."

"Whoops! They saw us coming!"

Neither looked terribly pleased about it. Going around or cutting through with spells would both take a chunk of time, and while they were struggling to get ashore, Katie's team could focus fire on Andrews. Alone on the rocking waves, he was a prime target.

But what Andrews did next, his opponents did not expect. He reached into his robe and pulled out a polished plank, half his height. Then he dropped it on the water and stepped aboard.

"Impetus!"

His spell activated, and his body shot across the lake's surface. The wind at his back, he skimmed across the water, moving far faster than before. All spells aimed his way hit far behind him, and the waves they generated only aided in his surge forward.

Team Aalto gaped.

"...?!"

"What in the...?! He's surfing?!"

"Don't let up! Keep attacking!" Pete roared.

But their barrage was to no avail. Andrews darted left and right, weaving through it all—and approaching the island.

"Wowwwww! Mr. Andrews abandons Lake Walking for lake *surfing*! Nimbly dodging through their barrage and heading to the shore!"

It certainly got the crowd hyped up. Garland was nodding, eyes on the screen.

"Aha, interesting. That approach really is better with choppy waters. But if you aren't a skilled hand with wind spells, you'd never pull it off."

"But Andrews's reputation precedes him! What now, Team Aalto?"

Not far from the island, Andrews started maintaining his distance, dodging spells. By this point, Katie's team had realized just how hard he was to hit.

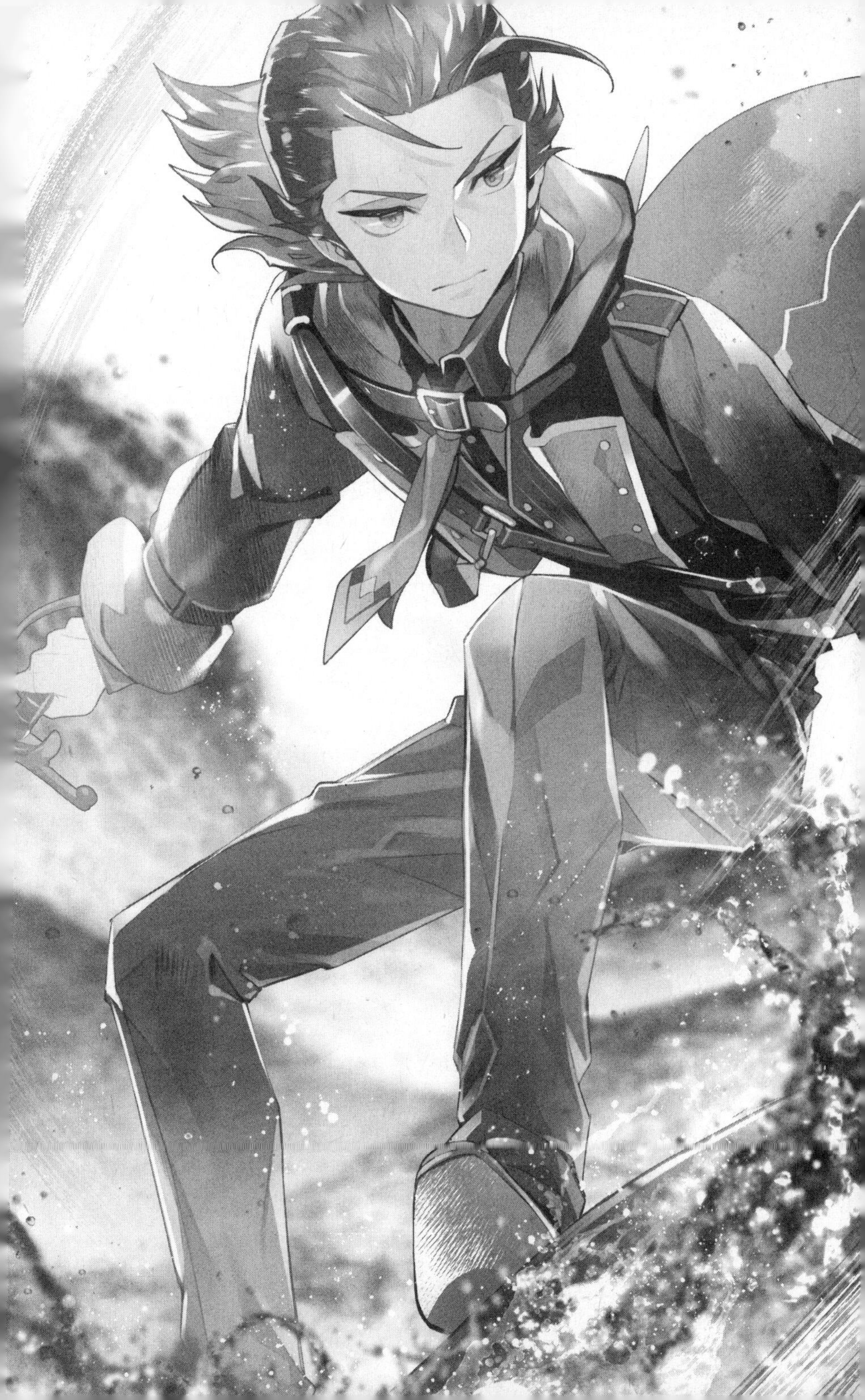

"So fast…!"

"Even if we do hit, it won't down him."

"Drop back to the island's center! Hurry, before they come ashore!"

They abandoned the shoot-out and fled to the interior. The barricades flanking the island burst apart, and two figures strode through the remnants of Guy's trees.

"That was a nuisance."

"Ah, dry land feels so sweet!"

Through the obstruction at last, Albright and Rossi stepped ashore. Andrews reached the beach in front and stepped off his surfboard.

Rossi shot him a grin. "Hanging ten? You will 'ave to teach me 'ow."

"Not as versatile as it looks. Most times brooms are faster."

With that curt dismissal, Andrews moved on. Katie's team had taken new positions at the center, and he stopped a good fifty yards out.

"We've eliminated our disadvantage," he said. "I'm afraid this won't last long, Ms. Aalto."

"…I'm not so sure," she replied.

Andrews and Rossi raised their athames to attack—but pillars of water shot up from the lake behind, followed by heavy footsteps.

"…Hrm?"

"Eh? Is this a joke?!"

They swung around, yelping. Seven feet tall. Maws lined with fangs. Ten-plus beasts, like crocodiles walking on two legs—leaving the water behind.

"What's this?! Tallgators congregating onshore?! Team Andrews is now caught between them and Team Aalto! They never saw it coming!"

"Well done, Ms. Aalto. You read the terrain flawlessly."

Garland looked pleased and was quickly reevaluating Katie Aalto. She clearly understood the nature of this field better than anyone else in the match.

*　　*　　*

Gazing at the magifauna behind Team Andrews, Katie whispered, "If you pay attention in magical biology and study the environment around, you can tell—what the apex predator on this map is."

"Tch..."

"*Progressio!*"

The moment they moved to break through the center, Guy's spell hit the ground. Another wooden barricade sprouted up. Since they'd always planned on surrounding them, he'd seeded toolplants accordingly. From behind that brush, he yelled, "Tough luck, but we ain't about to get in a duel with *you*."

"This is how *we* fight. As far as it takes us."

Unable to advance or retreat, Team Andrews found themselves subject to another barrage of spells—even as the beasts charged in from the rear. They were forced to deal with both at once.

"Ha-ha! Not 'alf bad," Rossi cried, dodging a fearsome set of jaws. "You 'ave not spent that long in Oliver's or Nanao's company for your 'ealth."

Yet even as he spoke, he fired a spell into a gaping maw. Electricity coursed through the beast's body, and it fell over unconscious. Another beast vaulted over the top of it, but Rossi kicked its jaw upward with his heel, and he used the body as a shield against Guy's spell.

"...But we 'ave not exactly been slacking off ourselves. If you think a trifle like this gives you the advantage—it will not end well for you."

More than a trace of bravado there.

"I'll handle defense against the spells," Andrews said. "You two finish these animals."

"Just a pack of nothings. Won't take long."

Albright wasn't sweating this any more than Rossi, but then something small darted out of the pack. It went right for his throat, and he dodged by a hairbreadth. He turned for a better look, but it was already hidden inside the throng. He had just barely caught a glimpse of a diminutive girl.

"*Tonitrus!*"

A spell from an entirely new direction—not from Katie's team. He canceled it with the oppositional and snorted.

"More nobodies mixed in. A mild annoyance."

The audience could clearly see all *three* teams going at it.

"Team Carste has been underwater this whole time, but they came ashore with the tallgators and joined the fray! Really taking advantage of the second-years' beast immunity!"

"If they were going to jump in, this is the place to do it. I imagine Team Aalto was prepared for that possibility. It was vital they hit quickly before Team Andrews managed to down anyone. They're well positioned, too. Team Andrews is being pummeled from all sides."

Garland was full of admiration for Team Aalto's plan. But as he watched the battle unfold, his frown deepened. In the time since the pincer attack began, half the gators had been eliminated...

"And they haven't wobbled... All three of them are just that *good*."

Despite having them perfectly caught in their trap, Katie's team hadn't managed to reduce their opponents' numbers. Naturally, that was starting to get to Team Aalto, but the barricade's defenses provided some small comfort. That meant the first to find themselves in trouble were the second-years attacking with the tallgators.

"...*Hah...hah...!*"

More specifically—Rita. Staying hidden and doing hit-and-runs was pretty similar to Teresa's real fighting style, but it was definitely not Rita's. She was hanging on because Teresa was adroitly keeping their foe's attention off her, but alone, she'd have long since been spotted and taken out. And frankly, that time was not far off. As the beasts dwindled in number, there were fewer and fewer places for her to hide.

She was at her limit. And as she sensed that, Albright dodged Teresa's strike, lost his balance, and left his back wide open. Her teammate had given her the chance of a lifetime—and Rita had no choice but to take it.

"...Now...!"

The distance was right. She'd been using spells, but those had all been blocked—so Rita slipped out from between the gators, her blade aimed for Albright's back, certain she had him. But her athame came up short—alongside a heavy blow to her stomach from his counter.

"Gotcha," Albright hissed, his eyes flashing.

"Gah...?!"

A back kick, the motion hidden by the folds of his robe—the same move Oliver had once used on him. The Lanoff-style Hidden Tail. He'd intentionally left his back exposed to set up this move.

"Impediendum. Hmph, the big one... The smaller would have been easier to carry, but no matter."

The follow-up spell took Rita out of commission, and he hefted her with one hand, thrusting her at the beasts. They all flinched. Their inability to harm second-years was now Albright's shield—but that provoked an unexpected reaction.

"Wha—?! You son of a bitch! Get your hands off Rita!"

"Augh! Guy, don't—!"

Unable to bear it, Guy blew off his teammate's restraints and vaulted over the barricade, coming after Albright directly. Using a younger kid as a meat shield was beyond his tolerance. Especially Rita, whom he'd been looking after from the get-go.

"Hmph."

As Guy charged in, Albright lightly tossed Rita to him. Guy couldn't very well dodge that. He caught her with one arm—and something hit him in the back.

"That was very you, yes," Rossi whispered in his ear. "But also very bad. You are in *combat*, remember?"

"...Rossi, you asshole..."

Guy managed one last curse before falling unconscious, still clutching Rita in his arms.

"That was brutal! Mr. Albright turning a falling second-year into an anti-beast shield! Mr. Greenwood couldn't stand the sight of that and vaulted over the barricade, only to get himself mercilessly mowed down! He's outta the match!"

"The magical beasts can't attack second-years, so this doesn't violate the rule against reckless pain and suffering. Use whatever you can—it may seem heartless, but if this were a real fight, it would be the right call. Mr. Greenwood's attempt to defend his junior is commendable on a personal level—but given the situation, clearly ill-considered."

Stern words from Garland. And he saw a clear shift in the balance of battle, too.

"As numbers dwindle, so does the pressure. They're no longer really surrounded—Team Andrews will make it out."

Guy and Rita were down, and only a third of the gators remained. There was no longer any need for Team Andrews to fight in the middle.

"Enough. To the next island."

"Hmph."

"As you wish!"

Breaking through the lines, they darted northwest, over the bluff to the water below. But as they landed, two burst spells erupted from the water around them. Not from behind but from the island ahead where two figures stood upon the shore.

"Are they serious? There is no point joining in this late!"

"Cowardly nobodies."

Rossi and Albright were equally contemptuous. Team Bowles had lost a member in the initial fight and only just come back for more. But attacking *after* Team Andrews escaped the island trap was clearly a blown opportunity. The three of them stalked across the rocking waters, perceiving no threat at all.

"Hmm?!"

But then a hand reached up from the water and grabbed Albright's ankle. Between his raw leg strength and Lake Walk skills, he tried to resist—but the water was too choppy, and his struggle lasted only seconds. Long enough for the follow-up strikes to reach him.

""Fragor!""

Katie and Pete were leaning over the top of the bluff they'd just vacated, firing spells after them. Rossi and Andrews quickly evaded, but with one leg secured from below, Albright didn't have that option.

"Tch."

It didn't even take a second. He quit resisting and let them drag him under before the spells hit. Two pillars of water erupted; the churn left Rossi and Andrews struggling to stay balanced, and those on the bluff took that as their opening.

"Now—!"

Katie, Pete, and Teresa all used Wall Walk to run down the cliff face, going for broke. The burst spells had left the water bucking, but while very uneven, the cliff face wasn't moving. They had the stronger foothold. And they could aim spells as they ran—while the churning surf left Rossi and Andrews too unsteady to do the same. Theoretically, at least.

"…Impetus."

"——?!"

"Huh—?!"

"——!"

Andrews's chant brought a gusts of wind that slammed the cliff runners in the back. He wasn't simply generating winds from the tip of his wand—he was summoning the atmospheric currents, generating gale-force winds from above the cliff itself. Katie did her level best to hunker down mid-cliff but was in no shape to aim a spell.

"Rahhhh!"

"*Hah!*"

Pete and Teresa took a different approach. They let the winds snatch them up, throwing themselves off the cliff and swinging right at Rossi and Andrews. The waves had Rossi off-balance and leaning backward, and Pete committed to a Rizett-style Hero's Charge—

"Whoop!"

—but just before his blade struck home, a sharp pain hit his belly. Rossi was bent way over backward, his palms on the water's surface; he'd gone into a handstand to kick Pete in the gut.

"Gah…!"

"So close, Pete. My old self might 'ave been done in."

Lake Walking on his hands on heaving surf, plus a bold kick to an airborne foe—both moves that required a lot of nerve and extraordinary talent. Pete was sent flying, landing on his back and sinking below the waves.

"Ngh…!"

"You're good… You must be the second-years' ace."

Teresa, meanwhile, had double feinted into a blow that Andrews *still* blocked. She backed off, looking for an opening, yet her foe remained impassive.

"But if your first strike fails, you've lost your shot at victory."

Even as his voice echoed, Teresa made to dart in—and a bolt struck her from behind.

"Guh…!"

She crumpled to the water's surface. The man who'd downed her was at her back, half out of the water.

"He actually dragged *me* under. That nobody's got guts, if nothing else," Albright grumbled, stepping back up to do a proper Lake Walk. Beside him bobbed another second-year—Dean, now unconscious.

His attack from below had momentarily pulled Albright into the water, but that wasn't enough to even the odds.

"Pete!" Katie yelled, vaulting off the cliff. She ran to where Pete was floating, pulling him to the surface. They could have stopped her, but Team Andrews no longer saw the point. They waited until the survivors of Team Aalto were both upright, then aimed their athames.

"More fun than I expected. Retrain and come at me again, Pete."

"...Why...you..."

But Albright's challenge was also a good-bye. Three spells at once, no means of resisting—Katie and Pete went down together.

"Oh, Mr. Reston and Ms. Aalto are both out! They hung in there for dear life, but that takes care of Team Aalto and Team Carste!"

"They made their share of errors, but both teams clearly had a very strong showing. This one simply must be chalked up to Team Andrews's ability to weather the storm."

Garland was already summing up the match before it officially ended. As he spoke, Team Andrews was moving quickly to the next island, easily finishing off the Team Bowles stragglers. When the buzzer signaled the end of the match, Glenda made the results official.

"And the two survivors of the last team are out! Team Andrews wins without a single casualty!"

That evening, the Sword Roses gathered in their base. Each had endured a tough battle.

"Oliver, Nanao, Chela, congrats on making it to the finals! Shame our team lost, though. Damn it all!" Katie was clearly still extremely frustrated.

But with that, cider mugs clashed. The table might have been divided between the victors and the eliminated, but Chela had praise for each of them.

"All three of you should be proud. You fought well, and the match was a joy to witness. Garland was showering you with compliments."

"Chela speaks the truth. You all did good work. They were just stronger. Rossi and Albright go without saying, but Mr. Andrews—the way he fought was a real eye-opener."

Oliver meant every word, and Nanao was nodding the whole time.

"Indeed, he crackled with spirit from head to toe, moving with unbridled aplomb. A feat accomplished with the certitude obtained after reforging one's self to perfection. If you ask me, Andrews now has the air of a true warrior."

"Yes, Rick's amazing! Oh, I mean…well, Rick *is* amazing, but… Katie, Guy, Pete, this match showed the fruits of your training, and you were in no way inferior."

Torn between pride in her old friend's accomplishments and joy in her new friends' performance, Chela was starting to waffle. But little of this was reaching their ears. All three of them were agonizing over their loss.

"…It's my fault," Guy began. "If I hadn't jumped out like that…"

"…If I were stronger—if I'd downed Rossi at the end, we might still have had a chance…"

"…The whole plan was mine. Ugh, if only we could rewind time…! I'm sure I could come up with something better now…"

Each voice was tinged with lament. Oliver looked them over, then straightened up.

Clearly, not one of them was interested in comfort or praise.

"You want more than words of encouragement, then?" he asked. "Very well. Let's try the harsh version."

His gaze shifted to the tall boy.

"Guy, as you're well aware, rushing out to save Ms. Appleton was thoughtless. In a real fight, you'd have died with her. And you'd have put Katie's and Pete's lives at risk. Your life isn't just yours—it directly impacts the survival of your comrades."

"Urgh…"

Guy hung his head, gnashing his teeth.

Oliver turned to the bespectacled boy next.

"Pete, the regret you voiced is not what I'd point to. Committing to a Hero's Charge in the endgame is not a bad choice. Without reducing your foe's numbers, you had no shot at victory, and in those circumstances, risks must be taken. What you need to look at was the battle on the island earlier. You were too focused on landing your spells, and the result? They were far too easy to predict."

"…Rrgh…!"

Pete was on his knees, his fists shaking.

And Oliver turned to the last of them, the curly-haired girl.

"Katie, your plan to use the field's ecosystem was a good one. I doubt anyone else in our year could pull that off. But if I must point out a flaw—I can't say you fully took advantage of the ecosystem. Frankly, in that situation—I'd have been using doublecant spells, hitting my enemy *and* the beasts at once."

"…But then…!"

That was a cruel blow, and it made her voice quaver. Oliver knew only too well how it hit her, but he wasn't ready to let up.

"I know you thought of it and decided against it. Even if the lethality of your spells is limited, you would never want to harm a creature caught up in the thick of your battle. But like with Guy, imagine if that were a real fight. Your reluctance to harm an animal prevents you from eliminating your enemy, and as a result, your companions perish. Naturally, if you're certain you could make the hard choice in a real battle, I have nothing more to say. But are you really ready to make that call?"

Katie's face fell. Oliver glanced over all three of them, eyes narrowing.

"Today's matches proved one thing. As mages, all three of you are growing at a dizzying pace. Chela and I couldn't believe our eyes. But watching you convinced me of something else—in due time, in some

way, each of you will act as mages do and put your life on the line...
And when that time comes, I don't want you hesitating. No matter
what you're fighting—or who."

There was a desperate entreaty in his voice. And all three felt the
weight of it. For a long time, they were silent, mulling over Oliver's
words.

At length, he let out a sigh and stood up.

"Enough pompous lectures. Time for my own regrets."

"...Huh?"

"Mm?"

"Oh?"

As his friends blinked, he pointed his white wand at the blackboard,
furiously filling it with letters. Katie's jaw dropped. There was a downright obsessive degree of detail, and every word of it was about mistakes he'd made.

"Every one of these—*every last one* is a mistake I made in this match!
Strings of little oversights that added up to horrific failures! You all
watched the fight, and I'm sure you saw things! Go on, turn the tables.
Treat me like your punching bag and pummel away! Do your worst!"

Oliver's words were a plea. He couldn't stomach laying into his
friends after all they'd accomplished. And Chela was the first to sym-
pathize with that. She smiled and kicked things off.

"...From start to finish, you were reliant on Nanao's and Mr. Leik's
adaptability. Your faith in them is commendable, but can you really
call that *leadership*?"

"Urgh...!"

Every bit as brutal as he'd asked for, but it still made him stagger.
And after seeing that, Katie shot up her hand.

"...Th-then I've got one, too... Um...Mistral's splinters are totally
not that hard to tell apart from the real one, you know? I spent the
whole time confused by why you were struggling with that."

"?! Wait, Katie, what are you talking about?! You could tell the whole
time?!"

"Y-yeah. I mean, the shadow splinters are just plain empty, but the more fleshed-out ones—the way the muscles move is all kinds of weird. Bipedal creatures' bodies are, like, far more complex."

Katie was clearly just speaking self-evident truths, unaware of how uncanny her observations were. Oliver couldn't keep his jaw closed.

Guy was grinning at that, and he fired another shot across the bow.

"For all your talk about real fights, you sure picked the fun option at the end. Did you *actually* need to fight Ms. Ames one-on-one? We couldn't see the fight itself, but I bet it would've been way easier if you'd regrouped with Nanao first."

"Gah…b-but they were watching for that! Moving back to the surface was risky! It was logically sound…!"

"If you ask me, after you dropped two from Team Mistral, forgetting about Team Ames and going after Team Liebert was highly questionable. You clearly underestimated the challenge of tackling that golem fortification," Pete added. "Or…no, you were freaking out about Ms. Asmus's sniping. But you knew full well only she could aim properly at that distance. You could have just left Leik on defense and been in no real danger."

"Aughhhh!"

Pete's words were a dagger to the heart and Oliver was left clutching his chest. Each of these points sparked debate and led to a detailed group analysis of both matches. Harsh criticisms flew like wildfire—but each one stemmed from touching kindness.

CHAPTER 4

The Tyrant

The lower forms' league matches proceeded without a hitch, and the next day was the long-awaited upper-form prelim. The screens showed the fourth- and fifth-years at the start point on the labyrinth's first layer, and Glenda was so worked up, you'd think they were in the main rounds already.

"The underclassmen showed their stuff, but now it's time for the upper-form league! The prelim round will be tried-and-true, a labyrinth trail run! They'll be starting on the first layer and heading for a goal on the third! The fourth-years get a five-minute head start!"

"We decided this is simply the best means of judging overall ability. Unlike the lower forms, at this point, teams have not yet been formed. Upperclassmen shouldn't need any help to get through something like this. The head start is only five minutes because like it or not, the gap between older students just gets that much closer. Although we are holding separate leagues for fourth- and fifth-years and sixth- and seventh-years."

"The fourth-years are racing across the quiet, wandering path like it's their own front yard! Nobody even needs to think about what pattern the paths have taken—their bodies already know! But this is the *combat* league! This may only be the first layer, but don't think you're getting through it humming a merry tune!"

Glenda was not wrong. The lead group was making swift work of the floor until they hit a room where five passages converged—and there they stopped. Where the exit should have been was a strange spiral tube, the whole thing writhing downward.

"Damn, a cave golem?"

"Can't just bulldoze through *that*."

The walls were swarming with golems and bristling with magic traps. The students grumbled—but they couldn't stop here. Each drew their athame and threw themselves into the obstacle before them.

In the stands, Nanao was pointing excitedly at the screen.

"Oliver! 'Tis the cave we passed through!"

"So it is. With the help of President Godfrey..."

Oliver nodded, vivid memories of their pursuit of Enrico and the captive Pete flowing through his mind. It had nearly cost them their lives, but that was nothing compared to the cave golem the upperclassmen were handling. Golems and traps positively teeming everywhere, the path itself roiling and coiling in all directions, the very ground beneath their feet unreliable. Could he and Nanao make it through even today?

"...If the first layer's already this bad, the upper-form leagues are certainly earning their name," Chela murmured.

"Gosh..." Katie gasped. "How bad is the *second* layer?"

And what followed was every bit as bad as they feared.

As the fourth- and fifth-year leaders made it out of the cave golem onto the second layer, they found the bustling forest covered in a red-tinged white fog.

"Erk."

"...Hoo boy."

Even upperclassmen came up short, clapping their hands over their mouths and noses. The forest seemed foggy because the air was *unclean*. And the source of this contamination was the immense amounts of pollen produced by the second layer's magiflora. Naturally, this was hardly harmless—at this density, plunging into it unprepared would leave you too intoxicated to stand in mere seconds.

"How horrid. Even at peak season, it doesn't get this bad."

"You breathe right, you can avoid the pollen. But with visibility this lousy…"

"Ain't nobody going fast here."

Everyone was grumbling about the conditions—but through the pollen fog, they could hear things stirring, followed by low growls. Sensing further obstacles, they drew their athame.

"And of course there's beasts out there!"

"Please take the lead!"

"You first!"

No one wanted to be first into the cloud, but soon enough, they'd all plunged in. Beset on all sides by beasts whose forms they could not even discern.

"The leaders plunge into the second layer! Pollen so thick, they can't even see! What a nightmare!"

"It may seem like a bad joke, but think of it as good training for poor weather. We worked closely with Instructor Holzwirt to create these conditions. It requires proper breathing techniques to filter out the airborne poison and finesse to maintain that while fighting off magical beasts. Both vital skills on the Gnostic hunts."

"Sound logic doesn't make it suck any less! But our upperclassmen don't mess around. For all the swearing, they're forging right on through! What a sight! You realize this right here is why people dismiss us as just a Gnostic Hunter training school."

"Hey, now."

Glenda was trash-talking her own school, and Garland's protests weren't all that strong. The audience was laughing out loud. This was the nature of Kimberly, just as it had been when Garland himself was a student here.

*   *   *

Unimaginably harsh conditions—and the upperclassmen making quick work of it, confident in their actions. The underclassmen in the audience couldn't take their eyes off it.

"*Ha-choo!* Just watching this is making me sneeze," Guy grumbled.

"Ah-ha-ha!" Yuri laughed. "Me too, me too."

"Breathing techniques to eliminate poison…," Pete said. "Oliver, can you do that?"

"I can, but when the toxins are that thick, it's hard to completely filter them. The fundamentals are just like the Perfume. You want to get through the pollen as fast as you can, but if you pick up the pace too fast, you'll get out of breath and be unable to maintain the technique. It's a tricky balance."

"If body, technique, and strength aren't aligned, you'll suffer for it. I'd be just fine, of course."

This came from a golden-haired girl stepping up beside them. Oliver glanced her way.

"Ms. Cornwallis. Belated congratulations on reaching the finals."

"Don't be too hasty. We're rivals now. And let me assure you—this time, *we'll* win."

Stacy pointed at him dramatically, and the servant behind her—Fay Willock—sighed.

"I said, *don't* start a fight… Sorry, Mr. Horn. We watched your battle and were both suitably impressed from start to finish."

"I wasn't *impressed*. I can do everything he did!"

"Don't, Stacy," Chela said gently. "Forgive her, Oliver. She just can't help but act like this before anyone she admires."

Chela was on Stacy and Fay's team for the duration of the league. Aware that she and Stacy were estranged half sisters, Oliver was just happy to see their relationship improving.

And her reproach did soften Stacy's tone a tad bit. She stepped closer to Oliver.

"You and Hibiya are one thing, but tell your transfer student to take the finals seriously," Stacy murmured, one eye on Yuri. "He's so shifty, it's positively vexing. Or is that the intent? He has secrets up his sleeve?"

"......Make of it what you will."

A very evasive answer. He'd just lectured Yuri on that exact thing, so she had a point. Stacy frowned, but before she could say anything else, Oliver turned the topic back to the match in progress.

"The leaders reached the end of the second layer. Almost at the climax."

"Oh."

"Huh?"

The end of the second layer—the Battle of Hell's Armies. A place the older students knew like the back of their hand—but today, they reacted like they'd never been here before. Two bone armies stood facing each other—infantry, cavalry, bestalry—the forces stretched as far as the eye could see. The scale was overwhelming, clearly an order of magnitude larger than ever before.

As the leaders reached the battlefield, gongs clattered, signaling the start of war. Both armies lurched into action. Beast riders left dust in their wake, mounted knights wheeled around the flanks, and the foot soldiers trudged inexorably down the middle like a mobile barricade. The fourth- and fifth-year students gaped at it from the sidelines.

"Hot damn! How many spartoi are there?"

"Might be nearly ten thousand. Definitely the most I've ever seen here."

"Are we supposed to win? We'll need numbers…"

"Don't worry—there are more inbound," one student said, glancing over their shoulder.

A moment later, another group of students emerged from the forest—quite a large one at more than thirty strong.

"…We'd better pick a plan fast," one girl said, rolling her eyes. "That'll force the stragglers to hook themselves to it."

"Leader gets to choose our strat. Maybe take down those ones first, then attack the ones over there, that sorta thing. Better make it snappy."

"Yeah. You want a chance to shine, right, candidate?"

The group looked to the front of the pack, where a fifth-year student was fussily wiping the pollen off his face with a handkerchief.

Not one to let that request pass, Percival Whalley drew his athame.

"Very well," he said. "Do as I say, pawns."

After a bit of prep, the fourth- and fifth-years waded into the unprecedented melee. Split into several squads, they began slicing their way through the skeletal forces. Oliver watched avidly from the stands. He'd assumed they'd be all out for themselves, but each was playing their part—delaying teams, divergence tactics, and surprise attacks abounded, all well-coordinated.

"…A pretty orthodox strategy. Someone's in command."

"Likely Mr. Whalley," Chela said. "He and his pack were right at the front of that lead party."

Oliver nodded. The prelim allowed for ad hoc group play, and anyone who wanted to take the reins on a task like this would need to have maintained a prominent position in the advance guard. Having a solid number of your own supporters around you was equally ideal. Whalley hadn't slacked on that front, but Chela's praise didn't stop there.

"He's a skilled leader. Perhaps he's the type who shines when in command of a large-scale battle rather than as an individual combatant. A rare caliber of mage."

"But he arranged this in advance, right?" said Guy. "Naturally, they're falling in line."

"We're including that planning in our appraisal," Oliver replied. "Convincing students from *this* school to fall in line with your plans is itself a considerable challenge. Just imagine if you had to convince, say, Rossi and Albright?"

"That'd be rough. I think I'd rather tame a griffin," Guy groaned.

The battle raged on, and the fourth- and fifth-years were getting steadily closer to the enemy general. Whalley's orders were controlling the flow, and any students who arrived late no longer had any way to interfere. There were likely several Watch supporters in the prelim, but in these years, at this stage, Leoncio's faction clearly had the upper hand.

"And that's all she wrote! The full quota crossed the finish line, and the prelim is no more! Congrats to anyone who made it to the main round. If you didn't quite make the cut, throw yourselves to your lamentations! Cry and wail away, for you have only your own inadequacies to blame!"

As the last student crossed the third-layer finish line, Glenda sounded the end of the contest. She showed no mercy no matter what year her subjects were in. The losers swore under their breaths and retreated, but she spared not a glance in their direction.

"They've gotta rework the course a bit, but in two hours' time, the sixth- and seventh-year prelim will be upon us! The core rules are the same, but the course difficulty is *way* higher! You know we're gonna see what Kimberly's best and brightest can really do!"

Two hours later, the sixth- and seventh-year students were on the first layer, ready for the prelim to kick off. Where the younger members of the upper forms had been nakedly competitive, the older members were comparatively subdued. Some even had pleasant smiles—but arguably, that just meant they were all so used to mortal combat that they needed no prior preparation. Surviving that long in this crucible would forge your mind into burnished steel.

"Don't assume a prelim will be *easy*," came a voice.

The speaker was perhaps the top student in the top year—the student body president, Alvin Godfrey. He was intentionally projecting his voice, making sure he was heard by everyone present—not just the students around him.

"Strike that—assume the *worst*. Don't get blasé and waltz in like this'll just be a few steps harder than what the fourth- and fifth-years faced."

"I'll bet."

"Our teachers are never *not* reprehensible."

Tim Linton and Lesedi Ingwe were nodding...and paying close attention to the next group over. Their main rivals—Leoncio's faction. Every bit as big a threat as whatever the faculty had waiting for them. Rules against direct interference were but tissue paper for students their age.

Catching their glares, Leoncio merely snorted, but the elf next to him sniggered.

"Don't raise your hackles, Lesedi," she said. "We won't interfere. The rules say we can't!"

"I ain't dumb enough to expect you of all people to become law-abiding. You make one false move, I'll shoot to kill. That's that."

Lesedi turned away, clearly done talking. If anyone ignored the rules and attacked, fighting back *was* allowed—if they chose to play it that way, this prelim could easily turn into an all-out war. Still, no one would actually benefit from that, so currently the two main powers were clustered around their respective leaders, keeping each other in check.

But even as the Watch glowered at their foes, a witch with bangs over one eye popped up beside them.

"Seek the largest tree for shelter," she said. "Mind if I join you?"

"Yeah, you do that," Lesedi replied, nodding. "You're a Watch rep. Don't want you accidentally dropping out here."

That worked for Vera Miligan, who quickly joined their group. As a candidate for the presidency, she was a prime target for interference—and having Godfrey's crew around her would make a huge difference in preventing that.

As each group tucked more people under their wings, Tim snorted.

"We group up like this, it ain't even worth trying to trip each other."

"That's not all the president's concerned about," Miligan offered. "There are worse—"

She broke off, spinning around. All eyes present converged on a single point: a seventh-year dressed in clerical vestments.

"Such hostility," he said. "You're still at one another's throats?"

"...There's your goal, Leik," Oliver said.

In the audience, they'd seen the warlock serenely join the line of older students waiting for the run to start. Yuri was up on his feet, his eyes feasting away.

"*That's* Rivermoore?! Yeah, he fits the descriptions! The man has *vibes!*"

"I know I suggested it, but for him to actually show up..."

Oliver's frown deepened, but Yuri was wriggling excitedly.

"Ohhh, I can't wait to talk to him! Where should I meet him?!"

"Settle down. Per the rules, when the prelim ends, all participants have to return to the school building. You can speak to him then. Even if that doesn't work out, do *not* go chasing him into the labyrinth."

Oliver hammered that point home again. Stopping Yuri's death wish took as much mental agility as any league match.

It felt like the light in the first layer had dimmed considerably.

The first to respond was the old student council's leader, Leoncio. He spoke to Rivermoore like one would to an old comrade.

"You're here, Rivermoore? Consider me surprised. These festivities don't often tempt you."

"I come and go as I please, if the reward is worth my while."

The warlock's blithe retort drew a frown from Godfrey.

"You're after the dragrium? The headmistress sure prepped a big carrot."

"But all *you* care about is how the election goes, yes?" Rivermoore sneered. "Hardly in the spirit of things."

At this point, however, Garland's voice echoed through the surveillance golems, warning of the ensuing start.

"No more chatter," Lesedi said, drawing her blade. "It's time."

A few moments later, the countdown began. The two factions would be in furious competition the moment the buzzer rang, and those in neither camp were staying well to the rear of it. Each and every one was jockeying for the slightest advantage.

"Three, two, one...start!"

The instant the match began, Godfrey ruined all of that. Pointing his athame at his feet, he yelled, **"Calidi Ignis!"**

The president's scorching inferno bored a hole beneath their feet, and while the walls still glowed red, Godfrey and his faction threw themselves in. A moment later, the other students followed suit.

"Wh-what a turnup!" Glenda cried. "President Godfrey ignores the designated path and punches right through the floor! Are they literally aiming for the shortest route to the second layer?"

The audience was hooting, but Oliver was rubbing his temples.

"He just... No, his output's somehow gotten even *worse*. He's now so powerful, he can just ignore the constraints of the labyrinth itself."

"Hot damn. Ain't that a bit *too* crazy?" Guy asked, crooking his head. "He could get through the prelim no prob without doing *this*."

"That's not the point," Pete said. "Everyone who entered can use the shortcut, and he's not trying to hinder them. Which means it's *not* about winning."

Through the hole he'd dug, Godfrey's crew landed in the passage below and took off running. Leoncio soon drew up alongside.

"Not the most elegant approach, Godfrey," he said. "Have you forgotten the unspoken rule of a labyrinth trail run? Break not what you need not?"

"I decided to ignore that this time. Just…can't shake an ominous feeling in my gut."

Godfrey glanced over his shoulder, making sure all the participants had dropped through the hole with him.

The old student council alchemist running behind Leoncio picked up his intent.

"Ah," Gino Beltrami said. "You're not trying to shorten your time; you're trying to prevent the stragglers from getting behind."

"Ha-ha! Lovely. I support it! Let's all hold hands and frolic across the finish line together."

Khiirgi let out a breathy peal of laughter; Lesedi side-eyed her. Godfrey had spied the next shortcut ahead, and he raised his athame.

"If I'm wrong, I'll make amends. Frankly, I hope I am… **Calidi Ignis!**"

And he punched a second hole, plunging in without hesitation—like he had the route planned ahead of time.

"…Th-they're bringing their commentators to tears!" Glenda wailed. "The president's power play is making the prelim butter smooth, and there's nothing worth seeing! Should we have made floor busting illegal, Instructor Garland?"

The sword arts master winced.

"Hard to argue with that now," he said. "But either way, we knew these years wouldn't struggle with the first layer. And the league format this time is all about the loosest rules we can manage."

"Even so, there are few things sadder than a commentator with nothing to say! How am I supposed to fill the silence? The president needs to consider *my* feelings!"

But however unfair the approach, the sixth- and seventh-years had cut right through the first layer, skipping nearly all of it. First place and last place could still clearly see each other as their feet carried them to the next obstacle.

"We've hit the second layer. If all we had to do was raze this forest, that would be easy—"

But as the Watch sped off through the brush, they skidded to a halt. In the skies above the forest were not the usual bird wyverns but dragons far larger, with much greater wingspans.

The president frowned. "...They've got *actual* wyverns here? What is this, the fifth layer?"

"Count ourselves lucky there's no lindwurms," said Lesedi.

"Don't be too sure. There might be anything in these woods," Tim muttered, glaring into the darkened forest. The second layer was always teeming with life, but today it was eerily silent. As if the wyverns were there to draw their attention away from the *real* threat—exactly the sort of trick the Kimberly faculty loved. After a few seconds' thought, Godfrey decided to be consistent—and *ruin* things.

"Fine. Tim—poison it."

The students behind them collectively gasped. Tim's smile grew extra diabolical, and he popped the flap on his hip pouch.

"Music to my ears! Back off, people! Don't breathe!"

The crowd was way ahead of him. A moment later, eight vials left Tim's hands, arcing upward—and exploding, releasing a mist into the air. Godfrey's crew quickly aimed their athames.

"*Impetus!*"

"*""""Impetus!*"""""

Their winds created an updraft, carrying the mist skyward. It soon reached the wheeling wyverns—and their shrieks echoed across the layer.

"The Toxic Gasser's poison at work! Hoo boy, is it a doozy!" Glenda was screaming a lot today. "The first wyverns it hit instantly fell from the air, and the rest of the flight are balking hard. And the forest below is withering away! What on earth was in that, Tim Linton?"

"Brewing a poison strong enough to work on dragons is a challenge for even the finest alchemist," Garland said, sighing. "I remember something I once heard Darius grumble: *'The boy can't make a balm for bugbites, but he's got a knack for poison alone that is downright bloodcurdling.'* But, uh, from him, that's a compliment."

Garland was watching all their work get demolished sight unseen—and nodding his approval. Given what lay ahead, the wyverns were but a herald.

Another round of vials burst above the students, and the winds carried the contents forward, tracing the vapor trails from Tim's poison. This neutralized the toxins, and Godfrey's crew started running down the path they'd made.

"Mr. President," Gino Beltrami began. "If you're going to expect my help with your poisons, I'd appreciate a word in advance."

The neutralizing agents had been supplied by the Barman's alchemy, and he had a right to grumble.

Racing past withered trees and the desiccated corpses of magifauna, Godfrey smiled.

"My bad, Mr. Beltrami. No one at Kimberly can handle Tim's poison but you."

High praise but accurate—Gino was one of the best alchemists on campus, and without him, Godfrey could never have risked the order.

"No need," Tim said with a snort. "We'd have been fine without it. I concocted a mild one just for the occasion. Anyone had accidentally inhaled, they'd have been fine—just a ninety-five-day high-grade fever accompanied by agonizing pain that'd leave them writhing for the duration. See, Mr. President, I'm *nice*."

"Yeah, that's...one word for it, Tim."

"Hmph." Leoncio snorted. "Dizzyingly reprehensible, but clearing out the wyverns was a boon."

Khiirgi sidled up to him. "You sure you should be ceding the lead?"

"I don't like it. But my instincts are aligned. The dullard's route is the *right* one here."

He clearly meant that, and she took the hint. Keeping an even distance from them, Godfrey set the pace, passing through the forest and bounding up the side of the irminsul. With the wyverns and beasts wary of further poison, nothing stood in their way. They crossed the peak in no time and headed down the branches to the base. The end of the second layer wasn't far off.

"...Almost to the Battle of Hell's Armies," Lesedi said. "Be ready— you saw what the fourth- and fifth-years had to deal with."

"I've got this!" Tim patted his pouch, grinning. "My next poison'll melt any bones."

The students at the back were no further away than when the match began, and a few minutes' run later, the leaders of the pack—Godfrey and Leoncio—barked an order.

""Halt!""

Both parties skidded to a stop. The unaffiliated to the rear sensed something amiss and followed suit. The front row was scowling dead ahead—and the reason for their sudden command turned to face them.

"Oh, you're here. Faster than I figured."

The magical biology instructor—Vanessa Aldiss. No signs of her usual white coat—she was dressed down, shoulders bare. Like she was out for a quick jog.

"...Instructor Vanessa...?"

"Just finished my warm-up!" she said, stretching both arms overhead. "Ya ready for this?"

Every student here was suddenly very conscious of the pile of bones behind her. There'd been ten thousand spartoi here for the previous prelim. In the two hours since, the formations should have been reworked, strengthened, prepped for their arrival—but instead…

"Sorry, Instructor. You mean…?"

"You're fighting me. Ain't brooking no complaints."

A pronouncement like the fall of a guillotine blade. Godfrey gritted his teeth. The bad feeling in his gut had been worse than he'd feared.

"Leoncio…no, everyone here. For just this fight—forget *all* our differences."

His words hit home. Not one person needed an explainer. They grasped his intent not with their heads but with their skin. Not with logic but with raw instinct. The thing before them was merely *shaped* like a woman—but its true nature was death incarnate. There was no discernible difference between them and the pile of bones behind her.

"You get it. And if you don't—it ends here. *All* our lives are forfeit."

The moment Vanessa appeared on-screen, the color drained from Glenda's face.

"Instructor, are you serious?"

"………"

Garland spoke not a word. He listened to the hubbub of the stands, an order echoing through his head.

"One change to the sixth- and seventh-year prelim. Make Vanessa the final obstacle."

Just past noon, the headmistress had summoned him to her office to issue this instruction. Garland couldn't believe his ears.

"…Wait a minute, Headmistress. Specifically, you mean…"

"Make them *fight* her. Make them fear for their lives. Make them all *commit* to the battle."

He had been sure she didn't mean it literally, but Esmeralda left him no wiggle room. The witch of Kimberly stood with her back to the windowsill, staring down at him.

"...Flush them out?" Garland said, his fists tightening. "Peel the deception away in the face of mortal peril?"

"Reevaluate *everyone*. Discover which students are capable of killing a teacher."

This was why the witch had offered unprecedented cash and prizes this league. To truly evaluate the school's top students would take no ordinary challenge—so they'd throw in the worst there was. There was no doubting her logic. And while Garland was searching for the words to argue it, she spoke again.

"And it'll let her blow off some steam. Since the beasts in her care were targeted, she's been ready to flip her lid. Let her go buck wild."

He'd sensed the same thing. Assailed by an unknown enemy, Vanessa Aldiss wouldn't remain docile for long. Before she erupted, they'd need to let her vent. But even so...

"*Can* she fight without killing anyone?"

Garland minced no words. He knew perfectly well no matter what beast he dragged up from the labyrinth's depths, it would be far less dangerous than facing Vanessa Aldiss in a bad mood. The headmistress knew that full well.

"Even she can tell the difference between food and her students," she said. "If there's risk—it comes if they make things *too fun*."

"Oh yeah, there were, like, *rules* to this thing. Uh, right—immobilize me or, failing that, land a good one. I feel like there was a bunch more fine print, but I forgot. Let's just keep it simple."

Far too simple for a regulated league, but Vanessa was already stomping toward them.

She glanced once over the crowd, then growled, "So...how hard a hit can y'all take without *breaking*?"

The students spread out at that question, putting distance between them, surrounding her from all sides. It might have looked like their numbers were an advantage, but this was little more than a desperate insurance. When somebody died, they'd take less collateral with them.

"...Hooooo..."

Manipulating his mana circulation, Godfrey unleashed the mana reserves within. Blue fire rose up from his entire frame—which just made Vanessa grin.

"Ain't seen you mean business in ages! That's what I'm talkin' about!"

"**Ignis!**"

"**Solis lux!**"

""""""""**Fortis Flamma!**""""""""

Godfrey's and Leoncio's spells went out first, and the rest followed suit. Subjected to their focus fire, Vanessa never even tried to dodge. Magic strong enough to vaporize a person reached her—

"Hup."

—and something vaulted out of the flash and bang. They *barely* perceived it at all. A girl had *just* cast—and her body went flying. Limbs torn off, planting themselves in the ground like gravestones, crimson spray coating the students on either side.

"Kah..."

With nothing left below the waist, the girl let out a grunt—accompanied by a gush of blood.

Poised with a massive fist extended post-swing, Vanessa said, "Whoops." The gleam of polished steel peeked from beneath her burning clothes. "Sorry, that was a bit *too* rough. I keep forgetting how squishy you kids are."

""""""""**Extruditor!**""""""""

No one screamed or shrieked—they just chorused the next spell. Concentrated pressure great enough to level a house descended on Vanessa. They'd learned two things from that first sacrifice—stacked spells would do her *no* harm, and her movement speed was beyond their capacity to see. They could not afford to miss a single movement, and thus could not use any spell likely to impede their vision. Without anyone suggesting it, they were all on the same page.

"Huh. This is, you know—like that time I went sea diving like, ten thousand feet down."

The pressure *was* roughly equivalent. Without so much as a counterspell, Vanessa started strolling—humming under her breath. A sight to boggle the mind but one they'd all seen coming.

"""""""Lutuom limus!"""""""

The ground under Vanessa's feet turned to sand, and between the pressure and her own weight, she sank to her knees in the blink of an eye. She folded her arms, frowning down at the ground.

"Oh, so *that's* the plan. Not half bad."

"""""""Impetus!"""""""

A current of sand down below dragged her under. But that was merely the opening shot. Layered spells followed, turning the area into a whirlpool of sand.

"Wh-what is *that*?" Guy whispered, his jaw hanging open.

The stands around them had gone silent as a tomb. No one dared to blink.

"...An application of convergence magic," Oliver answered. "Convert a chunk of ground to high-fluidity sand, then use numbers to get that sand moving in the same direction, creating a whirlpool-like flow. Only doable if everyone involved is *good*."

"But it is an extremely effective means of binding a foe. Even with Vanessa's brute strength, with the sand constantly on the move, she has nothing to brace against. With her head under, she can't chant. There's no way she can escape..."

Chela's voice trailed off. Her eyes were on the screen—where something had just shot out of the ground *outside* the manufactured sand sea.

*　　*　　*

An explosion roared behind them. By the time they turned, two students had already lost their dominant hands—and half their torsos.

"Wha—?"

"…!"

Their eyes locked on the same thing—a razor-sharp fin growing down the instructor's spine. There were sturdy tail fins at the base of her feet, and the entirety of one arm had mutated into a massive jaw. Vanessa Aldiss was no longer even the same *species*.

"Ain't swum the sands in *ages*. A real good workout!"

As she spoke, the fins retracted—she had no further need of them. A realization sank in: With the aid of those physical attributes, she'd literally *swum* her way free.

But they had no time to stand stunned. She was free of the sand's coils but not yet divested of mutations unsuited for life on land. The students, hoping that was an advantage, lunged their athames at Vanessa. From the front, from the side, from behind—in three directions, all aimed directly for vital organs. Anyone else would have perished three times over, but every single blade *bounced* off her body, not even breaking the skin.

"?!"

"No damage…!"

"Ha-ha! We playing with swords now?"

She let out a cackle. The dorsal fin fully retracted, replaced with multiple arms, each with a jagged blade at the extremity. Less humanoid or animalistic than *mantis*, these limbs parried the athame strikes, moving with the utmost precision and easily deflecting the onslaught.

"Oh no…!"

"G-get back—!"

"Gah!"

One student who'd failed to block was cut in half at the waist, chunks of flesh falling to the ground. The other two just barely managed to back off before sharing that fate, but now Vanessa was chasing *them*. Six bladed arms extended from her spine, her human limbs folded across her chest.

"Your weapons are so damn *dull*. My claws slice *way* better!"

"Rahhhh!"

But then a blow from one side knocked hard on Vanessa's brow. Lesedi Ingwe had taken two steps through a Sky Walk and unleashed a brutal kick from midair. The weight of the adamant in her toes lent blunt force to the blow, and the sound echoed like a log striking a bell.

"Good kick—but a bit feeble."

Vanessa hadn't even *budged*. Numb from the knee to her shoulder, Lesedi gritted her teeth. Just *what* had she kicked? She used the recoil to retreat, but two claw arms gave chase—

"""Extruditor!"""

Godfrey's and Leoncio's spells covered her, each forcing one of the arms off course. A narrow escape. Lesedi touched down and was already into her next motion.

A slight distance from the action, two alchemists were conferring.

"...Tim, go all out. I'll handle cleanup."

"Goes without saying!"

Tim hurled a vial, and it burst in the air. Gino's winds carried its contents. This poison was far more virulent than the one he'd used on the second layer—every other student ran backward as a mist of death assaulted Vanessa, consuming all life in its path.

"Linton's poison, mm? *Haaah!*"

But when she saw it—she *inhaled*. An intake of breath so sharp, it lowered the atmospheric pressure in her vicinity, ensuring that every drop of the toxin entered her lungs. Vanessa was silent for a few seconds, savoring it then she licked her lips.

"Mm, on the sweet side. Gimme another."

"What a monster...!" Tim wailed.

Vanessa made a move toward him and Gino, but massive roots shot out of the ground near her, coiling themselves around her frame.

"Huh—?"

Vanessa frowned down at the roots binding her. A few seconds later, she divined the nature of them, and her eyes shot across the group of students—to the one kneeling down, her athame inserted in the soil.

"Irminsul roots? Not often you bust out the elf magic, Khiirgi."

"No aptitude. Really takes a lot out of me," Khiirgi said with a sigh. Everyone knew elves as a species had high affinity with flora, a quality that traced all the way back to the dominion bestowed upon them by a god in ancient times. The irminsul, too, was an ancient species and highly compatible with such ancient arts. If the caster had the aptitude, it could easily be encouraged into rapid growth.

"Hoh…?"

Their prey secured at the tips, the irminsul roots stretched skyward. A hundred feet above the ground, Vanessa pried her way free of their bondage and was released into the air. Gravity took over, and she dropped like a stone—and every athame below was pointed her way.

"Now, keep her up! **Gravitor!**" Miligan roared.

*""""""""***Gravitor!***"""""""""*

The spells pinned Vanessa's airborne body, but the burden on the casters was tremendous. It felt like holding up a mountain, and every jaw clenched tight.

"So…heavy!"

"Brace yourselves! Hold her till your mana drains!"

"Ah, trying to keep me dangling? Not the worst idea!"

Vanessa was suspended faceup, but she flipped herself around. Both hands toward the ground, she extended her arms to cover the entire hundred-foot gap; her massive palms grabbed fistfuls of the earth.

"Don't even *need* to grow wings! I can just *reach*."

Once she had a good grip on the ground, she just pulled—and the students' spell was overpowered, dissipating. Vanessa dropped straight to the earth, but before she got back up—a shadow loomed over her.

"…Been a while since I put together one this big."

A man stood within the spartoi bones. In the skies behind him reared the head of a white snake every bit as towering as the irminsul roots. On closer inspection, the snake itself was made of an unsettling number of human bones—Cyrus Rivermoore had crafted this creature from the remains of the spartoi Vanessa had dispatched.

"It's an inferior assembly from the material available, but the shape's what matters. Jörmungandr—consume."

"Ha, that's a good one. Well worth *punching*!"

The sheer bulk of the bone snake slithered toward her, and Vanessa charged in with glee. Her right fist clenched, muscles to her shoulder swelling outward, growing horrifically oversize and overpowered.

"Rahhh!"

As the snake's head snapped toward her, her hook slammed into its cheek. The snake's cranium burst in a shower of bone shards, and that rippled down the length of its body like an electric shock, unraveling it entirely. A single hit had put Rivermoore's creation on the brink of collapse. She had her fist fully extended from the swing and was leaning way off-balance, her lips curled into a smirk.

"Ha-ha, my bad. Overdid it again!"

But even as her delighted cry rang out, sharp blows hit her sides. Two figures struck home in passing, and she blinked, looking down.

"…Mm?"

Twin gouges from her fore to her back. Godfrey and Leoncio turned toward her from twenty yards behind, athames raised.

"…I got a full inch down her right flank. You?"

"Same on the left. Timing the strike to a big swing was the right call."

They shared their results, both frowning. This was the first blood they'd drawn, but it was far from a decisive wound—It was dubious if she'd even register it as damage. And the same approach would likely not work again.

"…Oh! That's pain! *That's* how cuts feel!" Vanessa roared. "Ha-ha, confused me for a moment. It's just been so *long*!"

She slapped her wounds with both hands. Then she turned, facing the seventh-year leaders. The students spread out around them gulped—and every bone in her body started cracking, changing shape.

"I'm having so much fun! What more'll you—?"

"That's enough, Instructor Vanessa."

Her transformation ceased. Garland's voice was echoing through the surveillance golems above—like ice water dripping on Vanessa's head.

"I said no full-body transformations. And I'm declaring those two wounds legitimate. The 'good one' you were looking for—twice over. In accordance with the rules of the event, you will now retreat and allow the students to pass."

"...Yo, Garland. Since when do *you* get to boss *me* around, you whelp?"

Vanessa glared up at the golems. Her transformation resumed, with bone- or hornlike protrusions sprouting on her back.

"I ain't pulling out *here*! It's just getting *good*! The real fun is yet to come! Right, kids—?"

"You mustn't, Vana."

A rasp like the bleating of a strangled sheep. A black *thing* draped across Vanessa's shoulders. Like the darkest moment of night boiled to maximum concentration, from which emerged a girl's pale visage, unnervingly young.

"...Dia."

"I know it's fun, but Lu's right. Any more and someone'll break."

The curse instructor, Baldia Muwezicamili, was whispering in her ear. Her dark eyes scanned the group of students.

"You'll be so sad if your toys break, Vana. See, look! If you take good care of them, they'll all be there to play with again. Right, children?"

Her lips curled into a semblance of a smile that made every student shudder. Her voice, her gestures, her expressions—they were all equally cursed. She was here to stop Vanessa's rampage, but she felt more like a *second* threat.

"…Ha."

And that was likely why Vanessa rewound her transformation and switched back to human form.

Only then did it feel like they'd actually *survived*.

"I've lost interest. Suit your damn selves."

"Hee-hee-hee. I love it when you *listen*, Vana."

Vanessa turned on her heel and stalked off toward the surface. Baldia stayed clinging to her back. As the students watched them go, white glittering feathers fell toward them.

"These feathers will fall on those who excelled in that battle," Garland intoned. "Those with feathers may advance; those without must wait here for five minutes before proceeding. Anyone immobilized will be swiftly collected by the medical team. That is all."

They could already see medevac teams running in from the third-layer exit. Their members quickly set about treating the wounded. Nearly everyone injured was in critical condition, and a few of them were even not in one piece, but mages never died instantly as long as their brains and hearts remained intact. Once he was sure no students had crossed that line, Godfrey let out a long sigh and lowered his athame. He sounded relieved.

"…It seems—"

But a blow from behind cut him off.

"Your protection prevented fatalities. And that resulting relief is your least guarded moment, Godfrey."

Godfrey's head snapped around. Cyrus Rivermoore stood behind him, his athame embedded in Godfrey's back, seizing the unguarded second after a deadly battle.

"Rivermoore, you're—"

But as Godfrey spoke, the blade withdrew—and his knees crumpled. At the tip of Rivermoore's athame: a bloodstained lump of white.

"Like I told you—I'm here for a *reward*. A first-rate sternum."

"Godfrey!"

"What the hell was that?!"

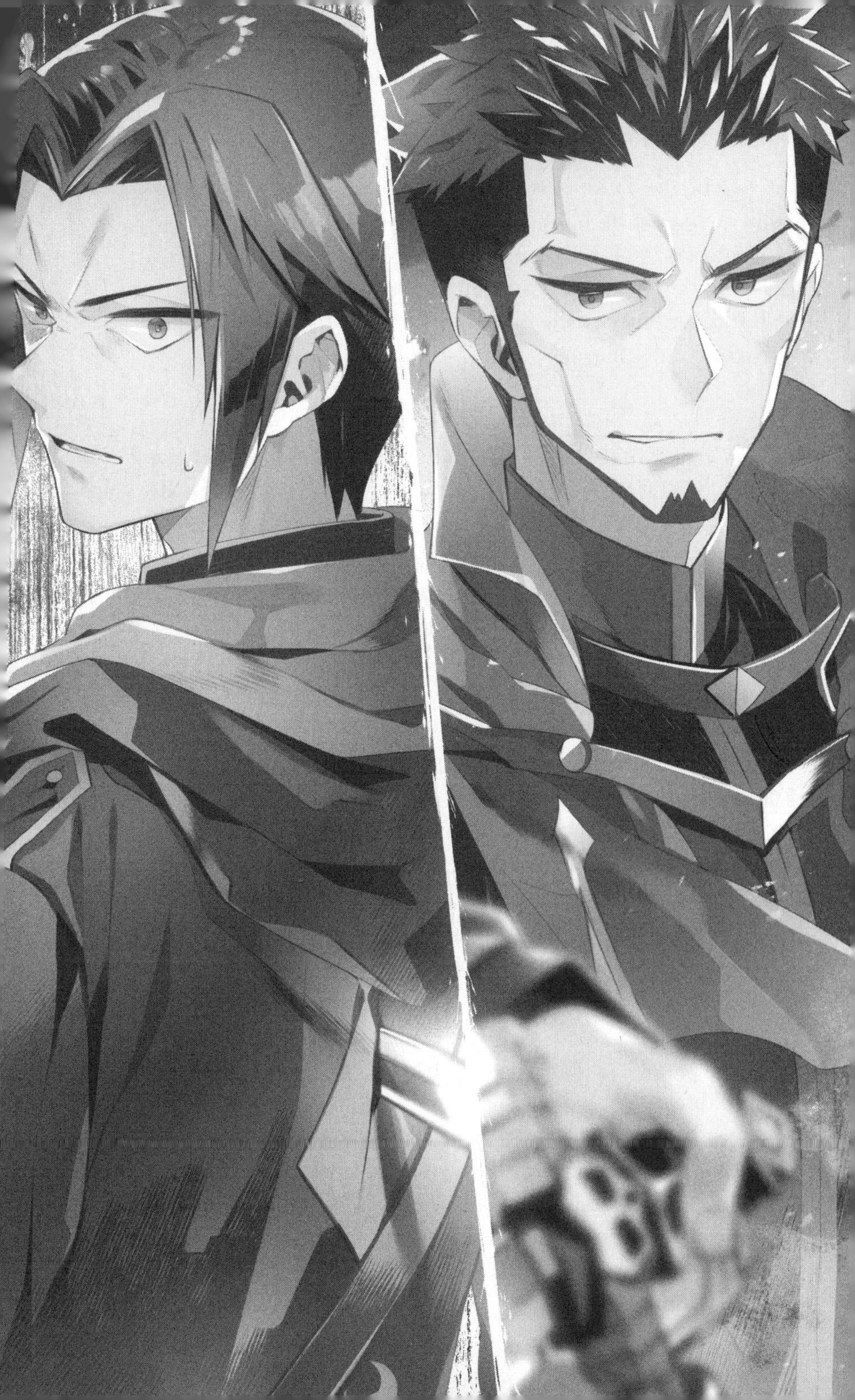

Lesedi and Tim saw red and charged in. The rest of the Watch was hot on their heels, but Rivermoore was already stalking away.

"My task is done. I'm dropping out."

With that, he broke into a run, throwing himself into the cave to the third layer. Not a single wasted motion. Clearly, he had no further use for the combat league.

First Vanessa's entrance, now this. The audience was left gaping in shock. And it fell to Glenda to put words to their emotions. Her voice shook.

"Mr. Rivermoore stabs the president in the back and bails! That's a clear rule violation! What is the Scavenger even doing?! If you're bailing on the league here, why fucking join at all?!"

She was so worked up, she forgot to keep her speech clean, but no one blamed her. Garland, scowling hard, barked orders to the staff on the scene.

Yuri was watching all this from the stands—but when he spoke, he *understood*.

"Ohhh…he never cared about the league in the first place."

Oliver clenched his fists tight. It was all too clear why the warlock had joined the festivities.

"He was waiting for his chance—to steal one of the president's bones…"

"Don't, Tim!" Lesedi yelled. "If you leave the course, you'll be disqualified!"

They were at the start of the third layer, and her compatriot had taken a step after Rivermoore, who'd immediately gone way off the path. It was impossible to give chase and stay in the prelim. That, too, was why he'd chosen this moment to act—but all Lesedi could do was grimace.

"...Rrgh...!"

Godfrey was hanging on her shoulder, barely keeping his feet moving. His breathing and mana circulation were in wild disarray, his face contorted in agony.

"Godfrey," Lesedi said. "What did he do?! He didn't *just* grab a bone, did he?"

"He got me good...," he rasped. "Took a chunk...of my etheric body with it..."

Bones were the basis of the flesh, and the ether was tightly woven to them. Anyone with expertise in that field could meddle with one through the other. And when that happened, treating the wounds was astronomically harder. A lost bone could be swiftly replaced, but lost ether was not so simple.

"Damn you, Rivermoore... No one wanted *this*," Leoncio spat, one eye on the man as he retreated.

Leoncio was leading the pack now. Gino shot him a disapproving glance, but he angrily shook it off—and picked up the pace.

END

Afterword

Hello, this is Bokuto Uno. A cacophonous salute and a bustling festival herald the opening of the third year.

Two years in this hellscape have changed our boys and girls beyond recognition. The six friends are not the only ones honing their skills. They're at the peak of the lower forms now; it is time to evaluate the fruits of their training. Is it any wonder they're all so committed?

Yet the students in the upper forms see things differently. The strings that tug on them prevent them from falling for the festival's thrall—but they are not any less active. Those in a position to lead the student body all the more so—walking a tightrope against the drives of the faculty, one may well forget to watch one's back. And the students at this school do so love to stab you there.

The Scavenger warlock claims his prize and exits the festivities. The answer our detective seeks now lies in the labyrinth's depths.

The dead are the past. Face that unwary, and you may well succumb. Take care lest you get dragged under—your lives are in your own two hands.

Post-Volume Special Feature

Reign of the Seven Spellblades: Kimberly Magic Academy Admission Contest

Winning Character Introductions!

Between the end of 2019 and the start of 2020, readers submitted original character creations to the Kimberly Magic Academy Admission Contest. Two character concepts were chosen to appear in this volume!

※ Some portions of the initial submissions may have been revised by the author during the writing process.

Submission by Kirigirisu!

Jasmine Ames

NAME:	Jasmine Ames
AGE:	Fifteen (Same class as Oliver & his friends)
GENDER:	Female
H/W:	~5'1", ~99 lbs.
APPEARANCE:	Red-brown hair, just past the shoulders. Eyes hidden but are a dark red, slightly downturned.
CLOTHES:	Standard Kimberly uniform. Wears a necklace bequeathed by her parents (for protection).
PERSONALITY:	Low self-esteem prevents her asserting herself. Dedicated.
MAGIC TALENTS:	Bad at nothing but excels at little. Her family's secret fake spellblade is something else in its own right.
OTHER:	Likes to read. Loves heroic legends and *shoujo* manga. Her family has history, if not as much as Chela's. They lament their failure to produce anyone of note, but a few generations back, they did develop an original spell.

※ Some submission details omitted.

Bokuto Uno's take!

This fencer with the hidden eyes fits right into that "strong but has pretended to be weak" trope. As I toyed with the original submission, she became one of her class's powerhouse characters. I imagine it was very tough hiding her talent for this long.

NAME:	Rosé Mistral
AGE:	Kimberly third-year
GENDER:	Male
H/W:	5'7", 137 lbs. (Pretty slender build)
APPEARANCE:	Upturned (liar's) nose but even features. Always smirking. Purplish hair.
CLOTHES:	Usually has his hood up. Otherwise, the standard uniform.
PERSONALITY:	Hard to get a read on. Eccentric. Never shows his hand. A liar—and thus, can tell when others are lying.
MAGIC TALENTS:	Frable allows creation of two to three splinters, one to two of which will explode. They can be detonated at will or when they're attacked. The explosion itself doesn't do much damage, just produces a big bang. Splinters can't use spells, so they have to use swords or other non-magical means. A magic known only to Mistrals, Frable is a portmanteau of Fragor and *double* (French for "twin").
OTHER:	Good at sleight of hand. Better than most at being sneaky. Primarily fights with magic. Not great at sword arts. Mainly buys time waiting for his chance to hit hard.

※ Some submission details omitted.

Submission by
ShiZu@yae!

Rosé Mistral

Bokuto Uno's take!

"I want at least one trickster this time"—and here comes exactly what I wanted. His inclusion immediately made the match infinitely more complex and had me puking blood. Pretty sure he's a very serious kid deep down.